HARD KNOCKS BOOK TWO

XAVIER COLD

MICHELLE A. VALENTINE

Xavier Cold
Copyright © 2016 by Michelle A. Valentine Books, LLC
Published by: Michelle A. Valentine Books, LLC
All rights reserved.

DISCLAIMER:
This book is intended for an adult audience due to strong language and naughty sexual situations.

Cover Art:
Letitia Hasser, Romantic Book Affairs
www.rbadesigns.com
(Stock photo purchased.)

Edited by:
Jovana Shirley, Unforseen Editing
www.unforseenediting,com

Edited by:
Editing 4 Indies
www.editing4indies.com

Interior Design and Formatting by:
Christine Borgford, Perfectly Publishable
www.perfectlypublishable.com

To Contact Michelle:
Email: *michelleavalentinebooks@gmail.com*
Website: *www.michelleavalentine.com*

Michelle A. Valentine Books

The Black Falcon Series
ROCK THE BEGINNING
ROCK THE HEART
ROCK THE BAND
ROCK MY BED
ROCK MY WORLD
ROCK THE BEAT
ROCK MY BODY

Hard Knocks Series
PHENOMENAL X
XAVIER COLD

The Collectors Series
DEMON AT MY DOOR
COMING SOON—DEMON IN MY BED

A Sexy Manhattan Fairytale
NAUGHTY KING
FEISTY PRINCESS
COMING SOON—DIRTY ROYALS

Wicked White Series
WICKED WHITE
WICKED REUNION
WICKED LOVE

"Do not be overcome by evil, but overcome evil with good."
Romans 12:21

Chapter
ONE

Xavier

A BUZZER GOES OFF, AND the sound of the steel bars locking me inside a ten-by-ten concrete cell echoes around the room. I hang my head, my hair falling down, cloaking the sides of my face, as I close my eyes and wish I could rewind the last few hours of my life.

Anna was right. I shouldn't have gone out there. I lost my fucking head, and now, there's no going back.

"Cold," the guard barks my name. "Let me know when you're ready for that phone call."

I scrub my hand down my face but don't make a move to answer the guard. Who the fuck am I going to call? I have no family, and I sure as hell don't want Anna to see me this way. It fucking guts me to know she had to witness my self-destruction in the ring and then the police carting me off in cuffs. I'd wanted to be a better man for her, but I failed fucking miserably.

I roll out the mattress assigned to me by the county jail and then busy myself with making my bed.

There's a clang on the bars behind me, and I find the same pudgy guard who escorted me into the cell, standing there with a pair of handcuffs.

"Inmate Cold, roll up. Looks like you're out of here. I need to cuff you and get you to discharge." He motions me over.

My mind rushes with the possibility of who came here to get me.

I turn around and stick my hands through the rectangular space between the bars. The metal clicks around my wrists.

"Arms back through," he orders after securing my arms together. Then he yells an order out to someone, "Open cell three two five."

When I turn around, the door to my cell opens. The man grabs the upper part of my right arm and then escorts me through the corridor. Snores come from the other prisoners as we pass by their cells, and I'm thankful that I don't have to spend even one night here. I'll forever be in Anna's debt for getting me out of here so quickly.

We head through a series of doors until we come to ones with the word *Discharge* clearly labeled across them. The guard leads me to a desk where a tall man with a Tom Selleck mustache is busy with filling out forms. He doesn't even bother glancing up at me. "Are you Xavier Cold, number seven, one, five, two, seven, three, seven, one?"

I clear my throat. "Yes, sir."

"Do you have any dress outs?" the attending officer asks while still working on the paperwork in front of him.

How the hell am I supposed to know if I have street clothes here or not?

"I'm not sure. I've only been here for a few hours," I answer honestly, remembering I was wearing my wrestling gear when I was booked.

"We'll check that," he tells me. Then, he picks up the phone on his desk, and asks whoever is on the other line to check on my street clothes for release. He hangs up the phone and then makes eye contact with me. "Do you have a ride?"

I nod. "I assume my girlfriend who posted my bail is still here."

He makes another note on his paperwork and a new officer

comes into the room with a stack of neatly folded clothes that I immediately recognize from ones I packed in my suitcase. Relief floods me as it's confirmation that Anna is the one here for me. No one else had access to get into my hotel room.

The guard that led me in from the cell unlocks the cuffs from around my wrists and then stuffs them back into a black pouch on his tool belt. "Good luck, Cold. I'm sure we'll see you again soon. The hot-headed ones always come back."

My fingers curl, and I resist the urge to knock that smirk off his face. Even I know better than to do that here.

"I need you to sign here and here, and then you can change into your street clothes." I quickly scrawl my name where he indicated and then grab my clothes.

"There's a restroom behind you. Go in there and change."

I hate taking orders like this, but I'm willing to do anything to get the hell out of here.

After I change, I come back out and the officer pushes himself up from his seat. "I'll escort you out."

We go through a few more doors, and then once a large gray steel door opens, I spot Anna standing in a very sterile-looking waiting room. The expression on her face can only be described as anxious as she bites her lower lip and strains her neck to get a look at me through the opening door.

Relief floods her face as our eyes lock. "Xavier!"

The door no sooner opens than I rush through it and wrap my arms around Anna, pulling her against my chest. I inhale deeply and close my eyes. Her fruity shampoo and perfume comfort me as I hold her tight.

"I'm so sorry. I'm so fucking sorry," I say over and over again.

I take in a shaky breath. "I fucked up. I know I did."

"Shhh . . ." she says, trying to soothe me as she tangles her fingers into my hair. "We'll get this figured out."

The way she says *we* warms my heart. So many times in my

life I've been tossed away, like I meant nothing. People don't stick with me, which is what makes me cherish Anna even more.

When I pull back, I see tears glistening in her eyes. One drop slides down her cheek, and I swipe it away with my thumb. "Please don't cry because of me. You know how it fucking kills me to see a frown on your face."

She sniffs. "I thought I lost you."

I cradle her face in my hands and whisper, "I'll always find my way back to you."

"Promise?"

I gaze into her eyes and answer with absolute certainty. "Yes."

Nothing is ever going to stand between us again. I'll do everything within my power to see to that.

I give her one more kiss. "Come on, beautiful. Let's get out of here before they change their minds and try to make me stay in this shithole."

"Okay."

I throw my arm around her, thankful for having her by my side, and I lead her outside through the heavy glass doors. Anna clings to me as we walk in step toward the parking lot, and I welcome her warmth. For a while in there, I wondered how long it would be before I could feel her pressed up against me like this. Good thing I'd put all that money into her bank account.

"Thank you for bailing me out," I say before kissing the top of her head. "I was fully prepared to spend the night there. I was surprised they let me out so fast."

Anna stares up at me. "That's the thing. I didn't pay to get you out."

I furrow my brow. "You didn't?"

"No. I fully intended to, but by the time I went to the hotel room to pick up my checkbook and clothes for you, the bail was already paid when I arrived at the jail."

My mind races with the possibilities of who could've paid my bail, but as soon as we step foot in the parking lot and I spot the black stretch limo, I no longer have to wonder.

Oh, fuck. This isn't good.

The back window slides down, and Mr. Silverman leans forward, so he can make eye contact with me. "Get in."

My heart races inside my chest. Going to jail for what I did to Rex was just the beginning of the punishment heading my way. My boss isn't going to allow my actions to slide. For all of his staff at Tension, he has a zero-tolerance policy when it comes to fighting outside the ring, so fighting on national television was a sure way to get my ass fired right here on the spot.

I lead Anna around to the other side of the car and swallow hard. This is the end of my fucking dream right here. Without wrestling, I have nothing, other than Anna. How long can I possibly expect to keep her in my life if I don't have a way to support her? It's not like there's a shit-ton of great paying jobs for a man with my background. Felons aren't likely any employer's first choice.

Anna lays her hand on my stomach. "No matter what he says, I'm with you."

I place my hand on top of hers and silently pray to God that she means it because there's no way in hell I can give her up now.

I open the car door for Anna and then slide in after her. The inside of the limo has lights around the top of the interior, making it easy to see Mr. Silverman's face as I sit across from him with Anna by my side. She takes my hand and gives it a small squeeze, reassuring me like she always does that she's here for me.

The boss presses a small red button on the console next to him. "Back to the hotel to drop Xavier and Anna off, please."

"Right away, sir," the driver replies. The car begins to move.

He adjusts the gray tie he's wearing and then locks eyes with me. "A couple of shows ago, I seem to recall having a discussion with you about following the script to a T and reminding you that I don't like lawsuits. It appears, that discussion fell upon deaf ears, seeing as how I just came down to bail you out of jail because you'd beaten one of my other employees unconscious during a live show."

There's no denying what he's saying.

I square my shoulders and lift my chin, ready to face the consequences of my actions head-on. "Yes, I did all those things, and while I'm sorry that it's landed me in some deep shit, I'm not sorry that I did it. Rex had it coming. He got personal and took it to a level that it should never have gone to."

"While I don't doubt that Rex was a son of a bitch to you, the cold, hard truth here is that we have rules in place for a reason. No matter what he said or did, you should've kept your cool."

"I know. I've been trying hard to work on my temper."

"You've put me in a predicament here, X. Both you and Rex are the future of my company—you, in particular. You've been the topic of a lot of marketing strategies now that Brian wants to step back and spend more time with his wife and little girl. We need someone who can takeover his role, someone the crowd will really get behind. I'm struggling with going against my company policy and trying to make all of this go away for you. I need to work it so that the company can still benefit from you."

My mouth drops open a bit. "Are you saying that I'm not fired?"

Anna bites her bottom lip, trying not to smile, like she doesn't want to show any excitement until it's confirmed that my dream hasn't been crushed.

"I'm saying that you are too valuable to fire. Your popularity means money for Tension, and that's good for business, which is why I bailed you out. I've got a meeting with some local connections tomorrow. I have to put a spin on this situation, saying that it was a match that got out of hand, that everything was actually a part of the show, and that the cops intervened when they weren't needed."

I roll my eyes. "Rex will never go along with that. He'll press charges just to see me suffer. That motherfucker hates me."

"I've already worked things out with Rex. He'll agree to save your ass, if I make him the next champion."

I should be grateful for this easy out, but I can't stop myself from being pissed.

The muscle in my jaw flexes beneath my skin. Rex getting the belt this way is soul-crushing. That championship should've been mine, and had I not lost my fucking head, I would be on my way to wrapping that gold around my waist. Instead, I practically handed Rex the belt on a silver fucking platter.

I always fuck up everything good in my life, which is why I'm holding on to Anna with both hands and doing my best to do right by her. If that means allowing Rex this short-lived victory to keep me from being behind bars, then that's the way it has to be. I need this job more than anything to support Anna and to prove to her that I can take care of her every need.

"The problem is"—He rubs his chin—"it doesn't seem like the mandatory vacation I sent you on was enough distance between you and Rex, so I'm suspending you, X. I have to make an example out of you, so the other employees see that, no matter who you are, they cannot pull stunts like this and walk away from this matter scot-free."

I hate the idea of not being able to work, but it's a hell of a lot better than rotting in jail or spending all my time on probation. My boss will get no argument out of me on this one.

I sigh. "For how long?"

"Three months," he answers matter-of-factly. "And during that time period, you will not be permitted in any arena where we hold shows. Hell, I don't even want to hear about you being in the same city as Tension while you're suspended."

I nod. "Fine. Stay the hell away—I got it. Anna and I will head back to Detroit until this is finished."

"No, only you. This suspension doesn't apply to Anna. She'll still be required to show up to every show as scheduled."

The thought of Anna being alone where Rex and Deena can get to her while I'm not there to protect her is more than I can fucking handle. I can't allow that to happen. I'm supposed to watch over her. How am I supposed to do that if I'm hundreds of miles away in another state?

"That's not going to happen," I retort. "If I'm not there, Anna isn't going. You don't need her."

"Fine." He shrugs. "That's on you, but I will fire her if she doesn't show up, and when your suspension is lifted, I will not allow her back into the building during any of our shows."

I narrow my eyes. "You can't do that. That's blackmail."

He releases a bitter laugh from the back of his throat. "Have you forgotten who you're talking to? I own Tension. I can do whatever I please."

I drag my fingers through my hair.

Fuck.

What in the hell am I supposed to do here? I'm damned if I do and damned if I don't. There's only one real option left.

My eyes lock with his. "Maybe I should quit then."

"To do what? A man with a temper like yours needs this job, so don't be ridiculous. Anna is imperative to the storylines. That's it. Play along and do as I ask for the next three months, and all will be forgiven. Then, you can get back in the ring and go after that championship spot."

I shake my head. I won't sacrifice being with Anna for the sake of my job.

I open my mouth to tell my boss this very thing when Anna leans forward and quickly glances at me before turning her attention to our boss.

"That's a generous offer, sir. We'll figure out a way to make it work. I will be at the shows. I don't want to jeopardize my privileges to be backstage with Xavier when his suspension is lifted. Being with him is all that matters to me."

"Anna . . ." I say her name like a warning.

She stares at me. "I know what you're thinking, but I'll be fine. I can handle things while you're gone. Besides, it won't be forever. We'll be apart for only a few days out of the month. We'll get through it."

"Listen to her, X. She's smart, and she has your best interest in mind."

I know she does.

Anna has been nothing but good for me. I trust her. I absolutely loathe the idea of her being at Tension without me, but what other choice do I have than to agree right now? Being hotheaded has done nothing but fuck things up for me, so I need to learn to be sensible. So, I'll put on a front that I support this until I can talk some sense into her.

"Fine. But after my three-month suspension is over, you have to give me a chance to win the belt."

I know it's ballsy for a man in my position to make any demands, but being the champion is something I still really want.

"Of course. The fans would expect nothing less. I'll see to it that whoever possesses the belt—"

"I don't want just anyone. I want Rex in the ring." That's one part of my deal that has to be crystal clear. There's only one person I want to see in that ring when I return, only one person I want to inflict some pain on while I strip him of the thing he values most in this world.

He nods. "That would make an epic showdown. I'll grant that request—as long as you heed my warning and stay away from the show until your suspension is over, and I've had time to promote the buildup of your return."

The car pulls up at the hotel and parks in front of the entrance as I mull over his stipulation. Staying away from Anna is the last thing I want to do. Not a day has gone by since I met her that we haven't been together, and as much as I don't like it, I know I have to allow this to happen. But I swear to God, if Rex fucks with her in any way, no one will be able to pull me off of him the next time.

"Understood," is all I say before I open the car door and let myself out. I stretch my hand to help Anna out of the car. "Come on, beautiful."

Anna clings to me as we head back to our hotel room. I kiss the top of her head as we wait on the elevator. As fucked up as this situation is, it could've been a hell of a lot worse.

Chapter
TWO

Anna

LOCKED AWAY IN OUR HOTEL room, there are no prying eyes.

I finally have Xavier all to myself.

I wrap my arms around him, needing to feel his skin against me.

When I saw the cops carting Xavier out of that fight in handcuffs, my entire world crumbled before my eyes. We'd finally been getting to a good place, and then all hell broke loose and shook up our world.

Kneeling down in front of Xavier on that mat earlier tonight was the worst moment of my life. I hated seeing him lose control, jeopardizing everything he'd worked for. That cut me to the core. It should've never gotten to that point, but Rex wouldn't back off, and Xavier isn't the type to back down.

The thing I hadn't expected was for Xavier to say he loved me. It crushed me—that the second he'd admitted how he felt about me, he was being hauled off to jail.

"You don't know how scared I was that I was going to lose this," I whisper as Xavier holds me tight and the events from the match feel like a distant memory.

He rests his chin on top of my head. "You don't have to worry about that. I'll find my way back to you . . . always."

His words make me melt right on the spot. If someone would have told me that the overly sexual beast of a man that I met on the plane would say words that make me swoon—obliterate my panties sure, but promising to always be in my life?—well, I never would've seen it coming.

It's like what had happened to him in the ring somehow changed his perspective on everything. He was always so reluctant to make any type of promises or commitments before, even once telling me that he wasn't the marrying type. This feels like a good step in the right direction for us, regardless of all the craziness surrounding us tonight.

Xavier rubs small circles on my back, and it causes me to sigh before I snuggle into his chest.

"You tired?" he asks.

It doesn't hit me until then how exhausted I actually am. Tonight's been stressful, and I'm sure, if I allow myself to close my eyes for even the briefest time, I'd fall asleep on the spot.

But I refuse to let go of Xavier. When I thought they would lock him up and throw away the key, the opportunity to hold him against me anytime I wanted felt like it was quickly being ripped away. So, for now, I choose to stay here, in his presence, breathing him in as much as I possibly can.

I tilt my head up and stare into his light-blue eyes. "I'm ready for bed, but I don't want to sleep just yet."

For the first time since the chaos of the day began, Xavier smiles, but it's not just any smile. It's the heart-stopping one-sided smirk that drives me out of my ever-loving mind.

"Have I turned my good girl naughty?"

I give him my best wicked grin. "Afraid so. I can't seem to get enough of you."

His large hands cradle my face. "Glad to hear it because I'm fucking addicted to you."

His lips press on mine, and I'm immediately lost in his kiss. The stubble on his face scratches my fingertips as I trace his jawline.

"I need you."

A wicked gleam is in his eyes. "Is that so?"

Xavier bends down and nips my lower lip. "You don't know how much it turns me on when you ask for it. It takes every ounce of willpower in my body to stop myself from throwing you down on that bed and ravaging every inch of your body for my pleasure."

At the very thought of what that would be like, my pulse races under my skin. "What's stopping you?"

"You're too sweet for that." He leans in and runs his nose along my cheek, causing my entire body to quiver with anticipation. "And because you're not ready to go there—to allow me to have full control—yet."

"How do you know?" I take a deep breath as my chest heaves. "You don't always have to be gentle with me, Xavier. If you want me, then take me. I want to please you."

Heat from his parted lips brushes against the sensitive skin on my neck, causing my toes curl. It's amazing how turned on this man can make me with a few simple touches and naughty promises of pleasure. No one else has ever made me feel this way.

"You sure about that, beautiful?" His eyes are hooded with desire.

"Yes." I slide my hand under his shirt, allowing my fingertips to dance across the toned muscles in his abdomen. "Don't hold back."

That seems to be all the permission he needs because his touch shifts from gentle to demanding in a flash.

His fingers thread in my hair as he pins my head in place so that he can crush his lips to mine. His slick tongue glides over my lips, begging for entrance. I open my mouth, and he thrusts his tongue inside, a low growl emitting from his throat.

To know he's enjoying this kiss as much as I am makes my

sex clench.

"I need you naked." Xavier's fingers find the hem of my shirt, his pinkie grazing the bare skin along my side, before he whips it over my head with more grace than should be allowed for such a big man. The pads of his fingers caress the mound of flesh spilling out of the cup of my bra before he reaches behind me and unhooks it with ease.

I expect him to work on removing the bra straps, but he instead grabs the backs of my thighs and picks me up. His long hair twists between my fingers as all the playfulness leaves his face, and things turn serious while his eyes search mine.

Xavier slowly rakes his teeth over his bottom lip in a deliberately sexy manner. "I love you so fucking much, Anna. Don't ever leave me."

"Never."

He presses his lips to mine, so tender that it almost feels hesitant. "You can stop me at any time."

Before I can question what he means, a shriek escapes me as he tosses me onto the edge of the bed. I bounce against the mattress, and Xavier immediately climbs on top of me. He kisses me fiercely, and it's obvious that our talking session is now over. He removes the white lacy fabric from my chest and then wraps his mouth around the taut pink flesh standing at full attention before him.

A tingle passes all the way down to my toes as he nibbles on one nipple and then moves on to the other. I tug his long hair as he works on popping the button of my jeans, and then he unzips them, like I'm a Christmas present he can't wait to unwrap.

"I want to taste you," he whispers against my skin before his tongue darts out and swirls around my nipple. "I want to suck your clit until you come all over my tongue."

Oh my.

My stomach flutters as that dirty-talking mouth of his comes at me in full force, telling me exactly what he wants to do with me.

He drags my pants along with my panties over my hips, leaving me naked before him. The thing about being naked in front of Xavier is, I never feel like I'm being judged, only appreciated and admired. He takes a moment for his eyes to gaze over my nude flesh. He pulls his shirt over his head, making his hair look even sexier than before—if that's even possible—and then he kicks off his boots before dropping his pants and boxer briefs to the floor, like he can't stand them between us anymore.

He climbs back on top of me, and I writhe below him.

"I need a little taste, Anna. You're going to come a lot tonight, and I won't apologize for it, so I hope you meant what you said because there will be no holding back on my end."

"Anything you want, take it. It's all yours."

Damn if he doesn't know what to say to me to get me to agree to anything he wants.

A smile flashes across his face before he pushes off me, grabs my hips, and flips me onto my stomach without any warning. The next thing I know, my ass is being yanked up into the air, and Xavier's tongue is drilling into my pussy from behind. My eyes roll back the moment the warmth of his mouth is on me. My legs instinctually open wider, giving him better access. He works my clit , driving me into a frenzy while his nose moves around my entrance, stimulating every inch of my folds. It doesn't take long before I'm crumpling the sheets in my fists while I teeter on the brink of ecstasy.

"Oh God, Xavier, I'm coming already. Ohhhh!" The cry that comes out of me could rival the most seasoned porn star as an orgasm rips through me.

He's never made me come that fast before. Usually, he takes his time with me, but tonight, he's doing what he said he was going to do—ravage me.

He slows his assault down and licks me one final time before he turns me back over.

He crawls on top of me and kisses my lips, allowing me to taste myself on him. "See how good you are? So sweet. I'll never have my fill of you."

I cradle his cheek in my hand. "And I'll never want you to. I want you—always."

"Don't worry. There's no way you're getting rid of me now. Like I told you before, this shit is fucking permanent."

"Good," I whisper against his lips as he circles his hips to coat his cock in my wetness.

He finds my entrance with the tip of his stiff shaft and then thrusts his hips, slamming into me hard, balls deep. Another moan spills out of me as I call out his name and dig my nails into the flesh of his back. He pumps into me a few more times before he slips out of me and stands by the bed. His hands settle on my hips, and he yanks me to the edge before grabbing the base of his cock and ramming it back into me.

"Mmm . . . so fucking tight. This pussy was made for me, and it's all fucking mine." The way the words come out of his mouth with a slight growl in his voice causes my toes to curl.

It's total caveman talk, but his possessiveness is such a turn-on. I love that he takes ownership of me.

A shiver of intense pleasure ripples down my spine as he continues to seek out his own release. This beast of a man before me is sexy as sin as his mouth drifts open while he uses my body to pleasure himself. My eyes roam down his chiseled chest before pausing on his abs, which are contoured to perfection, and then they move even further down to watch his cock work in and out of me.

He grunts as his tattoo-covered arms flex as he holds on to me. His penis slips out of me. Immediately, I miss his warmth, but it's quickly replaced when he flips me over yet again and shoves my right leg up further on the bed, spreading me open further while I'm on all fours on the bed. He rubs his cock against my folds, and a long moan escapes from my mouth. I'm so ready for him.

Xavier shoves my hair to one side of my neck, exposing the skin, before he kisses it. "You want me back inside you?"

"Yesssss . . ." I hiss because his touch feels so damn good. "Xavier . . ."

"You know I like to hear you say it. Tell me you want it, and I'll give it to you," he whispers in my ear.

"Oh God." My eyes roll back when he pushes the very tip inside me, but he holds back, so it's only a tease. "I want you, Xavier. Please, I need you inside me."

"That's my good girl," he encourages before he thrusts his hips, slipping the head of his cock inside me from behind.

This sensation is completely different from every other time we've done it. It's primal and raw and completely about seeking a release.

He pumps in and out of me. "So fucking amazing." He grips one of my hips with one hand and then twists the other into my hair. "Fuck, Anna," he growls like it's difficult for him to speak. "I'm not ready for this to end, but I can't seem to hold back when I'm inside you."

A familiar tingle starts to roll through me, and I know I'm only moments away from peaking again. "Don't stop."

He digs his fingers into my skin and slams into me so hard that the distinct sound of his skin slapping against mine echoes around the room.

It doesn't take long before my entire body is shaking. "I'm coming."

A string of curses pour from his mouth as he comes hard, and we get lost in ecstasy together.

He collapses onto my back and then quickly rolls off of me. He pulls me tight against his chest and kisses my forehead. "I'm never going to get enough of you."

I lift my chin, so I can gaze into his eyes. "I feel the same way about you."

He reaches up and traces my cheek with the pad of his thumb. "I don't want you to worry about our future together, Anna. I'm going to figure out a way to take care of you."

I furrow my brow, completely thrown off by this change of topic. "I'm not worried. I know that we have each other, and everything will work out for the best."

"I don't know how you always manage to be so damn optimistic about everything."

"It's because I believe in you. You've already proven that you have a way of making things better for yourself," I honestly tell him. "Besides, I still have my job with Tension. I won't make as much money as you, but every little bit will help, right?"

He sighs heavily. "I hate the idea of you going on the road without me. You shouldn't go."

"You heard what Mr. Silverman said. I have to go. If I don't—"

"I could quit."

The ease in the way he says it, like it's no big deal, shocks me, and I don't believe he really means it.

"But you love wrestling. How can you be willing to give it up so easily?"

His eyes focus on me. "Because you mean more to me—that's why. When I was in that ring and the cops were about to cuff me for nearly killing Rex, I came to the realization that I can't live without you. I love you more than my own life, Anna."

My heart does a double thump inside my ribs. It was a huge step for him to admit how he felt about me, and it's amazing to hear him say it again.

"I love you, too." I rise up and kiss his lips. "You are not quitting, and neither am I, for that matter. This will all blow over, and when it does, I want to be by your side all the time. We can't screw up my chances of going backstage. You have to trust me."

He's quiet for a second, and then he slides his hand up to cup my jaw. "I trust you with anything I have, even my life. I won't like it, but I know you need to go on the road."

It's easy to see how hard this is for him. The people in Xavier's life have never given him much cause to trust anyone, so I'm grateful that he's opening that part of himself up to me. There's no telling how things will work out, but whatever happens, we're in this together.

Chapter
THREE

Anna

AFTER WE GET A FEW hours of sleep, Xavier's cell phone rings, waking us up.

He groans and rolls over onto his side to reach for the phone on the nightstand. "Hello?" his voice growls. Then, he's silent for a few moments as he listens to whoever is on the other end of the line. "Understood." He lets out an exasperated sigh and then scrubs his hand down his face. "I'll be on the first flight back to Detroit tomorrow."

He ends the call and then lays the phone down. "We need to pack."

"What's wrong?" I push myself up onto my elbow and stare down at his beautiful face.

Conflict is raging in his eyes, and it instantly makes me curious about what's on his mind.

"That was one of the lawyers with Tension. Looks like Mr. Silverman did indeed get all the charges dropped, like he said, so I'm out of all the legal trouble."

Relief washes through me. "That's fantastic news. I told you things would work out."

The corner of his mouth pulls down into a one-sided frown. "There's a catch."

"Other than being suspended? We knew that was part of the

deal."

"It appears that the boss decided to add another stipulation after our conversation last night,."

I grimace. "What is it?"

There's a flutter in my chest as my nerves go crazy while my brain works in overtime, attempting to figure out what in the world Tension could ask of him. Mr. Silverman has already taken away his career by suspending him.

"He is fining me for my actions against Rex. On top of that, Tension wants me to not only pay out of pocket for the medical bills that racked up because of what I had done, but I also have to pay Rex for his pain and suffering."

My eyes widen. "You've got to be kidding. Can he even do that?"

Xavier nods. "Tension affords Mr. Silverman to be a very rich man, and he can do anything he wants, and if I want to ever get back in the ring, I have to do what he asks, or I can kiss my job good-bye."

I frown. "That doesn't seem fair."

He locks eyes with me. "The world isn't fair, beautiful, especially when it comes to guys like me."

"Is it a lot of money?"

I know he's well-off—the man obviously has enough to wire thirty thousand dollars into my bank account—but anytime you take a huge cut out of your account, it's got to hurt.

"They want a hundred fifty thousand dollars total."

My mouth drops open, and I swear, I experience my first heart palpitation. The amount is insane. I can't imagine paying that much money for a fine.

"Oh my God, that's a lot."

"It is," he agrees.

I know I shouldn't be nosy about his financial situation, but I can't stop myself from asking, "Do you have that much?"

"I do, but since I won't have any money coming in for the

next few months, it's going to put me in a tight spot for a bit."

"The money you put into my account is still there. I haven't touched it. Will that be enough to get us by?"

"You'll need that money to pay for your hotel when you go on the road. The company doesn't give you any reimbursement. It's a business expense. Besides, that's your money. I gave it to you. I won't allow you to spend it on taking care of us."

"That's ridiculous. It's *your* money. I told you it didn't feel right for you to pay me since we're in a relationship now."

"Anna . . ." he says my name with a bite of warning. It's his go-to move when he's decided that he's not going to budge on his opinion.

"No, Xavier. Stop being silly. If you need the money—"

"Don't," he says, cutting me off. "This isn't up for discussion. You'll need it. Trust me. Traveling all the damn time isn't cheap. That's where most of my money has gone to."

Being broke is something I can relate to. When I first moved to Detroit, I barely had enough in my bank account to feed myself. If it wasn't for Quinn helping me to get a job, I'm not sure what I would've done. With that being said, I did manage to make it without much money, so Xavier and I will figure out a way to get by, too.

The thought of Quinn sets my mind spinning on how we can save a little money. "Fine, but since we'll be squeezed for money until everything gets worked out, I think we should stay with Quinn and Aunt Dee."

Xavier raises one of his thick eyebrows. "That won't work."

"Why not?" I argue. "I know they won't care, and it will save us from spending money on two hotel rooms."

"Their place is small, Anna, and while it's fine for you to stay with them, I'm a big guy. I take up a lot of room and will wear out my welcome pretty fast."

"That won't happen." I do my best to assure him, but he simply shakes his head.

"It will. Trust me. I bounced around from place to place after leaving home, and that was why most people kicked me out. It's hard to become transparent when you're six-four and two hundred sixty-five pounds."

I sigh, seeing as how he won't change his mind about this. That leaves one other place in Detroit where we could stay for free—his house, the one he owns and refuses to talk about.

Xavier doesn't mention his family, and he's made it crystal clear that pushing him into talking about it won't benefit either one of us. The times following nightmares that wake him from a dead sleep are the only glimpses I get into his past with his family life. The house he owns is a touchy subject, so I'm guessing it has to do with his family. Based on the story he told me before, it's possible the house is the one his mother died in, and the memories are too much to bear.

I don't want to bring up things that could hurt him, but I worry if he doesn't face the darkness of his past, he'll never make peace with it. I want to be there for him, to show him that it's okay to let go of the stuff that haunt him.

"Then, we should stay at your place." It's wrong of me to push this, but seeing as how we are in a tough predicament, living in the house he owns seems like the logical choice.

Xavier blows a rush of air through his nostrils, and I instantly regret saying anything.

"I won't go back there." His words come out in an angry growl.

I swipe a strand of his wild dark hair off his face as I gaze down at him. The uneasiness in his blue eyes is clear, and I hate that his past hurts him the way it does. I want to help him heal.

"Don't," he whispers. "I can't handle it when you look at me like that."

I'm instantly taken aback. "How am I looking at you?"

"With pity," he says. "I fucking hate when people pity me, especially when it comes from you."

This conversation gives me a flashback to the time we had an argument over talking about his family once before. When we were in my old boss, Andy's, office back at the restaurant I once worked for, we had a huge blowup over me trying to get him to open up about his mother. He stormed out on me, and I had to chase him down to apologize. I don't want to repeat that situation anytime soon.

"I'm sorry. I shouldn't pry. I know that. God knows, you've told me enough times that you don't like to talk about your family. But if you don't let me see that part of you, how am I ever going to really know you?"

"I'm trying."

Those two simple words speak volumes, and it's true. He's come a long way from the man I met on the plane.

"I know you are, but I'm greedy. I want to know everything about you."

He adjusts his head on the pillow, and then his fingertips trace the smooth skin on my shoulder. "Are you sure about that? My past—it's the shit that horror stories are written about. I've spent my entire life trying to forget the shit that happened to me."

I stare into his eyes. "Maybe it's time to stop forgetting. If you faced the things that scare you the most, it might help those nightmares go away."

"Or it could make them fifty fucking times worse."

"How will you know if you don't try?"

The pad of his thumb drifts across my lower lip, and I can tell by the expression on his face that he's really considering what I just said.

"Okay."

"Okay?" I question, wondering exactly what he's just agreed to.

"We'll stay at the house I own—or at least try to. I haven't been back there since I was fifteen, so I can't promise you that

I won't change my mind when we get there. A lot of evil shit happened to me in that house, bad shit that I wouldn't wish on my worst fucking enemy, and I'm not sure I'm ready to face it."

"I'm proud of you." I lean in and press my lips to his.

His taut muscles contract beneath my touch as he wraps his arms around me and pulls me against his hard chest.

"What are you doing to me, beautiful? You're changing me in ways I never thought possible," he murmurs against my lips.

I don't say anything, honestly, I don't know the answer to that, but I do know the feeling is mutual. He's changed me, too.

Chapter
FOUR

Anna

THE PLANE TOUCHES DOWN ON the runway, and I'm surprised by how excited I am to be back in Detroit. The city hasn't been my home for very long, but it already feels like where I'm supposed to be.

I shoot a quick text to Quinn to let her know that we've landed. Afterward, Xavier threads his fingers through mine and leads me off the aircraft. I smile as I think back to that first time we met. Flying into this airport will always hold a special place in my heart.

The baggage carousel is crowded, and our bags still haven't come out of the chute yet. I lick my dry lips and swirl my tongue inside my mouth to try to relieve the cotton mouth I've got going on. When I turn around, I notice a little coffee stand, and my mouth waters.

"I'm going to grab something to drink. You want anything?" I ask Xavier.

He shakes his head. "I'm good."

Only one person is ahead of me in line, a handsome businessman in a fitted three-piece suit. His dark hair is short and perfectly styled into place. After he orders a coffee with two pumps of vanilla, he turns to step out of the way while the girl behind the counter prepares his drink. When he notices me, his eyes rake over my body, lingering a little too long on my chest, and then he gives me a lopsided grin. I do my best to ignore him, but it's hard when I can feel the heat of his stare.

"Next!" the girl behind the counter yells out as she hands Mr. Suit Man his coffee.

I step up to the counter. "I'll have a large iced coffee, please."

The girl pushes a couple of buttons on the register. "That's four sixty-eight."

I reach into my back pocket to grab a few dollars, but before I have a chance to pay, the stranger watching me swoops in and attempts to hand the girl a five-dollar bill. "It's on me."

I pull out my own money. "No, thanks."

That does nothing to deter him because he keeps his money out. "I insist."

My lips pull into a tight line. "I don't mean to be rude, but I don't want you to buy my coffee."

He smirks, and he turns toward the girl. She now looks completely confused on whom she should take the money from.

"Would you tell the beautiful lady to allow me the honor of buying her a drink?"

The dark-haired barista rolls her eyes at him, and when she turns her attention back to me, she takes my money.

"Thank you," I say to her.

I stand there, waiting for my drink. For some reason, a blunt no-thank-you didn't seem to work on the persistent business-man, as he is still standing next to me, but I do my best to pretend he's not there.

"I'm sorry. I think we got off on the wrong foot. I'm—"

"Leaving," Xavier's voice cuts the man off mid sentence.

As he takes in my tall, broad-shouldered boyfriend, the man's expression morphs from surprise to determination. His eyes narrow. "Excuse me?"

It's clear this man isn't used to being told no, and by antagonizing Xavier, it's also clear that he has a death wish.

Xavier rolls his neck and glares down at him with a stare so intense that it's downright scary. "Do you have a fucking hearing problem? I told you to beat it."

The man squares his shoulders. "I'll leave when I'm good and ready."

With a sharp tug, Xavier pulls me behind him. He has at least four inches and about sixty pounds on Mr. Suit Man.

Xavier's fingers flex into fists at his sides. "That's where you're wrong, motherfucker. You'll leave when I fucking say you will."

Flashbacks of what happened with Rex hit me hard. I will not allow Xavier to get into a fight in the goddamn airport because a guy hit on me.

I grab Xavier's wrist. "No. Don't be crazy."

Xavier jerks his gaze to me, and his thick eyebrows knit in confusion. "No?"

"No," I say again.

I stare into his eyes as I cling to him, remaining coolheaded in order to defuse this situation. The last thing we need is for Xavier to end up in handcuffs again for killing a man while defending me. Tension wouldn't be able to make this one go away because this guy isn't on their payroll.

Xavier swallows hard as the intense connection we always feel toward one another flows between us.

"Don't do something that could separate us again," I plead.

His jaw muscle flexes as he blows a rush of air out of his nose, attempting to calm himself.

Xavier directs his attention back to Mr. Suit Man. "You're lucky my girl here is a saint because I'm allowing you to walk away right now."

The man's face twists with disgust. "*Allowing* me? Do you know who I am?"

"No, and I don't give a fuck either."

The man opens his mouth again to fire off another snide

remark.

I can see in Xavier's eyes that his cool won't last long, so this time, I cut the guy off, "Mister, if I were you, I would leave while I could. He just got out of prison for nearly beating a man to death."

All the color drains from the man's face. He doesn't say another word. He simply heeds my warning and walks away.

Xavier never takes his eyes off his retreating opponent. "Fucking pussy."

I let out an exasperated sigh as I grab my bag Xavier wheeled over from the carousel and walk away from him.

"What?" Xavier calls from behind me as he gathers up the other bags and starts after me. "Are you pissed at me?"

"No—yes—I don't know. Don't you see the problem with what just happened?"

He releases one of the roller bags and grabs my wrist, halting me in place. "Hold up. I did that for you."

"No, Xavier, you did that for *you*. I was perfectly capable of fending off the guy's flirtatious behavior, and if all else failed, I would have walked away."

"I *did* walk away because you'd asked me, too."

"I shouldn't have to ask you to do that. There should've never been a confrontation to begin with. You need to trust me and stop fighting all my battles for me. I don't need you permanently ruining your career over me. If you threw everything away for me, that would kill me. You were damn lucky to get out of hurting Rex with only a suspension." Heat rises in my face, and I know my face is red.

"You think I give a shit about all that? You're what's important to me."

"Don't say that because you know it isn't true. You'd care if wrestling were no longer an option for you."

"It is true. I told Mr. Silverman I would quit if they tried to take you away from me, and I meant that."

I pinch the bridge of my nose. "And then I would feel guilty that you left Tension. Living with that kind of guilt would make a relationship between us impossible. You'd resent me."

The thought of not being with him crushes me, but I know myself. I could never get over being responsible for ending his career.

His eyes soften. "Don't ever talk like that. I can't lose you."

I close the distance between us and lay my hand on his chest. "Then, figure out how to control all that rage inside you before it destroys us both."

He wraps his fingers around my wrist as my hand rests over his heart. "I'm trying."

"I know," I whisper. I push up on my tiptoes and press my lips to his. "No more fighting. Let's go find our ride."

The first thing I spot when we step out into the summer heat is Quinn leaning against her silver Honda. Her lips curve into a smile as soon as her eyes land on us.

She throws her hands up and waves them like crazy as she dashes in our direction. She throws her arms around me. "Oh my God, I've missed you, cuz. I've got loads to tell you."

I laugh as her dark hair tickles my nose. "It's so good to see you."

"You want to pop your trunk, Quinn?" Xavier asks from behind me.

Quinn pulls back and then fishes her keys from the front pocket of her jean shorts. "Sorry about that. Almost forgot you were back there, X." She hits the unlock button on her key fob and then walks over to lift the trunk lid. "We should probably get you out of here before you get recognized."

Xavier chuckles as he loads our luggage into the car. "That would be ideal."

Quinn extends her left hand to me, and I immediately notice a little bling coming from her ring finger.

I grab her hand for a closer inspection. "Wow! Brock did an

excellent job. I love it."

She stares down at the diamond solitaire on her ring and smiles. "I do, too. I love that man so much."

"I'm so happy for you."

"Thanks, Anna." She grins. "I want you to be my maid of honor."

"Really?" I squeal. "I would love that!"

We instantly launch into another hug. This time, we are both squeeing. I am so incredibly happy for Quinn and Brock. Their relationship has been somewhat of a mystery to me, but they both seem committed to taking their relationship to the next level. It's plain to see that they have a lot of love for one another.

Once everything is loaded, I slip into the backseat of the car, giving Xavier the front because his legs are so much longer than mine. Quinn starts the ignition and then steers away from the curb to get us out of the passenger pickup area.

No one in the car says a word for the first few minutes of the ride. That's unlike my cousin. I'm surprised she hasn't fired off a million questions yet.

Quinn clears her throat. "Okay. I've tried to hold back from asking this question, but if I don't, I'm going to burst."

And there's the Quinn I know and love.

I'm almost afraid to hear what she's going to ask.

"Are you taking care of my cousin, X? I haven't heard from her in a couple of days, and then I get a text from her, saying to pick you guys up from the airport. What's the deal? I didn't think you guys would be back in Detroit for a while. Are you in trouble over that wrestler you beat up in the ring? Tons of rumors have been floating around the Internet, all mentioning the fight got out of hand and turned real."

"Quinn!" I scold her for being so damn nosy, but I know it's in her nature to pry. With her inquiring mind, she's like the epitome of a gossip magazine.

I'm not even sure if Xavier is allowed to talk about what actually happened, not that I think Quinn would run off and reveal the truth about the situation to anyone. Tension has done a lot to get this incident swept under the rug, so I don't want Xavier to say anything that might jeopardize that.

Quinn glances at me through her rearview mirror. "What? Can I not ask that? I just want to make sure that you're safe with him, Anna. You're my cousin, and it's my responsibility to look out for you since you're new to this whole living-on-your-own thing."

I smile and place my hand on her shoulder. "Rest assured, he's taking good care of me."

In the rearview mirror, I spot her eyes stealing a quick glance at Xavier before turning back to the road.

"That's good to hear. I would hate to be forced to figure out a way to kick the big guy's ass," she says.

Xavier turns his head, and a playful smile lights up his side profile. "Threats of violence? Really?"

Quinn shrugs. "We Cortez women stick together. If you fuck with one of us, you'd better be prepared to have your eyes clawed out because we work in packs."

This earns her a full-on deep rumble of a laugh from him. "Remind me never to piss either one of you off then. I'm partial to my eyesight since these eyes allow me to view Anna's beautiful body."

"Aw," Quinn gushes. "That's so sweet, but you are completely avoiding my question."

I bite my tongue to keep myself from saying anything. It's not my place to tell Xavier's business, so I sit back and give him time to address her.

"It's like this, Quinn," Xavier starts. "I'm so damn good at my job that everyone who watched my last live match is now convinced that I actually hurt Assassin."

"But you didn't?" she questions as she turns onto the

freeway.

Xavier shakes his head. "No. He was hurt because I hit him a little too hard, but what happened in the ring had all been planned out, and it was a part of the show. I was just an idiot who's strength hurt someone."

She's quiet. At first, I don't think she buys his story, but then she nods with a thoughtful expression on her face.

"That seems plausible. It looked real though. Hell, even I bought into it because I know that you've had some beef with him in the past."

"How do you know that?" he asks, clearly intrigued at how Quinn has that information.

I know he's probably thinking that I told her about the Rex situation, but I didn't. Quinn was always too worried about my sexual relationship with Xavier for me to even discuss his workplace drama with her.

She shrugs. "The Internet. I'll admit that I proficiently stalked you before I granted you the okay to spend a lot of time with Anna."

Xavier turns his head toward my cousin, and a smirk crosses his face. "I'm glad you're looking out for her. It's good to know that Anna's safety is a priority for us both."

I smile, thinking about how two of my favorite people in the world want to protect me. It's nice to know that they love me that much.

We make small talk as Xavier directs Quinn off the freeway and through all the streets leading us to Nettie's diner. We turn the last corner, and the restaurant comes into view. It's standing just the same as we left it a few weeks ago with its white brick exterior and the blue sign hanging over the entrance that simply reads, *Diner*. This is Xavier's comfort spot, the place that feels like home to him, which is why he leaves his motorcycle parked in the shed at the back of the building.

Nettie and Carl are two people he trusts. They are more like parents to him than friends.

Quinn parks in the diner parking lot. "I'll wait here and then follow you to where you are staying to drop off your luggage."

"Sounds good," Xavier tells her before he opens the car door.

His lean frame towers over the vehicle as he steps outside. He folds the passenger seat forward, extends his hand to me, and helps me get out of Quinn's two-door coupe.

"We to get the key to the house." His strong arm snakes around my shoulders as he leads me inside. "We need to at least go inside and make sure that Nettie knows we'll be in town for a while."

I laugh. "You'd better, or Nettie might give you that spanking she threatened you with the past couple of times she saw you."

The corner of his mouth turns up into a grin. "She's been threatening me with that for years, and she's yet to make good on it."

"She might just surprise you one day."

He gazes down at me with what can only be described as a you-can't-be-serious-right-now expression. "I'm pretty sure I can take her if she comes at me."

"I don't know," I say in a singsong voice. "According to Carl, he can take you. If you mess with Nettie, he might just step in."

Xavier throws his head back and laughs as he pushes open the door to the diner. "I'd like to see him try."

The sound of his laugh catches Nettie's attention, and her face lights up when her eyes land on Xavier. She races out from behind the counter and bear-hugs him. His impressive arms make Nettie appear so tiny as he squeezes her against his chest in a loving embrace.

It's sweet how she treats him like a son. I'm glad that he's had Nettie and Carl looking out for him all these years.

Nettie pulls back, but she's still holding Xavier in front of her by gripping his arms. "You're back already? Not that I'm complaining. You know I always love to see you. I'm surprised because I didn't expect to see you again for a while since your vacation just ended." Her gaze flicks over to me, and her grin widens when she notices me standing next to Xavier. "Anna, honey, it's good to see you, too."

I grin. "How have you been, Nettie?"

"Oh, can't complain too much, sugar. Business has picked up a little, so Carl and I have been busy, which is great. We could use our busboy back to help out around here." Nettie winks at Xavier.

"The way things have been going, Nettie, I might take you up on that offer."

She tilts her head and studies his face. Xavier sighs under the weight of her stare.

He and Nettie have such a connection that she's able to read the hesitation on his face, and she instantly knows that something is wrong.

Nettie clucks her tongue. "I know that expression. You going to tell me what's wrong, or am I gonna have to pry it out of ya?"

"It's work," he admits. "I fucked up, Nettie."

Her face softens. "Well, we all do from time to time, honey. Come on in here and let me fix you something to eat while you tell me all about it."

"No, Nettie. We really can't—"

"Of course you can," she completely cuts off Xavier's attempt to explain that Quinn's waiting out front for us.

She jerks her head toward the cooking area on the other side of the counter so fast that her braids whip around her face. "Carl, get your butt out here."

"Hold your damn horses, woman. I'm coming," Carl calls from the other side of the door that leads back into what I've learned is the stockroom / office / break room.

The gray-headed cook swings open the heavy wooden door that separates the front of the restaurant from the back. Carl's eyes light up as soon as he spots us. "What up, X? You back already? Did you get canned over that match going south the other night? I saw that on TV. Man, you really fu—"

"Hush, Carl. Don't be jumping to conclusions like that. He's done told us over and over that everything is scripted. None of them boys really fight."

"Actually, Nettie, Carl's right," Xavier admits. "I got suspended for losing my shit and attacking Rex in the ring."

Nettie's mouth gapes open while Carl shouts, "Told ya!" behind her.

"What?" She's shocked by the news. "I thought you was done with all that fighting bullshit when you turned legit. You know the trouble that comes with laying your hands on another man. You should know better."

"I know. The guy has been giving me shit for months, and I let it all go, but he crossed the line when he started fucking with Anna. I wasn't going to allow him to hurt her or take her away from me."

It stings, hearing him admit out loud that I'm the reason he lost his head in the ring, and it's all the more reason I need to do everything I can to get him reinstated as quickly as possible. I won't be able to live with myself, knowing I ruined his career.

Nettie's gaze drifts over to me for a split second before returning to Xavier. There was uneasiness in her expression that makes me wonder what she's so worried about. "So, the two of you will be in town for a while?"

He nods. "Yeah, and that's why I'm here. I need my bike. Anna's cousin picked us up from the airport and is waiting out front. She's going to follow us over to my house on Sycamore to drop off our luggage."

Nettie's mouth drops open. "You're going to stay on the Block? You sure you want to go down there?"

"I don't have any other option. Tension is fining me a hundred fifty thousand dollars. I have to pay in order to keep my ass out of jail."

"You have to pay that man? I wouldn't do that. That's too much damn money."

"I have to. Giving that asshole money to go along with the explanation Tension created about the situation is far better than sitting in some cell or serving community service. If I don't pay him, he won't go along with the story that me beating his ass was a stunt gone too far."

"So, you're going to stay in your grandmother's house? Are you sure you can handle that? You couldn't even handle coming to her funeral when she passed away last year. How are you going to deal with living in a place surrounded by her things and all the memories they hold?"

It's the first bit of information that I've learned about the house Xavier owns. It's obvious that something about his grandmother strikes a nerve with him, which explains why he never wants to discuss the house that's in his name.

"Paying all this money plus getting no pay during the suspension will nearly break my bank account. I won't have the extra money to live in a hotel. There's no other option."

Nettie's lips roll down into a frown. "If staying at that house overwhelms you, come back and stay in your old bed in the stockroom."

Xavier gives her a small smile. "Thanks, but I don't think both of us will fit on a twin mattress in a broom closet."

"You come to us if you need *anything*." Nettie reaches over and takes my hand. Her smooth brown skin is warm as it connects with mine. "That goes for you, too, Anna. Things get out of control, you let me and Carl know."

"I will. Thank you," I tell her.

Nettie pulls back and sighs. "Be careful down there, Xavier. Things have changed a lot. Bishop's running things around the

Block now, and when word gets back to him that you're staying down there, he's going to come looking for you. I don't want to hear one peep about you getting mixed up with him again."

"Don't worry. I've learned my lesson on messing around with those guys. I don't plan on going back to that life anytime soon."

She slightly narrows one eye. "Better not. You've pulled yourself out of that gutter, and if you mess around and get tangled up with Bishop, old Nettie here is going to whip your butt."

"Trust me, Nettie. As soon as this suspension is lifted in three months, I'm out of there, and you can go back to checking on the house while I'm gone."

That answer seems to satisfy her. She lifts her hand and pats his cheek. "Don't be strangers while you two are in town. Come in and eat whenever you want—on us."

He lays his hand on top of hers while it rests on his face. "Thank you."

Nettie takes in a long breath. "Let me go grab your keys from the office. I'll be right back."

Xavier reaches down and threads his fingers through mine. It sounds like going back to his old stomping grounds is going to be rough for Xavier. I'm not exactly sure who this Bishop person is, but from the worried expression on Nettie's face when she was warning Xavier to stay away from him, I'd say he's bad news.

Chapter
FIVE

Xavier

THE RUMBLE OF MY BIKE'S engine echoes off the tightly knit houses in the run-down neighborhood that I once called home. Everything is just how I remembered it, except most of the tiny two-story houses now have boarded up windows. I never thought I would be back on this street—never wanted to either—but here I am, moving back into the one house I swore I would never set foot in again.

If it weren't for my mother making me promise her to always be here at this house so that she could find me, I would not have bought the shithole my grandmother had owned. I felt obligated to buy it when the church she'd left it to put it up for sale. I never had any intention of living in the place that's the center of most of my nightmares, but it's where I figured Mom would find her way back to if she were an angel. Mom always came back here when she was fucked up on drugs. It was like she could find it even if she were out of her mind.

Every time I think about my mother, my mind always wonders about how things would've been different for me if she weren't an addict. When I was young, I knew I wasn't like the other kids at school. In my neighborhood, having a junkie as a parent was common, but most didn't have to contend with a lunatic grandmother who was hell-bent on beating the demon out of them.

My bike bounces a bit when I turn into the driveway. The concrete is cracked and riddled with holes from years of neglect. If it weren't for Nettie and Carl maintaining the place, I'm sure the rest of the place would be in bad shape, too.

I stare up at the brown house, and I zero in on the rusted wrought iron railing caging in the front porch like a prison. Quinn's Honda parks directly behind me, and the girls get out of the car.

Quinn shields her eyes from the evening sun as she tilts her head up to examine the house. "You sure the two of you will be safe staying here? The neighborhood isn't known to be a beacon of safety. Every shooting on the local news comes from this part of town."

"He was raised here, Quinn. I'm sure Xavier wouldn't bring us here if he thought we'd run into trouble."

Anna's sweet for saying that, but she's aware this isn't the safest place after the conversation we had with Nettie earlier.

I think the pep-talk is more to ease Quinn's mind than her trying to get me to admit how horrible this place is.

Quinn turns to Anna, and her lips pull into a frown. "I don't like the idea of you being down here. This place is the epitome of concrete jungle. The whole kill-or-be-killed mentality is very real in this neighborhood. It just doesn't feel right, leaving you somewhere like this."

Anna places her hand on Quinn's forearm in an attempt to reassure her again. "Please, don't worry. Xavier will be here with me. He'll protect me."

Warmth spreads through my chest as confidence rings in her voice.

I place my hand over my heart. "I'll guard her with my life."

"You'd better," Quinn says. "I know where you live now."

"This isn't exactly home," I reply coolly as my eyes narrow at the house in front of me.

Quinn glances over at Anna and raises her eyebrows. It's clear that she wants to know the story about me and this house, but Anna doesn't say a word. She just simply shakes her head.

"Okay then, maybe we should get your bags unloaded." Quinn walks around to the back of the Honda.

After gathering Anna's and my luggage, I head for the front door to face the demons of my past.

Chapter
SIX

Anna

XAVIER SETS THE BAGS DOWN and then fishes a set of keys from the pocket of his jeans.

My breath actually catches when he twists the knob and pushes open the front door. I don't know what I'm about to walk into, but the tension floating in the air is so thick that I can feel it pushing down on my shoulders.

From what I can tell, Xavier is dreading going inside.

When Quinn steps up onto the porch, Xavier turns his head in her direction. "Thanks for the ride and for bringing our bags, but I think we've got it from here."

Xavier turns to head inside, leaving Quinn and me alone on the front porch. The second he's out of sight, Quinn grabs my arm and drags me back down the steps toward her car.

"What are you doing?" I question.

"I don't like this. He's being weird, and this house . . . it's *scary*, Anna. The neighborhood isn't exactly the kind of place you want to be when it gets dark. I think you need to leave him here, and you come and stay at my place. We can share my room, and if you need something to take your mind off of X, you can help me and Brock with the wedding."

I pull back, halting Quinn in her tracks and she releases me. "I'm not leaving him, Quinn. He needs me."

Her lips pull into a tight line as she studies my face. "Are you sure? It feels wrong to leave you here."

"I've never been more certain about anything in my life," I honestly tell her.

That earns me a small smile from her. "You love him."

It's not a question but a statement. I should've known that Quinn would be able to figure out how deeply I care for Xavier before I even had a chance to tell her. She's excellent at reading me.

"I do," I admit. "I love him so much that it scares me—like, it's hard to breathe when I think about not being with him."

"Damn, cuz. You've got it bad. I understand though. We Cortez women tend to do crazy, irrational things when it comes to the men we love, so I know there's no dragging you away from this place, no matter how much I don't want you to be here."

I nod. "Thank you for understanding. I promise, I'll be safe."

She reaches out and grabs my hand, giving it a little squeeze. "I meant what I said earlier. Things get rough, you call me. I don't want you over here, stressed or in a dangerous situation."

I curl my fingers around hers. "I will."

She quickly wraps her arms around me and then whispers in my ear, "Love you."

"Love you, too."

Quinn pulls back and gives me a small smile before turning on her heel and walking to her car. I wait until she's buckled up inside and cranks the engine to life before I swallow hard and make my way back up to the front door to find out what is awaiting me on the other side.

I take a hesitant step inside and allow my eyes to adjust to the dim room. The curtains in the living room are drawn tight, and the only light entering the room comes from the open door. There's a steep staircase leading to the second floor in front of me, and the rest of the living room is set off to the left. The furniture is dated but appears to be in pristine condition un-der the plastic covers. A round woven rug covers the hardwood floor that appears to run into the dining room attached to the living room. Our luggage is sitting on top of the rug in the cen-ter of the living room, and there's no sign of Xavier anywhere.

I close the door behind me and begin to explore. On the wall are several pictures of a rather pristine lady wearing a wide-brimmed hat. She reminds me a lot of the upper-class women who attend horse races. In most of the pictures, the woman is with a dark-haired beauty with soulful brown eyes. When I look at this woman, there's no mistaking the resemblance to Xavier, which probably means this is the mother he lost when he was only eight years old.

"You hungry?" Xavier's voice cuts through the otherwise si-lent room. "We could go out and eat since we don't have any food here yet."

"I'm not hungry just yet." I continue to study the pictures on the wall, and my curiosity needs confirmation to what it al-ready knows. "Is this your mother?"

Xavier blows a rush of air out of his nose before walking over to where I'm standing. He stares at the pictures, and in-stead of answering my question, he moves in to take the frames off the wall. "I forgot all these were up here. I should've had Nettie take them down a long time ago."

I wrap my fingers around his wrist as he reaches for the next picture. "You don't want to leave them?"

"No," he replies instantly. "I don't like to be reminded of the past."

Since I've known Xavier, all I've done is push him to talk about his past even though he's warned me over and over again that the topic of his family was off-limits, so I'm curious to find out more about them.

I watch as Xavier pulls all the pictures off the wall, one by one, before tucking away the memories that haunt him into a storage closet not far from the front door.

Once he's satisfied that all the pictures are gone, he turns and surveys the room. "I don't like looking at her."

I'm not sure who he means, but I'm trying not to get him aggravated by asking too many questions.

He lets out a long sigh, like he doesn't know what to do with himself in this space. It's clear that being here is a struggle for him. I'm beginning to have my doubts about talking him into facing his past. It might not be such a good idea.

Lord knows I do my best to keep from facing my past. Last I spoke with my father, he was angry, and I pissed him off even further when I told him I was staying with Xavier. As far as I know, I'm still not welcomed at home, and since the day Father showed up in Atlanta, I've not heard a peep from anyone in Portland.

I'd shocked them all by running away the way I did, but I couldn't see another way out of the situation with my controlling family. I hadn't wanted the life they had planned for me, and the only way to stop that from happening to me was by breaking free.

And, man, did I ever get freedom.

My eyes have been opened to the cruel realities that others, like Xavier, have faced. His life is, by far, worse than mine, but I respect the hell out of him for finding his own way and making something out of himself on his own terms.

I slide my arms around his waist and snuggle up against him. I'm not sure what's going on in that head of his, but I want him to know that I'm here, and he can count on me.

Chapter
SEVEN

Xavier

IT'S HARDER THAN I THOUGHT, walking back into this house. Everywhere I look, I'm reminded of something horrible that happened. If anything good ever happened, I sure as hell don't remember it.

When I look at the couch, I picture Mom lying there, strung out, after returning from a bender. That image in my head leads me back to the moments that make up my nightmares.

If I didn't love Anna so damn much and have this over-whelming desire to protect her and see to her every need, I would've rather lived on the street again before coming back here. But that life—the hardness of it—isn't for Anna. She's much too pure for that, and I'll be damned if I'm the man who taints her light.

She clings to me, not saying a word and not pushing me for more information about the house. I appreciate that.

I'm not ready to spill all my secrets to her. God knows, it was hard enough, telling her about the death of my mother. There's no way I want Anna to know that the woman in those pictures, the one with the seemingly sweet face, is at the very center of all the things that haunt me.

Nettie is the only person on this earth whom I've ever told about the beatings I received at the hands of my grandmother, and that wasn't by choice. She figured it out when she tried to wake me up from one of my nightmares, and I took a swing at her. I didn't make contact—thank God—but it scared her. I could see it in her eyes. It made her question taking in a kid off the streets. Desperate to stay with her and Carl, I confessed everything about my life. She didn't like what she heard, and she begged me to turn my grandmother in, but I knew that wouldn't do any good. To the community, my grandmother was a saint. She gave to every charity, smiled all the time, and was loyal to her church. No one would've ever believed me. They would've taken one look at the raggedy street kid in front of them and accused me of lying. That wasn't something I wanted to deal with. After that night, Nettie never brought up my past again, and it bonded us together. She never had any kids of her own, and I suppose I was the next best thing.

I have to get out of this house. I've been here for only a few short minutes, and I already have the desire to run out of here as quickly as I can.

"Ready?" I ask Anna.

She nods. "Let's go."

Once we're on the bike, relief floods through me. I'm grateful to be out of that fucking house. The bike rumbles to a stop, Anna peels her body off me and hops off. I balance its weight between my thighs as I grin and reach over to unfasten the buckle beneath her chin. My fingertips lightly trace her skin, causing her to instantly blush. I love the way the slightest touch from me affects her. It's nice to constantly have confirmation that I can turn her on so quickly with such a simple move.

She pulls the helmet off her head and hands it to me. I throw the kickstand down and then set the helmet on the handlebar before I swing my leg over the bike to get off.

When I turn around, I catch Anna staring at my ass, and it causes me to chuckle. She jerks her eyes away, embarrassed that I caught her looking.

One corner of my mouth pulls into a lopsided grin. "See something you like?"

The blush on her cheeks deepens, and she shrugs sheepishly. "I can't help it. Your body . . . it's pretty fantastic."

I tuck two fingers into the waistband of her jeans and pull her against me. I gaze down at her pouty pink mouth, and all that crosses my mind is the thought of kissing her. "You keep saying things like that to me, beautiful, and I'll toss you back onto this bike and take you right here in this parking lot."

Her eyes widen, and her mouth falls agape. "You wouldn't."

I slide my bottom lip between my teeth as I contemplate carrying through on my threat. "You're right, but that's only because the thought of any other man seeing you naked drives me out of my fucking mind."

"You don't have to worry about that because this belongs only to you."

"Mmm . . . I like it when you say that," I admit.

"What?" She blinks slowly as she gazes up at me.

"You saying that you're mine."

"I'll always be yours."

When I hear those words willingly come out of her mouth, my heart does a double thump. I didn't have to bring her to the edge of orgasm and force her to admit she was mine seconds before I made her come.

My cock jerks in my jeans, and if we don't change this conversation, I'll throw her sweet little ass back on this bike and find a place where we can be alone.

I sigh and then reach down and grab her hand, pulling my brain out of the sex daze it entered. "Food. We came here for food."

"Right." She giggles. "I nearly forgot."

I lead her into the diner. Nettie is busy wiping down the counter, and Carl is throwing food around on the grill.

Nettie glances up at me and smiles. "I'll be right there,

sugar."

"Take your time," I call to her as I guide Anna to my favorite corner booth. "Hey, Carl," I toss over my shoulder before I slide into the booth.

"What up, X?" he replies as he flips a steaks onto a plate.

Anna slips into the booth, and then I slide in across from her. I study her face as she reads over the menu. Her dark hair is down and a little wild from the ride here, but she looks as beautiful as ever. Her green eyes move around from one page to the next as she reads. Those eyes of hers are the first things that caught my attention on the plane. They stand out so much against her tan complexion that it's impossible not to notice them. When she looks at you with them, you know how sincere she is. You can read it in her eyes.

"I think I'm going to have—" Her eyes flick to mine, and she pauses. "Why are you looking at me like that?"

"How am I looking at you?" Is it possible to tell that I'm thinking about her by the expression on my face? I'm typically pretty damn good at hiding my emotions.

"I don't know," she says. "You look like you're lost in thought."

I stretch my hand across the table and take her hand in mine. "I'm glad you're here."

That makes her smile and seems to appease her curious mind.

It doesn't take long for Nettie to make it over to our table. She focuses on me when she asks, "Did you get settled in?"

The real question she wants to ask is, *Were you able to handle going back into that house?*

I kept my shit together when we were there, mostly to make Anna feel safe. There was no way in hell I wanted to peel back the curtain on my whole fucked-up psyche in front of her.

Her seeing my nightmare freak-outs is bad enough.

I don't deserve a good girl like Anna to stick by my side, but

I'm glad she's here, and I plan on keeping her forever.

I lean back and throw my arm over the top of the booth. "We did. Things are going to be fine."

I hope my actions are enough to reassure Nettie so that she won't worry, but I can tell by the pointed look she's giving me that understands it was harder for me than I led on.

She sighs and then moves to change the subject because she knows me well enough to expect that I'm not going to elaborate any further on the situation. "You still on that protein diet, honey?"

"No. Seeing as how I don't even have a gym to work out at right now, my training is on hold until I can get back to it."

"So, you gonna have a cheat meal then? Your favorite?"

I lift one shoulder in a noncommittal shrug. "Sure. Why not?"

"Carl!" Nettie yells over her shoulder. "Pancakes for our boy."

"Damn it, woman. Can't you write the stuff down and then come over and give me the letter about what to cook?" Carl complains as he works at pouring out batter onto the griddle in the kitchen that's visible to all the customers.

"You know it works better when I tell you what to cook as we go," Nettie fires back. Then, she quickly repeats the same scenario with Anna's order. "You know, Xavier, Cole took over his daddy's gym. You ought to go check it out. He'd be glad to see you."

Damn. I've only been here a few hours, and already, Nettie has dragged me down memory lane more today than she has in the past few years.

Cole Parker is one person from the old neighborhood I wouldn't mind seeing. We were tight back in the day because we'd broken out of the street life at the same time. It bonded us because we'd pissed off the crew that ran The Block.

Nettie and Carl had made it clear that if I wanted to stay

here with them, I was to have nothing to do with the people I used to hang with. And Cole—well, his father was in his life, and when he'd gotten word that Cole was getting mixed up with the wrong crowd, he'd intervened.

It's good to hear that he's doing all right for himself.

"Thanks for the heads-up, Nettie. I'll check it out."

The sound of Anna's cell ringing catches my attention. She fishes it from her back pocket, and her eyes widen as she glances down at the caller ID. Her hand flips the phone around for me to see the words *Tension Writers* illuminate the screen.

"Should I answer it?" she asks in a voice that's only a few octaves above a whisper.

More than anything, I want her to answer that phone and tell whoever is on the other end of the line to fuck off and that she's not coming back to the show without me, but we both know that wouldn't be a wise move.

"Answer it," I advise her. "There's no way around talking to them."

She sighs and then hits the green phone button on the screen. "Hello?" There's a pause as she listens to person talking. "Okay. I understand that, but—well, no, but—"

I curl my fingers and then flex them back out, trying to stop myself from making fists and pounding on the table. Whoever is speaking to her is being rude as fuck. They keep interrupting her, and it's pissing me off. They have about two seconds to change their attitude with Anna, or I will jerk that phone away and make the person on the end of that line wish they'd never rung her number.

Nettie must see the aggression on my face because she places her hand on my shoulder. She leans down next to me and speaks only loud enough for me to hear, "Calm down, baby. Let your girl handle this. She's smart. She'll make the right move."

Her words sink into my brain, and I and take a deep breath.

"Trust her. She's a good one." Nettie kisses my cheek before rushing over to Carl.

Nettie gets me. She can tell when I'm about to lose my shit. Then again, she's had years of practice with me, learning the signs.

"All right. I understand. No, it won't be a problem. Yes, I'll be there." Anna pulls the phone away from her ear and stares at the screen. She blinks a couple of times and then lays it down in the center of the table. She flicks her gaze up to mine. "It seems I was supposed to be at the show tonight."

My lip curls of its own accord as I find myself fucking appalled that they wouldn't even give her a few days with me to get shit sorted out before they expected her to be back at work. "That's horse shit. If they wanted you there, they should've made that call on Tuesday and put it on your schedule."

Her pink lips pull into a tight line. "I didn't really have a schedule, remember? I just officially became a part of the show when I stood beside you for that match. They probably figured that I would be there with you tonight."

"Just because you're with me doesn't give them an excuse not to tell you if you are expected to be at a show. I was given my schedule long before I was sent on vacation to Detroit. It required me to be at every show Tension put on."

She frowns. "According to the head writer of the show, Vicky, I'm to attend every show for the next month—every Thursday, Saturday, Sunday and Tuesday show."

A rush of air forces its way out of my nose as I scrub my hand down my face. "Fucking Rex. This has his name written all over it. He's fucking Vicky, so she's his puppet. He's doing this to fuck with me."

"Don't let it." Anna grabs my hand that's resting on the table. "Don't give him that power over you by losing your cool. He knew, if he pushed your buttons enough, then you'd go berserk on him and ruin your shot at being champion. He got exactly what he'd wanted, so don't help him out any further by losing your head over this. You can trust me, Xavier. No matter what Rex does or says, you will never have to worry. You have my heart, and nothing will ever change that."

"Promise?" I know it makes me look like a pussy, needing to hear her say that, but I've been through so much. I wouldn't be able to handle ever losing her.

She sets her eyes on mine. "I swear on my life."

The honesty and goodness shines in her eyes, and I believe she means what she says. I relax a little, but the tension is still rolling through my muscles.

I glance down at my watch and notice it's nearly time for Thursday Tension to come on, and I wonder what the writers have planned for tonight's show.

I glance over at Nettie, who is stacking clean glasses behind the counter. "Would you mind turning on Tension?"

"Sure thing," Nettie answers as she grabs the remote from under the counter and flips the channel.

A few minutes later, the unmistakable promo music for Tension begins to play, and the familiar clips of me and some of the other guys who work for the company appear on the screen. It's a wonder that they haven't yanked me from being one of the faces on their trailers, seeing as how I've been giving them problems for quite a while now.

My back straightens a bit when Mr. Silverman's music blasts through the speakers. The camera zooms in on him as he steps through the black curtain and onto the metal grating ramp leading down to the ring. His thin lips rest in an emotionless line, and his gray eyes appear hard and focused beneath his neatly trimmed silver eyebrows and hair.

Fuck.

This can't be good.

"Does he make appearances often?" Anna asks.

I can't force my eyes off the screen. "No, hardly ever. He rarely shows his face, even backstage. Typically, the only time he comes out is to fire or promote someone."

"Oh," she says, the surprise in her voice apparent.

I know that quick-witted brain of hers has a list of questions.

"Are you saying that we've been seeing him more than most of the other athletes?" she asks.

I nod. "I've seen him more the past couple of weeks than I have my entire career. I've been making a lot of waves, so I'm sure he felt compelled to check out the situations for himself."

The crowd screaming and booing as Mr. Silverman pulls the microphone to his lips draws my attention back to the screen.

"I'm sure many of you are wondering why I'm here tonight," he says.

I sure as hell am.

"I'm here to dispel some of the rumors I saw floating around social media after Tuesday's show. I felt they needed to be addressed in order to end all the secondhand gossip. What you saw occur in this very ring earlier this week was in fact real. Phenomenal X did lose his head and beat Assassin mercilessly in front of a live television audience of millions of people. X was carted out of here in handcuffs, but Assassin refused to press charges."

The crowd murmurs with confusion as he allows them to digest what he just said.

It doesn't surprise me one bit that they are taking the truth of the situation and spinning it in a way that works with a storyline. It's how things are done in Tension. They often use things that happen in our real lives to create stories for our characters in the ring, which is why it's in each athlete's best interests to keep their personal life on lockdown. Allowing a devious writer like Vicky to know any of your secrets is definitely a bad move.

Take my relationship with Anna, for instance. Vicky and Rex used it against me, and from what I've gathered, they are far from finished.

"Now, I know a lot of you are asking yourselves, *What does that mean for Phenomenal X?*" his voice cuts back through the diner. "I've suspended him for three months."

The boos for my suspension are loud and clear.

"That means, until his suspension is lifted, X will not be eligible to compete in any fashion for the world heavyweight title. For the next three months, he's not even allowed to be in the same city as Tension. I gave him strict orders to stay away while Assassin heals." He looks around the arena and then faces the camera head-on. "To make up for the tragic accident that nearly ended Assassin's career, when he's ready, Assassin will be guaranteed a shot at the title."

My nostrils flare, and I know that this wouldn't even be up for discussion right now if I didn't hand Rex this opportunity on a silver platter.

"When X returns, as long as he remains in good standing with the company and learns to control himself, he will be granted a title rematch shot with whoever currently holds the title—whether that be with Brian Razor Rollins or Assassin."

The crowd erupts with cheers, and it's clear to anyone watching that they're still backing me. I was fully prepared for the fans to turn on me after what I had done. It would've served me right, but that isn't what's happening.

"Assassin is expected to be back in the ring soon. He's suffered a broken nose and a few cracked ribs, but it could've been much, much worse had it not been for the quick reaction of Tension's security team, other wrestlers, and, of course, the esteemed Atlanta Police force who were on hand." He pauses for a moment. "Now, without further ado, I give you Thursday night Tension!"

Hard rock music plays, and I know that's all the information I'm going to get.

With both Rex and me out of the picture, it puzzles me why Vicky wanted Anna to be there tonight. The only storyline with her character would involve either Rex or me, and seeing as how he'll be out for a while, there was no need for Anna to show up.

They just wanted her there to fuck with me. I know it.

"Damn that Rex," I mumble as the show begins to play.

I'm not sure if I'm going to be able to handle her on the road without me. She hasn't even left yet, and I'm already driving myself crazy about it.

Anna sighs across from me, dragging my attention back to her.

"Something wrong, beautiful?"

The way she's chewing on the corner of her lower lip is a telltale sign that she's nervous. Whatever is on her mind, she's scared to talk to me about it, which has my brain running wild with possibilities.

"Um . . ." She swallows hard, and her lips pull into a tight line. "There was one more thing Vicky told me when she called."

"What was that?"

Anna twists her lips. "They want to start that love-triangle story between me and Rex to get things geared up for your return."

My fingers ball into fists, and I thump one fist on the table, causing Anna to jump. "No. I told you before, that's not fucking happening. You call Vicky back and tell her that you quit."

"You know I can't do that," she whispers. "I need this job. We need the money, and above all else, I don't want to lose the privilege of going on the road with you when your suspension is over."

"I don't give a shit about the money, Anna. Those mother-fuckers are not going to use you against me. I won't let that shit happen."

"Xavier—"

"No, Anna," I snap, rage filling every inch of me. "You're

not going."

"Yes, I am," she argues. "I told you earlier to trust me. If you would take a moment and calm down—"

"You're mine! You. Are. Mine."

Her eyes widen. "I'm not a possession to be controlled. I came to Detroit to get away from one man who wanted to control my life. Don't make me leave you, too, Xavier."

The monster inside me rears its ugly head, and before I say something to Anna that I don't mean, I shove myself out of the booth.

"Where are you going?" Anna asks.

I can't answer her as I storm out of the diner. I can't even look at her right now because I don't understand how she doesn't see my side on this. I can't have Rex trying to touch her without me there to stop him. I won't allow him to take her away from me—ever.

Chapter
EIGHT

Anna

"XAVIER!" NETTIE YELLS HIS NAME as he shoves the front door open and disappears through it. She turns back to me, a frown etched into her face, as she carries food to my table. She sets a plate of pancakes in front of me. "I swear, that boy has a temper and a half on him. What's he so pissed for?"

I sigh as I stare at the plate she puts in front of Xavier's now empty seat. "Tension wants me to pretend to be Rex's girlfriend to up the angst for Xavier's return to the show. They think a love triangle will get the crowd behind their rivalry."

Nettie leans her hip against the side of the booth. "I see where my boy would take issue with that. He's used to things he loves being taken away from him."

It breaks my heart that he would believe that for one second. "He should realize that I'm not going anywhere."

She tilts her head as she stares down at me. "It's hard to trust something good is going to stay in your life when you've been through what he has. He's never had something worth losing, like what he has with you. Be patient with him. I know it's hard, but if you love him, be there for him. He's waiting for the bottom to fall out of your relationship, for you to leave him like his mama did."

"It's awful—what happened with his mother. The story he

told me was the most heart-wrenching thing I've heard in my life. I can't imagine waking up in your dead mother's arms. What that must've done to him as a little boy—"

Nettie's gray eyebrows shoot up. "He told you about that?"

I nod. "I don't think he really wanted to. He had a nightmare, and it all just sort of came out."

"Well, honey, if he's opened up to you that much, you're really bringing him out of the darkness where he has kept himself secluded. It took years before he let me in. He needs you. Don't give up on him, especially now that he's back in that house. Being there is going to test your relationship." Nettie stares down at Xavier's plate. "I'll get this boxed up and have Carl give you a ride. He has a key to the house."

After Nettie boxes everything up, Carl struts over to me and twirls his car keys around his index finger. "Ready, girl?"

I follow Carl through the diner and eventually out the back door to the parking lot where an old dark blue Cutlass is sitting under the streetlight. He walks over to it, and then he manually unlocks the passenger door and opens it. I haven't been in a car that didn't have automatic locks before.

I slip into the seat, and I am instantly surprised by how well kept the vehicle is. While it's dated, it still appears to be brand-new.

I run my hand along the dashboard as Carl gets behind the wheel. "This car is in great shape. What year is it?"

"Nineteen eighty-eight. It's a classic, like me." He wiggles his eyebrows.

I laugh as he pulls out of the parking lot and onto the main road. The song playing on the radio reminds me of those old R&B songs that Father used to play before he turned his life over to Jesus. I haven't heard this kind of music since then. When Father decided to give his life over to the Lord, he banished all music in our house, except for secular songs, so my exposure to anything other than that is limited.

I tap my finger along to the beat as Carl hums the tune.

Eventually, he clears his throat and asks, "Where are you from exactly, Anna?"

"Portland," I answer easily. "Born and raised."

He nods with a thoughtful expression on his face. "How'd you end up here in Detroit with X?"

"Oh, um . . . I have family who live here, and I met Xavier on the plane ride from home to here when I moved."

"So, you don't know much about the neighborhood you're staying in?"

I pick at the chipping nail polish on my fingernails. "Not really—only that my cousin says it's not the best area."

"She's right. At one time, it was a decent street to live on, but it's overrun with thugs now, so be careful when you are there alone. People will come right up to your front door and beg you for money, so they can get high. Drugs are bad over there, thanks to Bishop and his crew down on the Block."

The name catches my attention. "Nettie mentioned that name before and told Xavier he'd better stay away from him."

"X would do good to heed her warning. Bishop was a small-time dealer who had kids working for him, but now, he runs things. Nothing goes on in that neighborhood that Bishop doesn't know about, so it won't be long before he comes sniffing around X, trying to get him mixed up in some crazy deal."

Since Xavier doesn't give me much information about himself, the only way I've learned about him is through Nettie and Carl, and Carl doesn't seem to mind spilling all kinds of details about Xavier's past. This might be a good time to poke around a little more.

"I know Xavier lived on the streets for a while, and Nettie said he ran with a gang for a bit. Was it Bishop's?"

Carl nods. "Yeah, it was, but X was only involved with him for a couple of years. When he tried to go straight, Bishop kicked him back on the streets with no money. That's when he robbed us." He chuckles, like remembering the time he took Xavier down greatly amuses him. "Nettie took him in and gave him a bed in the stockroom, and the boy actually turned himself around. Studied and got his GED. Then, he started working out at Tough's Gym with his buddy, Cole. It's a wrestling gym, and Xavier took a shine to it. As you know, the boy went legit and entered the wrestling circuit, and the rest is history."

I sit in silence and ingest all the information Carl just laid on me. That's the most knowledge about Xavier's past I've ever been given in one sitting. "Wow. I didn't know all that."

Carl adjusts his body in the seat. "I'm not surprised. X never was one to flap his gums too much. That kid has always kept to himself. It took Nettie years to really get to know him."

"They seem close."

"They are," he confirms as he turns the corner. He drives down the street to Xavier's house.

The lights are on, and when Carl parks in front of the house, I spot Xavier sitting on the front porch steps, like he's waiting on me.

I cradle the boxes of food in my hands. "Thanks for the ride."

Xavier's outside my door, opening it, before I even have a chance to make a move for the door handle.

"Anytime," Carl replies as I step out of the car.

Xavier leans down, so he can see inside. "Thanks for bringing her back."

Carl pokes his head out, so he can see Xavier's face. "No problem, brother. You need anything else, you be sure to let us know."

"Will do," he says before shutting the door. He shoves his hands deep into his front pockets while the Cutlass drives off.

We stand alone on the dark sidewalk, neither of us saying a word.

"Look, Anna. I, um . . . shit. I've been sitting here on this porch, thinking of ways to tell you how sorry I am, but none of the apologies I came up with in my head sounded good enough for how I left you. What I did . . . it was beyond fucked up. I left you stranded because I couldn't control my temper. There are times, like tonight, when I almost convince myself that I should let you go because I'll never be a good enough man for you. You deserve so much better than me."

I hate it when he does this—bashes himself. It's like he doesn't understand how I see him through my eyes.

I reach up and place the palm of my hand on his cheek. "Don't ever doubt that you're a good man. Since I've known you, all you've wanted to do is protect me, even in the messed up ways when you take things overboard with all the fighting. How could I ever fault you for that?"

He closes his eyes, like my touch causes him physical pain. "I'm trying so hard, Anna. I really am, but I don't think I'll ever get things right."

I chew the inside of my lower lip. "Do you love me?"

"With every inch of my soul," he answers without hesitation.

I smile up at him. "Then, you're doing it right. Everything else is fixable. You just have to stop lashing out all the time."

His face is a mixture of relief and sadness. "That's the hardest part. I don't know if I can control this rage inside me. There has to be a man who's more deserving of you, and I'm afraid that, someday, he's going to swoop in and steal you away from me."

I train my gaze firmly on his. "That's never going to happen, which is why you need to trust me. Have faith in me that I'm going to do right by you."

Xavier presses his forehead against mine. "I'll try."

I shake my head. "There's no trying on this one, Xavier. Without trust, a relationship has nothing. I don't want us to fall apart because we keep having the same damn fight all the time."

"You're right. I will work on that. I'll do whatever it takes to keep you in my life."

He leans in to kiss me, but the sound of a motor closing in behind me rips his attention away. He narrows his eyes, and I turn around in time to spot a black Escalade whipping into the driveway.

Xavier tugs me behind him. "If something happens, run inside, lock the door, and call the cops."

"Who—"

The passenger door pops open, cutting me off, as a short black guy wearing all black clothes and a bandanna wrapped around his head hops out of the Escalade.

The guy looks close to Xavier's age, but the top of his head is bald, like he shaves it down to the skin. The menacing snarl on his face reminds me of the one Xavier does when he makes men shake in fear of him. That expression must be one that's learned easily around this area. Even though he's barely taller than me, I sure as hell wouldn't want to meet this guy in a dark alley.

Two other men flank the short man's sides—both of them taller than the man who is clearly the leader of the group and as intimidating as Xavier.

Xavier rolls his shoulders. "What are you doing here, Kai?"

Kai lifts his chin, and if he's scared of Xavier, he's not showing it. "You think you can just roll back into the Block, and I wouldn't hear about it? Shit don't work like that here, X. There ain't nothing secret round here. You know that."

Xavier lifts his chin. "Yeah, so? What are you going to do about it?"

My mouth gapes open, and my heart bangs against my rib cage, as I fear for Xavier's and my safety. Since we've set foot in this neighborhood, I've been warned about how dangerous it is down here. Now, I'm thinking maybe I should've heeded

Quinn's warning and left this place with her.

Xavier stares down at Kai, and just as I'm preparing myself for the battle of the century, a huge smile breaks over Kai's face, and he steps toward Xavier with his hand up in a greeting.

"Damn. Same ole, X. Haven't lost your edge."

Xavier reaches up and locks hands with Kai as he leans in for one of those chest-bump hugs. "How you been, man?"

Kai pulls back and lifts one shoulder in a noncommittal shrug. "Ah, you know, same ole. Hustlin', making shit happen."

Xavier nods. "I heard. Bishop's running things now? What happened to Tiny?"

A devious grin crosses Kai's face, and one of the guys beside him chuckles darkly.

"Tiny went on a . . . *permanent* vacation," Kai says.

Xavier doesn't even flinch at this man's admission, but all my blood drains down into my toes.

Holy shit.

These are legitimate thugs—the kind authors write stories about, the kind who are ruthless and will kill on a dime and then laugh about it. And Xavier seems at ease with them.

It makes me really wonder about his past. He told me once, he should be in jail for some of the things he's done, and now, after meeting Kai, it's scary to know he was serious.

Now, I see why Nettie was freaking out about Xavier meeting back up with this Bishop person.

"Fuck, enough about all that. What about you, man? We've all seen you on TV, getting famous and shit. We know you have to be fucking rollin' now."

The muscles in Xavier's back tense beneath my touch, and I can tell he doesn't like where this is heading.

"Nah, man. I don't make as much as you all think," Xavier says.

Kai tilts his head. "Now, see, that's not what Bishop found out. According to last year's tax return he had pulled on you,

you've got some money."

I peek up at Xavier's face, and see his jaw muscle flex. "That's all gone. You think I'd be staying here if I had money?"

Kai suspiciously eyes Xavier and then flicks his gaze to the house before looking back to Xavier. "You could be telling the truth . . . but maybe you're just trying to fuck with me. Either way, Bishop wants to see you. He wants to talk business."

Xavier shakes his head. "Not interested."

Kai jerks his head back, and his eyes widen. "Not interested? You do realize that you're refusing Bishop."

"I don't give a fuck who it is. I'm not fucking getting mixed up in the shit that goes down around here."

"Don't be fucking stupid, X. I'm telling you, as a friend, get in this fucking car right now. Don't make me put you in there."

"We both know that will never happen. Don't try me, Kai."

Instead of backing down, Kai takes a step, closing the space between himself and Xavier. "You've been out of the hood for too long. Maybe you need to be reminded about how things work."

Xavier's fingers flex at his sides, like he's readying himself for a fight. "Fucking try it."

Kai stares up at him and smiles, causing my breath to catch.

"Go in the house, Anna," Xavier orders.

Kai's eyes snap to me and then flit between me and Xavier. It's like he's just noticing me for the first time. "That your girl, X? She's fine. Maybe Bishop needs to meet her, too. What do you say?"

"Lay one fucking finger on her—"

"And you'll, what? Kill me?" Kai smirks. "We both know you don't have the stomach for that. Words are only a threat when someone will actually carry things out."

A primal growl rips up from Xavier's throat as he draws back his fist to crush every bone in Kai's face, but before he can make contact, all three of the men rush toward him at the same time. Xavier struggles against them and lands a solid right hook into a guy's face, causing him to stumble back in a daze.

The other two struggle against Xavier, and they are having a hard time restraining him.

"Get the girl," Kai orders the man who is still shaking his head, attempting to get his bearings.

"No!" Xavier roars. Then, he blasts the next goon in the face.

Kai, realizing Xavier is free, takes a step back.

Blood trickles down Xavier's face from a cut above his left eye, but he doesn't seem to bother him. "Anna! Get in the house."

"I won't leave you!" I cry.

"Get in the fucking house."

I stand there, frozen. There's no way I'm leaving him out here, alone with these guys. I might not be strong, but I will help him anyway I can.

Kai laughs. "You've lost your touch, X. Seems you can't even control your bitch."

Without warning, X delivers a hard fist into Kai's face, causing his head to whip to the side.

Kai traces his lips with his fingers and then spits a mouthful of blood onto the ground. "Is that how it is now?"

Xavier nods while his chest heaves. If looks could kill, Kai would already be in a body bag.

Kai steps around the front of the truck. "This isn't over, X."

Xavier allows the men to throw around their promises of retribution and doesn't make a move to attack them. Rather, he stands firm in full-on protection mode until the men lock themselves inside the Escalade and drive away.

Chapter
NINE

Anna

ADRENALINE IS STILL FLOWING THROUGH every inch of my body. "What in the hell was that all about?"

Xavier swallows hard. "Old friends."

I crinkle my eyebrows inward. "Those were your *friends*? My God, Xavier, I would hate to see your enemies."

"This was a mistake, coming back here. We should leave." He starts toward the back of the house.

"We can do that. Quinn and Aunt Dee will let us stay there," I remind him as the loose sections of blacktop on the driveway crunch beneath the soles of my shoes.

He sighs as he walks over to his bike that's parked next to the back porch. "We can't do that either. We'll go to a hotel."

I'm still holding the Styrofoam containers from Nettie in my hands as he bends down to chain the bike to a post that's sunk into the ground as part of the porch's foundation. The material of his dark jeans stretches perfectly over his sexy ass, and I appreciate the view, but I refuse to allow his body to distract me. We've got a serious situation here.

"You said that we couldn't afford to do that."

"I'll figure it out."

"Well if you won't stay at my aunts, then we're staying here. It's the logical thing to do."

Xavier pushes himself up and rolls his shoulders back. The thin material of his black button-up shirt strains against his biceps. All of his clothes seem to fit extra tight, probably due to his sheer size, but it looks good on him because his body is so defined.

"Did you forget what just happened here?" he asks.

"No, of course not."

He sets his eyes on me. "Then, you know why we need to go."

No matter how badly he wants to leave this place, Xavier needs to realize that staying in a hotel for three straight months will hit his bank account hard, and we can't do that—unless he thinks we won't be safe.

"Will those guys hurt us if we stay here?"

Xavier's blue eyes darken. "They'll never touch you."

I stare into his eyes, knowing he means that. He's proven time and time again that he would never allow anyone to hurt me, so I'm not afraid for my own well-being, only his.

I take a step toward him to close the distance between us. "Will they hurt you?"

"No. I'm too valuable to them. They think I'm a walking ATM. They might threaten me, but they know, if something happens to me, the cops would be all over them."

"Then, we should stay. I'm not afraid, as long as I have you to protect me."

"I'll always guard that beautiful body of yours."

I smile at him. "There's my bodyguard who's always looking out for me in this city."

"You know it." He smiles back at me, clearly amused that I remembered his promise to be my personal bodyguard from all the pricks in Detroit.

My eyes drift to the cut above his eye where the blood has crusted over. "We should go in and look at that eye of yours. I might not have your bandaging ability, but I use a Band-Aid like no other."

He chuckles as I'm sure he's thinking about the time he cleaned up my knee at Larry's. "I have to see this skill of yours."

"Well, come on. Nettie sent home your food." I start to take a step toward the house, but I pause when I notice that Xavier is still stuck in place.

He pushes his long hair back from his face as he stares up at the house in front of him. "I'm dreading tonight."

He doesn't have to say any more than that for me to understand that he's talking about his nightmares.

I reach over and take his hand, causing his eyes to drift down to mine. I stare into the blue pools of his irises and say, "They always say, the first step is the hardest, and I can attest to that. I was always afraid to leave home even though I hated how overbearing Father was. Making the decision was the easy part, but taking that first step on the plane was tough. I don't regret doing it though because it was the right decision. It led me here to you. Whether you realized it or not, you helped me through the roughest day of my life on that plane. You were kind to me. You saved me. Now, let me be here for you. If it becomes too much for you in there, lean on me, please, the way I've leaned on you."

Xavier swallows hard and cups my face into his hand before he kissed my lips. "I'll try, but this place absolutely brings out the beast in me, and I don't want to accidentally unleash on you."

"You won't," I whisper. "I trust you."

He leans his forehead against mine. "You don't know how badly I want to be a good guy for you, Anna, because that's what you deserve. You shouldn't have to live in this ghetto hell with me."

I place my hands on his cheeks. "I don't care where we live, as long as we're together."

He closes his eyes but doesn't say anything else. I don't push him either. If there's one thing I've learned about Xavier Cold, it's that he doesn't do well when he's ordered around. He operates on his own time.

We stand there for a while before Xavier releases a heavy sigh. "We should probably go in and figure out where we're sleeping." He grabs my hand and leads me up onto the back porch.

I tilt my head. "I just assumed we'd be sleeping in your old room."

Xavier's muscle twitches beneath the skin of his jaw. "We can't do that."

"Oh," I say, deflated.

I was looking forward to seeing the room where Xavier had spent his time as a little boy. "Will you at least show me your old bedroom?"

"That's not going to happen either."

I furrow my brow. "Why not? Don't you want me to see it?"

He unlocks the back door. "It's not that, Anna."

"Then . . . I don't understand." I'm completely confused.

"I never had a room. Not every kid had a room like you, Anna. I wasn't blessed with a family who actually gave a shit when it came to me. I was lucky to be fed. Things like toys or a bed to sleep in weren't things my grandmother thought I deserved."

Pressure snakes around my heart, and I swear, it feels like it's breaking. I know this might be crossing the line in regard to what he's willing to say about his family, but I can't stop my brain from wondering, and it will eat at me if I don't get this out. "What about your mother? Didn't she—"

"Anna . . ." he says my name with a bite to it.

"I'm sorry. This subject is off-limits—you've told me that so many times—but I want to understand you better. I want to know about your past."

"My past is fucked up. You know that. You've seen the way

it affects me, firsthand, so you should understand why I don't want to talk about it." He opens the door and stares inside the house. "Can we not do this right now? Talking about it and being here—I can't do it."

"I'm sorry. I shouldn't have pushed. I'll try to stop doing that."

He sighs and turns to me. "I wish it wasn't so damn hard to talk about my past. I want you to know me, but there are some demons that your goodness shouldn't be exposed to. I don't want God to look down at me, pissed that I tainted one of his angels with my darkness."

My eyebrows knit together. "I'm no angel."

"You are to me." Xavier threads his fingers through mine. "Come on, beautiful. Let's find a place to sleep."

He reaches inside and flips on the lights to the kitchen. The cabinets are dated, and there's a green-topped table with metal legs sitting in the middle of the small space. Like the living room, the chairs have plastic over them. We walk to the table, and I set the food down before we move into the living room. It's the only other room I've seen in this house.

Xavier then leads me to the stairs, and we head up. My hand trails up the wood paneling as we reach the second floor. It's no bigger up here than the first floor. There are three doors at the top of the stairs, and all of them are closed.

Xavier points toward the door directly across from the stairs. "Bathroom. It's the only one in the house. The door to the right of that one is my mother's old room, and the other door is Grandmother's room." He turns toward me. "The only thing I ask is that you not go into Grandmother's room. I've never been in there, and that's one door I want to always stay closed."

My eyes wander over to the room in question, and I zero in on a padlock, sealing the door shut. "Is that why there's a lock?"

Xavier shakes his head. "She put that on there. She didn't want anyone in her room."

"Were you curious as to why she kept it locked?"

"No," he says flatly. "The thought of defying her never crossed my mind. I didn't want to pay the consequence. Things were bad enough as they were. I didn't need to create mischief to bring any more hell down on myself."

I swallow hard. "She sounds horrible."

"Yeah, but if you ask any of the neighbors around here about her, they'll fucking sing her praises like she's Mother Teresa."

"They obviously didn't know her."

He nods. "You got that right. She put on a face for the public, for her church, but she was no sweet old lady behind these walls. Her true nature came out here, where no one else but me could see it."

My eyes burn, and there's no way I can stop the tears from falling from them. I sniff, and it catches Xavier's attention. His eyes flit down to my face, and the corners of his mouth turn down.

He slides his thick index finger under my chin and then tips my chin up, so he can set his gaze directly down on me. "It kills me when you frown. You know I hate that."

"What you must've gone through . . . I can't . . . it breaks my heart." I have a hard time getting all the words out.

"Don't," he whispers with a slight growl in his voice. "Don't cry for me. I'm not worth it."

"You are worth it," I manage to squeak out between sobs. "You're one of the best people I've ever known."

He squeezes his eyes shut, like my words physically cause him pain. "Anna, I'm not. I've done horrible things."

"It doesn't matter. I've told you that. I love you for the man you are now. I don't care about your past. I love you, Xavier."

Without warning or permission, he crushes his mouth down on mine. Fire courses through every inch of me as I press myself against his sculpted chest. I claw at his shirt as he backs me up to the wall. His fingers find their way under my shirt, causing a shiver to run down my spine. His cock hardens beneath those tight jeans, and it presses into my belly as we continue to devour each other. His tongue probes my mouth, and I'm so turned on that I can't see straight. Between my legs, I ache, and I know only having him inside me can give me any relief.

"God, Anna, you taste so good," Xavier murmurs as he slides his hand down my thigh. Then, he hitches my leg up onto his hip.

I toss my head back and moan as his stiff length creates friction through my jeans. He kisses a trail down my chin, leaving fire in his wake, and then he licks the soft skin of my neck.

This man has the ability to turn me on with the slightest touch, and there's nothing more I want right now than to feel every inch of his bare skin pressed against mine.

I grab the hem of his shirt and push up. He drags it over his head, making his hair a sexy mess. I thrust my fingers into his thick hair and kiss him. The taste of him dances across my tongue, and I can't get enough.

Xavier's fingers work quickly to pop the button on my jeans, and then he unzips them before his hand snakes inside my panties.

The moment his digit makes contact with my most sensitive flesh, I bite down on my bottom lip. "Xavier . . ."

"Mmm . . . so wet and always so ready for me," he growls into my ear. "I can't wait to feel that tight little pussy of yours wrapped around me."

The delicious torture on my clit continues, and my head falls back and bumps into the wall. "Oh God." It's all I can manage to get out before he flicks my clit one final time, and I come against his finger.

My entire body shudders as he pushes my pants and panties down in one quick swoop. My fingers fly over his belt. I need to feel him moving inside me.

"Patience, baby. I'm far from done with you yet."

He bends down and pulls my shoes off, one by one, and tosses them to the floor. I step out of them as he pops up and then slowly slips my shirt over my head.

One finger traces the mounds of flesh on my chest while his other hand reaches behind me and unhooks my bra. I stand there, completely naked, in front of him, and his eyes take their time in raking over every inch of bare flesh exposed to him.

"So fucking beautiful and all fucking mine."

Goose bumps erupt across my skin at the sound of his possessive words. It turns me on to know he claims me as his own, and the way he looks at me makes me feel like the most desired woman in the world.

He gently pinches my chin and then rubs his thumb across my lips. I open my mouth, wrap my lips around his thumb, and suck as I stare up at him.

I want to taste him.

He seems to know what I want to do because he drops his hand from my face, and I lean in and kiss his neck just below his chin. The scruff tickles my nose as I work my way along his neck before I turn my attention down to that toned chest of his.

I drop to my knees in front of him and unzip his pants. When I push his boxer briefs along with his jeans down, his cock springs free. I run my hand along the silky skin before popping the head into my mouth.

Xavier sucks in a quick breath through gritted teeth. "Fuck . . . Anna."

The way he says my name encourages me to keep going because I like seeing him lose control.

I work faster, bobbing my head, taking as much in as I can. I feel proud of myself for resisting the urge to gag when he hits the back of my throat.

He runs his fingers through my hair and holds it away from my face, so he can watch me. "If you keep that up, I'll come in that pretty mouth of yours, and I'm not ready for this to be over."

My tongue darts out, and I lick his length one final time before he pulls me back up to face him. The wood paneling scratches my back as he pushes me against it and hitches my right leg over his hip.

The head of his cock presses against my entrance. He crushes his mouth into mine, and I close my eyes as he slips into me.

"Mmm . . . yes!" I breathe as he pulls back and then slides into me again. "So good."

"You like that?" he whispers as he continues to pump in and out of me. "You want more? Harder? Deeper?"

My mouth hangs open, and he bites my bottom lip.

"Tell me."

"Yes. All of it. Just keep going." The desperation in my voice surprises me.

Xavier grabs both of my thighs, lifting me off my feet with ease. I wrap my legs around his waist, and he pushes inside me even deeper.

"Fucking perfect. You were made for me."

His pace picks up, and sweat slicks his skin as he pounds into me.

The constant attention to my pussy causes that familiar tingle to erupt, and I cry out as an orgasm rips through me hard. "Xavier. Oh God. Yes."

His movements become more rigid. He buries his face into the crook of my neck and bites my shoulder as he finds his own release. "Fuck, Anna. Shit." Tremors ripple through his entire body as he comes down from his orgasmic high.

He pulls back and presses a soft kiss to my lips. "I love you, Anna."

I stare into the eyes of the man I love without a doubt, and there's no question that this is who I was made for, the man I'm supposed to spend the rest of my life with.

Our love—it's unbreakable.

Chapter
TEN

Xavier

THERE'S NOT MUCH SHELTER FROM the brutal Detroit winter under a freeway bridge, but it's the best place I can find to sleep without being harassed by the cops all night long.

It's been a month since I packed all my shit into one tiny bag and split from Grandmother's house. The beatings were becoming too severe, and if I stayed, I would've ended up really hurting the old lady—or worse, killing her. At fifteen, I'm already twice her size, so all it would've taken was me losing my head and hitting her back harder than I'd meant to, and my ass would've been locked up.

So, I decided taking my chances out here on the streets is a much better option.

Footsteps crunch along the gravel, and I pull the only blanket I own around me even tighter to keep the person from trying to snatch it from me. I really don't feel like fighting over this thing again tonight.

The steps grow closer, and a flashlight shines right in my face, blinding me. I hold my hand up to shield my eyes as I squint.

"What do you want?" I ask in the roughest voice possible to try to scare whoever it is.

"Holy shit! Xavier? Is that you?" A voice that sounds vaguely familiar sounds excited to discover he actually knows who I am.

Still doesn't mean I trust them.

"Yeah. What of it?"

"Damn, man, I thought you were dead. It's me—Cole," the voice says.

But I still can't see the person because of the light.

"Cole?"

"Yeah. Oh, shit. Sorry."

He cuts the flashlight off, and soon, my eyes adjust back to the darkness.

Standing there is Cole Parker, a scrawny black kid with braids who used to sit with me at lunch from time to time. Beside him is Malakai Johnson, mostly known as Kai around the neighborhood. Kai and Cole are both in my grade, but Kai is a well-known troublemaker who runs with a local gang, and Cole is more laid-back. I never even knew the two of them were friends.

"What the hell are you guys doing here?" I ask, my voice groggy. "Don't you two have someplace to be?"

I don't want them here. I don't want them asking any questions about how I ended up here. That's something I don't want to discuss with anybody.

Kai shrugs. "Home? What home? If you call that shithole foster house where I live a home, then you can fucking keep it. If there wasn't already a rap sheet a mile long attached to my name—shit, man—I'd be right out here, next to you."

I nod but then direct my attention back to Cole.

"I have a pretty good home, but I'm a rebel, and I like to break the rules."

Kai shoves Cole's shoulder. "You're trippin'. You're spoiled."

Cole doesn't argue. He only laughs in response. He shoves his hands deep into his front pockets. "You really don't have any other place to go?"

I frown and shake my head. "No."

"Is your family searching for you?"

"Definitely not." I sigh. "The only person I've got is me."

Cole whips his head in Kai's direction and says, "You should take him to Bishop."

Kai raises his dark eyebrows but turns his attention to me. "Slingin' ain't for everybody, but I know a guy who is looking to expand his crew. Once you're in, you won't be sleeping under bridges anymore."

I glance up at the concrete pillars holding up the freeway where cars have been zooming over me all night long. While selling dope has never been on the top of my priority list, a warm place to stay is something I would be willing to sell my soul for right now.

"I'm in. How soon can I meet this Bishop guy?"

"Shit. I can take you to him right now," Kai says with a smile. "Bishop is my older cousin."

I shove myself up from the ground, and my cold, stiff legs take a minute to stretch out. Once the blood is flowing through them and I feel like I can walk without falling over, I stuff my blanket into my backpack. "Let's go."

I might be jumping into fire, but at this point, I really don't give a fuck.

MY EYES SNAP OPEN, AND I gasp. It takes a moment for me to figure out that it was just a dream because it'd felt so real. While reliving one of the lowest points in my life wasn't exactly a nightmare, it's not something I like to dream about.

I haven't dreamed about that night in so long, and I have no idea what brought it on tonight, but I'll take those dreams over the nightmares any day.

Anna's head is resting on my shoulder as she lies on top of me on the floor of the living room. There wasn't anywhere I could bear to sleep in this place but in the spot in the corner where I always slept when I was a kid.

She stirs and lifts her head. "You all right?"

My hand strokes her hair. "Yeah, I'm good. Go back to sleep."

Anna's breathing evens out, and I fight the urge to hop up and begin doing push-ups to stop myself from thinking about the times that haunt me.

Chapter
ELEVEN

Anna

I STAND OUTSIDE QUINN'S CAR, hesitant to leave Xavier alone. "Are you sure you don't want to come with me? Designing a wedding invitation shouldn't take too long."

"That's totally a chick thing. Go have fun," he says.

"What are you going to do all afternoon?" There's no way I can hide the worry in my voice.

Xavier slides his index finger under my chin. "No frowning. I'll be fine. Besides, I'm going to go check out Cole's gym."

I smile and poke at his chiseled abs beneath his tight T-shirt. "Don't want these to get all soft, huh?"

A wicked grin spreads across his face. "Hell no. My girl seems to like them, so I need to keep her happy."

I bite my lower lip. "They are pretty damn sexy, but I would love you with or without them."

That earns me a genuine smile.

"You'd better go before I stop you from leaving."

A familiar tingle erupts in my belly, and I can't help myself from asking, "How would you plan on doing that?"

He leans in and presses his warm lips to the sensitive flesh below my ear. "I have my ways."

I inhale deeply, attempting to keep my body from going into overdrive. The spiciness of his cologne mixed with a scent that is one hundred percent all Xavier flow through my senses, making my mouth water.

He pulls back, takes in my face, and then chuckles. "See?"

I shake my head at his amusement of his ability to turn me on so quickly. "On that note, I'm leaving." I open the car door. "I'll see you when I get back."

He kisses me. "Be careful, beautiful. You have any problems, call me."

"I will."

Warmth spreads over me as I buckle in, and Quinn backs the Honda out of the driveway. I love how protective he is over me. It's a complete turn-on, even during the times when he takes it too far and I explode at him for being so reckless. It's a good feeling to know he cares so much about me.

"Damn, Anna." Quinn's voice pulls me out of my thoughts. "He's got it so bad for you."

My cheeks tingle as my mouth spreads into a smile. "The feeling is mutual. I can't seem to get enough of him."

She laughs. "And to think, it wasn't that long ago when I had to threaten you to get a pair of lady nuggets when it came to X."

"I can't believe it was ever so hard to come out with how I really felt about him."

She shrugs. "You didn't want to get hurt. On top of that, you'd never been around someone like Xavier. Uncle Simon made sure to keep guys like that far away from you."

I tense at the mention of Father's name, and while I don't agree with how he treated me or the way my family back home expected me to live my life, I do miss them.

"Has Aunt Dee heard from Father?"

"Oh, yeah. She's been on the receiving end of his wrath ever since he came to Atlanta. He's so pissed at X. He blames X for your rebellion and not coming back home."

"That's absurd. Xavier isn't the only reason I don't plan on going back."

She nods as she stops at a red light. "I know that, but you know Uncle Simon needs someone to blame for why you aren't going back home."

"Nothing is ever his fault. He doesn't see a thing wrong with how he treated me. I mean, who in their right mind tries to force their daughter into marrying a man she doesn't love just because it fits their plan for how they want the world to perceive their family?"

She presses on the gas pedal, and the car moves again. "The whole Jorge thing was completely fucked up. It never seemed like you ever really liked him."

The relationship I had with Jorge is nothing like the one I have with Xavier. Jorge felt more like a friend, someone I enjoyed being around. I didn't long for him with every inch of my being when I was away from him. It's the complete opposite of how I feel about Xavier. When I'm not with him, he's always on my mind. They're two totally different feelings.

"I don't think I ever loved Jorge—at least, not in the way you should love the person you're going to marry. Being with Xavier has opened up my eyes to a lot of things."

Quinn giggles and then suggestively wiggles her eyebrows. "I bet. That man is sex on a stick. I can only imagine what he's like in the bedroom. He's probably all primal and demanding."

I nudge her arm. "Quinn! Oh my God, I can't believe you just said that."

"What? It's true, isn't it?"

Heat creeps up my neck and then spreads into my cheeks. I know I'm blushing something fierce.

Quinn flicks her eyes in my direction before she squeals. "I knew it. I knew having sex with a known bad boy would change everything for you."

"It's changed *everything*," I say. "Being with him, I feel things I didn't know was possible. He's so intense and a bit scary sometimes, but I find comfort in him. I feel like he could protect me from the world."

Visions of what happened last night flash through my head. I want to tell Quinn about Kai and the whole situation, but she's already worried. If I tell her, knowing her, she wouldn't take me back to Xavier. She'd demand I stay with her and Aunt Dee, which wouldn't be a possibility for me because Xavier wouldn't stay there, and I couldn't be without him. So, I keep it to myself.

I need a change of subject, so I don't rattle on too much and let things slip. "So, this wedding . . . do you have your colors picked out?"

Quinn instantly begins firing out all the things she's planning to do. It's nice to see her so excited and, above all else, happy.

Chapter
TWELVE

Xavier

I PARK MY BIKE ON the sidewalk outside of Tough's Gym. The three-story brick building towers over me, and aside from appearing even more run-down than the last time I saw it, it looks exactly the same—rough.

No one would ever figure a world-class wrestling training facility rested behind these walls. Some of the finest athletes who have ever trained to be in the ring came from this gym, including me. This place taught me that hard work and discipline combined with strength could get you far in this business. I owe Cole's father a world of thanks for allowing me to train here practically for free.

I swing my leg off my bike and adjust the waistband of my sweatpants. I stand outside the front door, staring up at the place where I used to spend every waking hour when I was a kid, wondering what it's going to be like inside.

I take a deep breath and push open the door.

The stairwell is dark, dingy, and covered in tattered posters of wrestlers who went pro. I smile when I get to the top landing and spot a fairly new poster of me hanging beside the door.

"You know that ugly motherfucker?"

I turn and find Cole sitting just down the hall in a single chair with a cell phone in his hands. He pops up from the chair and walks in my direction, wearing a huge smile.

I clasp my hand in his and then nod to the poster. "Yeah, I might've seen this guy a time or two."

He laughs. "It's good to see you, X."

"You, too. I see you've cleaned up a bit." I nod to the fade on the top of his head that's replaced the braids he used to wear.

"Can't say the same for you. What's up with all this long hair? I thought you weren't going to do that."

I push my hair back from my face. "I know, but once I started growing it, I liked it."

Cole smiles. "I can hear Dad now, saying, *I told you to grow your hair out.*"

We both laugh, remembering all the times his dad would get on my case about my nearly bald scalp.

"He was right. It does add dramatics to the ring and exaggerates movements," I admit.

"He was known to be right from time to time. Come on in. Check out what I've done to the place."

Cole opens the door, and I follow him through.

Fresh gray paint covers the walls and the old wooden floor, causing the red on the ring ropes and punching bags to pop. A few guys are here training, but none of them notice me because they are so fixated on what they're doing.

"Wow," I say as I throw my hands on my hips and continue to look around. "You've cleaned this place up."

"It's amazing what a little paint and scrubbing will do. Dad never had time for all that. He was too focused on training."

I turn to my friend, and I see pride in his eyes. "You did good. Frank would've been real proud."

Cole claps his hands together, and I know it's his way of getting off the topic of his dad. From what I've gathered from Nettie, his father's passing is still pretty fresh, seeing as how it just happened.

"You here to train or just look pretty?"

"Do you have the time?"

"For you, there's always time, as long as we're done by three. I work second shift."

I drag my shirt over my head and toss it over a weight bench before I begin stretching. "This isn't your full-time gig?"

"Not yet, but I'm hoping to get there one day. I've got a wife and a little girl to support, so I can't be living here like Dad did. I had to go out and get a real job."

I grab a jump rope off the wall and begin jumping in a slow rhythm. "Makes sense. So, what do you do?"

"I'm a cop," he says simply.

My eyes widen. "A cop? Are you fucking with me right now?"

He crosses his arms over his chest. "I never joke about my job."

"What about Kai and Bishop?"

"We have an understanding. They keep their shit away from me, and I won't bother them."

I lift my eyebrows. "I never saw that coming from you. A cop . . . wow."

"Ten years ago, I wouldn't have either, but when I figured out that running with the crew was the wrong thing to do, I wised up. What they were doing wasn't right, and I didn't want any part of it. So, to protect myself, I changed everything about me. Being a cop is the most opposite of those guys that I can get. Plus," he adds, "they know they can't fuck with me or my business and get away with it. I won't pay them their fucking protection fee, like they demand from the rest of the local businesses around here."

"It's good that you stand up to them. More people need to do that."

"They do," he agrees. "But you know how intimidating those guys can be. Hell, when you ran with them, even as a teenager, you were scary as hell. That's why Bishop liked having you as his muscle."

I shake my head. "I look back at myself during those couple of years of my life, and I don't like what I see there."

Cole nods. "But you were smart enough back then to realize for yourself all the damage the crew was doing, and you walked away even though you knew you'd be living on the streets again. That was brave as hell. I only got out because Dad threatened to send me to military school."

I think back to that time period. Kai was right. Bishop made sure I had everything I needed—food, nice clothes, and a bed—to entice me to stay and do his dirty work. I got caught up in having things I'd never had before, but when things went from simple drug dealing to hurting people for money, I couldn't take it. I was done, and I walked away. After spending two years with Bishop and his crew, I went back to living under that freeway bridge.

I'm not sure what I would've done if Nettie and Carl hadn't intervened in my life. I'm a better person because of them.

All this talk about the old days has me curious. "When's the last time you saw Kai?"

"I haven't talked to him in a long time, but I've seen him around while I've been out on patrol."

For a moment, I debate on making Cole aware of the situation that happened last night, but I decide against it. There's no need to bring him into the situation. I won't put him in danger, but it's good to know that, if the shit gets too hot to handle, there's someone on the force I can trust.

Once both Cole and I are warmed up, I climb into the ring. Leaning against these ropes, I feel at home. Countless hours were spent in this very ring with Cole and his father, working on all the moves that are now trademarks of my style. Cole's father helped me figure out ways to harness all the rage I felt inside and put it into punishing my body in and out of the ring. It's one of the main reasons I'm able to take so much punishment. In an odd way, I enjoy the pain.

Cole swings his leg over the middle rope and then bounces around on the balls of his feet, like he's ready to box me. "Let's see what you've got, X. I've been dying to get back in the ring with you after watching you on television and seeing how much you've improved. I've been studying the new moves you've coined."

I laugh. "Don't worry. I'll take it easy on you."

Cole lunges first, and we lock up, but I get out of his hold with ease.

"Damn. How the hell did you get even faster?"

I wave him on. "Try again."

We repeat the same thing over and over, and each time, I get the best of him.

Eventually, Cole gives up and leans against the corner ropes. "Things have definitely changed. What else is different with you?"

I throw my elbows over the top and lean back. "Nothing, man. Same ole. You know."

"What about that girl I've seen you with on Tension? That real?"

I bite the inside of my lower lip. "Yeah. Her name is Anna."

"She's cute. Did you meet her through Tension?"

"No."

"Then, how'd she get on the show?"

I sigh and then go into detail about how I met her, and before I know it, I'm spilling everything to Cole about my situation with Rex. It feels good to get it off my chest.

"Shit, X. She worth all the trouble?"

"She is," I confirm without any hesitation. "I'd do anything for her."

Cole lets out a low whistle.

"What?"

He shrugs. "I never thought I would see the day when

Xavier Cold fell in love. You're not exactly known for keeping the same girl for very long."

"What can I say, man? Anna's different."

We finish training, and the muscles in my body burn. I needed this. It really helped bring things back into focus, and I realize that Anna was right. It would hurt like a motherfucker if I could never wrestle again. I'm glad she's kept a level head in this situation. I want her by my side when the suspension is lifted.

Cole walks with me down the stairwell, and I notice the sun is about to set.

Once we get outside, Cole turns to me. "Stop by whenever you want to train. I'm here most days."

I reach out, and we clasp hands. "Thanks, man. I appreciate that."

When I turn to walk to my bike, I notice Kai and another rather large man from his crew, leaning against the black Escalade that was at the house last night. My shoulders stiffen of their own accord while Cole stills next to me.

Kai is making good on his threat. The beef we had last night isn't over. Going with him to see Bishop is the last thing I want to do, but if I don't go, Bishop won't stop coming at me. Leaving with him in front of Cole will give me a little peace of mind. Kai's not stupid enough to kill me if a cop can place me with him last.

I turn toward Cole. "I'll see you tomorrow."

Cole doesn't try to talk me out of going with Kai. He knows as well as I do that there's no shaking Kai or Bishop in this city.

If going with him right now keeps Bishop away from Anna, I'll do it.

I'd do anything to protect her.

I near Kai, and a knowing smile spreads over his face.

He looks like he's won the battle. "I see you've come to your senses. 'Bout time."

"Shut up, and get in the fucking car," I snap.

I open the door of the Escalade and hop into the backseat while Kai and one of the other guys get in the front. The engine rumbles to life, and my heart races in my chest, as I'm about to face my past head-on.

Chapter
THIRTEEN

Xavier

THE SUV COMES TO A stop just outside an old building. It appears to be an abandoned factory of some type, which is common in this city. When the economy went south a few years back, most of the big businesses left, leaving it even poorer than when they had been here.

"We're here," Kai says before opening the door.

I follow suit and get out, wondering what in the hell we're doing. I'm not sure if he brought me to this abandoned building to kill me.

Kai notices me staring up at the building and laughs. "You can stop that shit that's going through your mind. Just because your bitch-ass punched me in the face doesn't mean I'm going to kill you, no matter if I should or not. Bishop wants to talk. That's all."

"About what?" I ask briskly, not liking all the secrecy.

Kai lifts his chin. "It's Bishop's place to tell you, but trust me, you won't want to turn it down."

My jaw muscle clenches as I try to figure out if that was a threat or not. "And if I say no?"

Kai sets his gaze firmly on mine, his dark eyes almost appearing black. "Trust me when I say, you won't want to do that. Now, come on. Bishop doesn't like to wait." He heads toward a metal door leading into the building with me close behind. Before he opens it, he turns to me and smiles. "This is going to blow your fucking mind."

I tilt my head as he opens the door, and music wafts outside, sounding like a party with the hip-hop bass thumping. We walk through the large open space and then round a corner before heading through a set of double doors into a room illuminated by blue and purple neon lights.

It has the feel of a nightclub, complete with a bouncer, who happens to be the other guy who showed up at the house last night.

His eyes narrow as I pass by him, and I notice he has a split in the center of his lip, no doubt caused by me. He doesn't say anything though. He just remains on the stool he's sitting on while guarding his post.

"What's up, G? How are the ladies looking tonight?" Kai asks the man, like having me with him is no big deal.

The man's gaze flicks from me to Kai as they clasp their hands together. "Some hot asses in the spot tonight."

"Good lookin' out, playa. I'll see you later." Kai grins at me after he speaks to the bouncer. "This way, X."

We finally make it into the main room, and the man who drove us here disappears into the crowd of bodies in front of us. This place is like a full-on underground nightclub. A few topless girls dance on a small stage in the center of the room and men stand around throwing money at her.

"Where the hell are we, Kai?"

"We're at Bishop's place. He got tired of going to bars where he couldn't control who came in and out, so he made his own spot. It's the hypest place in town."

"What's all this got to do with me? Bishop has all the money he needs. I don't owe him any money, and I never snitched on anything that had gone down while I ran in his crew. Why can't he just let me be?"

Kai turns and shrugs. "Look, X, we've known each other for a long time. Things have changed since you've been out of the game, and the thing you have to get through that thick skull of yours is that Bishop gets what he wants. There's no refusing him, and there's no walking away when you have something he needs."

"Like I told you before, I don't have any money."

He gives me a stop-fucking-with-me look and then motions for me to follow him. "Explain that to Bishop."

He weaves us in and out of the writhing bodies on the dance floor until we come to a sectioned off area with two men standing guard, both about my size. Bishop has certainly upped his protection. Back in the day, I was his only hired muscle. Bishop can afford a lot more than one bodyguard nowadays.

"Stay here," Kai orders as he slips past the men.

My eyes stay trained on Kai as he struts over to a plush black couch, and I spot Bishop sitting between two women. Kai leans down and whispers something into his ear, and Bishop's eyes snap in my direction.

A huge smile sweeps across his face as he shoves off the couch and walks in my direction with his arms out. "Phenomenal X, my man. What's up?"

He looks older than the last time I saw him. The last ten years haven't been kind to him. His light-brown skin has a few lines etched around his eyes, and his signature goatee is graying. The Afro he once sported is gone, replaced by tight braids against his scalp. The black pin-striped suit he's wearing is perfectly tailored to fit him. The tiny bowtie wrapped around his neck and the glasses on his face finish off the outfit. He looks like a pimp to some high-class hookers.

I raise my chin and stare down at him. "What do you want from me, Bishop?"

He cocks his head to the side. "Is that any way to talk to an old friend, to someone who helped you out when you were at the lowest point in your life?"

While that might be true, he sure as fuck didn't do it out of the goodness of his heart. Every scrap he gave me, I earned it by doing his dirty work, like beating money out of people who owed him.

When he sees there's not going to be any open-armed reunion, his smile disappears, and he motions toward the couch where he just came from. "Come in. Let's talk."

"You're wasting your time, Bishop. Whatever it is you want from me, the answer is no. Like I told Kai, I don't have any money. I have nothing of any value to you."

He squares his shoulders and meets my stare head-on. "As you can see, money, I have. What I need is a legitimate name, so I can open a business—a real nightclub—to pass my money through. And seeing as how you're on the straight and narrow now, I think you're the man I've been looking for."

It's common practice in the drug world to have businesses to make the large amounts of money moving through hands appear clean, and I have no desire to get mixed up with anything that could hurt my wrestling career.

I lick my lips. "No, not going to happen."

Bishop's eyes flit to Kai, who shrugs.

"I told you, man," Kai says. "This isn't the same X who ran with us."

Bishop sighs. "I was hoping things wouldn't have to get nasty, but I need this, X. I *need* you to do this for me, and I'm afraid I won't take no for an answer."

Even though the threat doesn't sound so menacing the way he presents it, there's no doubt in my mind that it's a vicious one. I need to tread carefully with what I say next because Bishop seems to have quite a bit of power around here now. That still doesn't mean I'm going to give in to him though.

"I'm sorry. I can't help you out. I'm not the right partner for you," I say.

Bishop shoves his glasses up the tip of his nose. "Are you close to that *bitch* of yours?"

Anger rolls through me, and I clench my fists at my sides. "Don't," I growl. "She's off-limits to you."

"Now, that depends. If you agree to do as I've asked, then your Anna won't be touched by me or the crew, but refuse"—Bishop lifts one shoulder as he pokes his bottom lip out a fraction—"and it'll be open season on her."

"Touch her, and I will fucking kill you."

Bishop throws his head back and laughs. "There's the X I knew."

There's nothing more I want at this very moment than to bash his face in with my fists, but I've got enough sense to know that if I do that—Cole being a witness to seeing me take off with Kai—I won't be walking out of this place.

"Here's the situation, X. *You're going* to cooperate with me and help me get the nightclub going. You will invest some of your money, and your name will be on all the legal stuff."

My nostrils flare as I allow him to talk, knowing full well that I'll never go along with what he says.

Bishop straightens his suit jacket. "Now all of that is taken care of, sit down with me, and let's have a celebratory drink."

"No. I'm good."

"All right then." He gives Kai a pointed look before turning back to me. "Your ride will be out front."

I begin to head back the way I came when Bishop's voice stops me dead in my tracks, "Tell Anna hello for me."

I flex my fingers, and as hard as it is for me to walk away, I know I have to.

Wandering through the bodies to make it to the exit, the only thing I can think of is how thankful I am that Anna will soon be back on the road and far away from this city. As much as I hate to admit it, I would much rather risk her being around Rex without me than her being here in this city with me while

Bishop has her in his sights.

I shove open the metal door leading outside, and I find a white Mercedes waiting with the engine running. The windows are tinted, so I can't tell who's waiting inside.

The passenger window rolls down, and a familiar face leans over and smiles.

"Hello, X."

Angie Martinez, a girl I used to fuck around with back in the day, is sitting behind the steering wheel.

I scrub my hand down my face. "You've got to be fucking kidding me."

"Get in," she says.

I glance around, but there's no other option for a ride, so as much as I don't want to, I open the car door and slide into the passenger seat of Angie's car.

She smiles and I can't help but to notice her too-tight skirt, showing off more leg than should be legal. Her dark hair flows loosely around her shoulders in big waves, and her face hasn't changed a bit since I saw her ten years ago.

"Where exactly am I taking you?"

"Tough's Gym."

The car rolls forward, and Angie's gaze slides over to me for a brief second before turning back to the road. "You look good, X. Glad to see you're doing so well. I've missed you around the Block."

I fold my arms over my chest, wanting to cut to the chase. "What are you doing with Bishop, Angie?"

She sits up a little straighter in her seat. "I'm not *with* Bishop. I work for him."

I shake my head in disgust. "What happened to getting out of here and going to college?"

She shrugs. "I didn't see the point in spending time hitting the books when I could work on the Block and make four times as much as I could at a regular job."

"A negative of a regular job isn't prison time though," I retort.

"Still righteous, I see. You're the only person I've ever known who actually left here and made something of himself. The rest of us who try always find our way back."

"Then, you didn't try hard enough to stay away."

Angie parks the car outside of Tough's Gym, and I don't waste any time in getting out of the car.

She's right behind me as I walk toward my bike. "Where are you staying? Maybe I can swing by a little later to keep you company."

I turn around to tell her there's no way in hell that's going down, but before I can get the words out, she kisses my cheek.

I grab her wrist before she can reach up and touch my face. "No, Angie. It's not happening."

She pokes her bottom lip out. "You've never told me no before."

"I've met someone," I tell her.

Her eyes scan my face, taking in my serious expression. She slowly pulls out of my grasp. "You love her?"

I nod. "I do."

Angie adjusts the blue top she's wearing, and her lips pull down into a deep frown. "She's a lucky lady." She takes a step back. "Good-bye, X."

I stand there, watching Angie hop into the car.

I have no doubt that my rejection hurt her. Back when we used to mess around, she made it clear that I wasn't the only man in her life, which was why I never took her seriously. We never loved each other.

I never knew what love was until I met Anna. She's my heart.

Chapter
FOURTEEN

Anna

SEVERAL SHADES OF COLORED TULLE line the table from the aftermath of Quinn picking her wedding colors. She points to a piece of violet tulle and holds it up next to a pale yellow one. "Perfect. It's so girlie. Don't you love it?"

Aunt Dee smiles at her. "Aye, they're lovely. I can't wait to see them paired next to your dress."

"My dress!" Quinn's excitement is evident. "Oh my God, Anna, wait until you see it. We need to figure out a time when we can go get you fitted for your dress."

I lay the fabric down on the table. "Oh, it'll have to be sometime in the middle of next week. I have to fly out to Seattle to meet up with Tension for a show on Sunday, and then I have to stay there for Tuesday's show."

Quinn's eyes widen. "Seattle? You do realize, being that close to Portland, Uncle Simon might just pop up."

I sigh. "I know, but if he shows up, I'll handle him."

"I don't doubt that, baby girl," Aunt Dee says as she adjusts the scarf wrapped around her head. "From what I heard, you shocked the hell out of him when he showed up in Atlanta. He wasn't prepared for you to speak to him that way while you were defending your relationship with X. It's hard for my brother to realize that his little girl is all grown-up."

"It took some real guts, telling him off like you did in Atlanta, cuz," Quinn adds. "I wasn't sure if you'd be able to handle facing Uncle Simon because of how hell-bent you were to avoid him when you first got into town, so major props to you for actually growing a little backbone."

"Thank you."

Standing up to Father was one of the hardest things I've ever done in my life, but I'm glad I made it clear that I'm in love with Xavier. Father should know now that I never plan on returning to Portland to marry Jorge. Xavier completely has my heart.

I glance at my cell phone. "I can't believe it's nearly five already."

"Five? Shit." Quinn pops up from her chair like someone lit a fire under it. "I have to be at work in forty-five minutes. Let me go get changed, and I'll drop you off on the way, Anna."

"Okay."

The moment Quinn leaves the room, Aunt Dee sets her brown eyes on me. "I know I harp on this every time I see you, but have you thought about calling your father? My poor brother has been going out of his mind since he discovered you're in love with that hunky fighter."

"He's a wrestler," I correct her.

She tilts her head. "Is that different?"

"Very much so. Not only does Xavier have to be physically in shape, but he also has to be able to follow a script and put on a show for the fans. Fighters just step into the ring and focus on inflicting physical pain on their opponents. Wrestling . . . it's a mixture of physicality and acting."

"Quinn told me you're a part of the show now. Does that mean, you'll have to fight someone in the ring? You know your father will go ballistic if he sees that on TV."

"I'm not trained for that, so that will probably never happen—" Something she said just registers in my brain. "Are you saying Father watches Tension?"

"Every time it's on," she confirms. "He told me it gives him peace of mind to catch glimpses of you. He worries about your safety."

"I didn't know he did that. He hates wrestling."

She reaches over and lays her hand on top of mine on the table. "That might be true, but he loves you even though it doesn't feel that way to you at times. He's harsh, and I'm in no way condoning his actions toward how he was trying to force you to live your life, but I do understand his grief about missing his only daughter. I don't know what I would ever do if Quinn wasn't speaking to me."

"I don't think that would ever happen. Quinn loves you too much."

"At one time, you loved your father, too."

"I still love him. I'm just mad at him right now."

"Then, promise me, when you're both ready to let your anger go, you'll allow him an opportunity to apologize to you. Simon is a good man, but it's hard for him to see that he's not always right about things. He's been that way since we were kids. When he saw that I was never going to bend to his will, he eventually gave in and stopped trying to change me. He learned to love my crazy ways even if he didn't fully understand them."

"You think that will happen between us? Right now, I feel like he hates me for running out on Jorge and for embarrassing the family."

Aunt Dee smiles. "He loves you, sweet girl, and love always conquers everything."

Quinn comes bouncing in the room, wearing a work uniform that says Property of Larry's. "Ready, Anna?"

"Yeah." I push myself out of my seat at the table and stretch my arms over my head, attempting to ease the stiffness in my back from sleeping on the hardwood floor last night. "Can I ask for a favor before we go?"

"Anything," Quinn answers instantly.

"Can I borrow the air mattress I slept on while I was here?"

Quinn furrows her brow. "Sure, but why do you need it?"

At first, I think about telling her the truth—that Xavier couldn't bring himself to sleep in his mother's bed or on the couch in the living room because his mother had died on it—but I decide to keep Xavier's heartbreaking past to myself.

"The bed at the house is like sleeping on the floor. The air mattress is much more comfortable."

"Okay. Let me grab it out of the closet for you." She dashes off and then returns with the portable bed and the sheets and blankets that I used on it. "I figured you might need these, too, since I know they fit the mattress pretty well."

I wrap my arms around everything. "Thank you. This will help so much."

Quinn smiles. "Awesome. Now, let's get on the road before I'm late, and Andy jumps all over my ass."

I laugh as I follow her out the door, and I throw a good-bye to Aunt Dee over my shoulder.

We load the stuff into her trunk while she prattles on about Larry's. "Things are so much better since Alice's bitchy ass has been fired. Andy promoted me to shift supervisor. Can you believe that? He says he knows he can count on me."

"Congratulations! That's awesome news."

"Thanks. The extra money has really come at a good time. Paying for a wedding is expensive."

We hop in the car and the mention of the cost of what it takes to get married causes the corners of my mouth to pull down. Father sank a pretty penny into the wedding he and Mother were planning for Jorge and me, and that makes me feel guilty because my family doesn't exactly have a lot of money to spare.

She fires up the car. "Uh-oh. What's wrong, Anna?"

"Nothing's wrong." I forgot how well she could read me.

"I call bullshit on that one," she throws back at me as she

pulls out onto the road. "I know that look. That beautiful face of yours is incapable of disguising sadness, especially those green eyes. They are, as people say, the windows to your soul."

I turn to stare out the window in an attempt to hide my emotions from her, but the moment I do, something catches my eye and causes my jaw to drop open.

"Xavier?" I whisper his name.

"He's the problem?"

"No . . . yes . . ." I tumble over my own words, not realizing I said it out loud. "I mean, I see him."

"Where?" She gasps when I'm sure she spots the same scene I'm witnessing in front of my very eyes. "Oh, hell no."

She jerks her car over to the side of the street where Xavier is standing, bumping her tire on the curb in the process.

Quinn turns to me. "Are you going to kill him, or do I get the pleasure? Don't let him get away with that shit, Anna, or so help me, I will revoke your lady nuggets."

"Oh, I've got this one." I fling open the car door. "Keep the motor running."

"Will do," Quinn says.

I hop out and march in Xavier's direction. My heart thunders in my chest as adrenaline flows through my veins. A million things I want to scream at him pop into my mind as I head right for him. I take in a shaky breath when I pass the girl who just kissed my man hops into a white Mercedes.

Who in the hell is she?

Xavier immediately holds up his hands in surrender, and I can tell by the shock on his face that he didn't expect to see me here. "Anna . . . it's not what it looks like."

"Save it. I know what I saw. You kissed her!" Tears burn my eyes as betrayal rocks through me.

Flashbacks of the night when Deena was strutting around Xavier's hotel room in nothing but some lingerie flip through my head. He hurt me once. What's stopping him from going behind my back again to sleep with someone else?

I swat the tears away as my stare bores into him, waiting on his explanation for allowing another woman to kiss him. Xavier reaches for me, but I smack his hands away.

"No. Don't touch me. Explain yourself."

His crystal-blue eyes soften. "Anna, please, calm down."

"Oh my God. This is *her*? How do you even put up with it?"

I whip around to find the source of the female voice bashing me, and my eyes land on the gorgeous Latina woman who I saw with him moments ago.

She is standing between the open driver's door and the car as she focuses her gaze in our direction. "Seriously, X, what do you see in her?"

Pain from the truth of her words slices through me. Many times, I've questioned what he sees in me when he can obviously have any woman he wants.

"Get back in the car, Angie," Xavier orders. When she doesn't move to follow his order, he adds, "Now."

Angie shrugs. "I think I would rather stay here and watch you talk your way out of our kiss to your little girlfriend."

"We didn't fucking kiss," he fires back at her. "You kissed me. It's not the same thing."

A wicked smile crosses her face. "You didn't exactly tell me *no* either. If this girl is going to be with you, she should learn that you're not exactly a one-woman kind of guy."

"Shut up, Angie. This doesn't fucking concern you."

I flinch at his tone. It's the same tone he took with Deena. Is this how he treats a woman when he's done with her? Will he treat me that way one day?

"Fine," Angie sighs. Then, she flips her long dark hair over her shoulder. "But if you change your mind about my offer from earlier, you know where to find me." With that, she slips into her car, slams the door, and pulls out onto the street.

I stare up at Xavier and fold my arms. "Another old friend?"

"Don't worry about her," he replies without a speck of emotion on his face. Then, he reaches for me, but I step back before he can touch me. "Come on, let's get out of here."

I lift my chin. "No. I'm not going anywhere until you explain to me how you ended up standing on a sidewalk, kissing some old girlfriend."

"She was never my girlfriend."

"Then, just another girl you made a special *arrangement* with, like Deena?"

"Something like that."

"Will that be *me* someday—just some other woman you once had a fuck-buddy relationship with?"

He scrubs his hand down his face. "How many times do I have to explain to you that you're different? You're nothing like the women I've been with before."

"How do I know you didn't feed them the same lines you've been feeding me? I won't be able to handle you breaking my heart, Xavier."

"That's not going to happen."

"Then, explain to me why you were with her," I demand, wanting the full truth from him.

His face twists and I can tell he's holding something back from me.

"I can't do that," he says.

My heart crumbles, and I clutch my chest in an attempt to hold it together. "If you keep things from me, how am I supposed to ever trust you?"

"There are some things you don't need to know, beautiful," he answers coolly. "Just be satisfied with what I can tell you."

I square my shoulders. "That's not good enough."

Seeing that I'm not getting anywhere with this, I take a few steps away from him, toward Quinn's car. "Come find me when you feel like telling me the truth."

He stands there with a blank expression, but makes no

attempts to chase after me.

Devastated, I turn and race to the Honda, not daring to look back.

I close myself inside. "Drive."

She doesn't question me, just shoves the transmission into gear and slams on the gas.

"Holy shit. What happened back there?" she asks.

I rest my head in my hand. "I'm not even sure."

"Who was the woman?"

I pinch the bridge of my nose. I would like more details about that myself. "Her name is Angie, and apparently, she's a woman from his past."

"His *past*? Are you saying that's an old girlfriend?"

"*Girlfriend* is a pretty specific title, one Xavier never uses when it comes to women he's been with."

"You mean, she was an old fuck buddy of his? What the hell was he doing with her?"

"He wouldn't tell me. He said it was basically none of my business." Repeating it out loud causes my lower lip to quiver. "Do you think he—oh God."

The tears can't be stopped now. The very thought of Xavier being with another woman causes a sharp pain to rip through my chest, and I gasp for breath. My hand covers my mouth as I attempt to stop from crying, but it's no use. This hurts so damn bad.

"Oh, Anna." Quinn reaches over and takes my hand. "I'm sure he wouldn't do that. Xavier might be a big brute of a man, but he's not stupid. He wouldn't risk losing you over some random piece of ass."

"He's done it before with Deena." I take a deep breath.

Quinn's brows furrow. "I know this sounds like I'm siding with him, but that situation with Deena was technically before the two of you were together. Do you really think he'd pull that shit now that you are official?"

"I didn't think he would, but what other reason would he have to be with her and not explain the situation? I saw her kiss him, and he did nothing to deter my doubting mind from thinking the worst when I confronted him about it."

"What *exactly* did he say?"

I sniff as I try to steady my breathing. "That there were some things I didn't need to know about."

Quinn twists her lips in an obvious show of questioning thought. "Do you trust him?"

"Yes, but sometimes, it's hard because of all the secrets he keeps from me. He rarely opens up about himself, and I'm always left with millions of questions that he refuses to answer. Seeing what I did just now . . . it shakes my faith in our relationship. What in the hell will he be doing behind my back when I'm on the road? Now, I know I'll worry the entire time."

"Then, you need to tell him that. Honesty in a relationship is always the best policy. Trust me on that one. It took me and Brock a while to get on the same page, but now that we're there, things are so much better."

"That's easier said than done, Quinn. Xavier doesn't like talking about his past. He gets angry whenever the subject comes up. He . . ." I hesitate for a moment, but I decide that a little insight into Xavier's past won't hurt. "Xavier really had it rough as a kid. The things he's told me—they break my heart. If he keeps that to himself, what else will he keep from me?"

She's quiet for a moment and then says, "You need to talk to him, tell him how you feel."

Tears streak down my face. "What if he refuses to open up and come clean about why he was with that girl?"

She frowns. "If he can't give you complete honesty, as much as it hurts, it might be time to face the possibility that Xavier isn't the right man for you."

My heart squeezes as the reality of her words hit me full force. As much as I don't want that to happen, I know Quinn has a point. I can't live my life going through pain like this be-cause Xavier refuses to let me into what's going on with both his past and present issues.

One thing is clear. Xavier and I need to deal with this issue before it completely tears us apart.

Chapter
FIFTEEN

Anna

SITTING AT THE BAR AT Larry's, Bar and Grill is actually a pleasant experience now that Alice is gone. Most of the booths are full, which is great because Quinn can use every spare penny she can come up with to help her finance the wedding.

Since I was here last, Tyler has moved up from fry cook to bartender. Brock misses him in the kitchen, but Tyler has been smiling all evening, and the customers really seem to enjoy him waiting on them.

"You want another drink, Anna?" Tyler asks as he wipes down the counter next to me.

I stare down at the nearly empty glass in front of me, seeing I only have a few good drinks left. "Yes, please. It's delicious."

Tyler grins. "I might have to cut you off soon."

"Why?" I ask, completely confused. "I love this fruity Sex on the Bay."

"You mean, Sex on the Beach?" My mistake earns a little chuckle from him. "You're getting lit. You've definitely reached your cutoff point. Andy will have my ass if I allow you to get too drunk, sitting out here."

"Andy won't care. I'm a paying customer now." I wave him off and accidentally knock over my glass. I grimace when I see the mess I just made. "Oops. Sorry."

I attempt to reach for the glass, but Tyler is much quicker to grab it.

He then blots up the spilled liquid. "I think we should hold off on that last drink and maybe try some food."

I sigh, completely deflated that I'm not getting another drink. "Okay. I'll take a hamburger."

"You got it." Tyler works on punching my order into the computer.

I glance over to Quinn, who is busy flirting with Brock through the window where the orders are sitting, waiting to be picked up by the servers.

They are adorable together, really in love, and if it weren't for worrying about embarrassing Quinn in front of a roomful of customers, I would call them out for being so darn cute.

Quinn notices me watching the two of them and quirks an eyebrow before she stops beside the bar. "Hey there, cuz. Looks like you're in a better mood."

"I am." I grin and then reach for my glass. My bottom lip pokes out a bit when I realize it's empty. "There might be something to this drinking thing. I can't stop smiling."

She turns to Tyler. "How many have you given her?"

He flings a dish towel over his shoulder and then runs his hand through his thick blond hair. "She just finished her sixth."

"*Six*? Damn it, Tyler. I said loosen her up a bit, not fuck her up. She won't be able to walk out of here if you give her any more."

Tyler defensively holds his hands up. "Hey, that's only two drinks an hour. I think I've paced her pretty well."

"That's an acceptable pace for someone who's used to drinking." Quinn sighs. "Anna doesn't drink. Last time I took her out, two drinks had her feeling pretty good."

"Hey," I interrupt before a hiccup slips out. "I think I'm doing fine. I only had one little accident when I knocked over that glass."

Quinn pats my arm. "I know, but you haven't tried to stand up in a while, and when you do, all the liquor is going to hit you. I want you to sit here for the next thirty minutes while I finish my shift, and then we'll go home."

I raise my hand and flick my thumb up. "You got it. I'll stay right here."

"Okay." She snickers and instructs Tyler to watch me and try to sober me up.

A coffee is placed in front of me, and I glance up at Tyler, wearing a frown. "I don't really like black coffee. Do you have iced coffee?"

He shakes his head and then lays a spoon and four creamers next to my cup. "That's about the closest you'll get to sweetened coffee around here."

I open the creamers and dump them in my cup. "You're so nice, Tyler."

A bashful smile spreads across his face as red creeps into his cheeks. "So are you." He's quiet for a few moments and then asks, "Are you still seeing Phenomenal X?"

I raise my brow. "You know who he is?"

"Of course I do. I love wrestling. X is a badass in the ring."

"That he is." I sigh. "He scares the shit out of most men."

"That's why I never dragged up the courage to ask you out once I found out you were seeing him. I knew I would never have a shot."

I stir my coffee as my mind drifts to when I saw Xavier earlier. "We're kind of in a fight right now."

I admitted that a little too easily, and then it hits me that Quinn is probably right about me being drunk. Typically, I wouldn't have divulged that information.

Tyler braces his hands on the bar across from me. "What about?"

I shrug. "He allowed another woman to kiss him."

Tyler raises his eyebrows and then shakes his head. "Man, if he's messing around on you, he's an idiot."

The corner of my mouth lifts into a small smile. "Thank you. That's sweet."

"It's true. Any man who has you would be an idiot to mess things up. Not only are you really nice, but you're also the prettiest woman I've ever seen." He sighs and then lays my bill down. "I hate to give you this, but you know Andy would shit a brick if I didn't make you pay."

"It's okay. I don't mind paying." I reach for the small white paper lying on the bar, but someone reaches over my shoulder and takes it before I can get my fingers on it.

Standing next to me is a broad-shouldered man with brown hair who is covered in tattoos from the neck down. He's wearing a smile that causes his dark eyes to twinkle. "I got this one."

"Oh, um . . ." I hesitate, knowing that situations like this make X to freak out. "Thank you, but I really should pay for that on my own."

The man slides onto the stool next to me, still holding my bill. "Consider this a welcome-to-the-neighborhood present."

I raise my eyebrows. "What makes you think I'm new?"

His eyes search my face, like he's trying to think of an answer to my question. "I've never seen you in here before."

My lips twist. "That's funny because I used to work here. Surely, you would've seen me then if you were a regular."

He nods and then runs his hand through his mussed hair. The blue shirt he's wearing catches my eye. On the sleeve of his shirt, there's some sort of weird symbol that has a scythe, a dollar symbol, and a square on it. The interesting pattern is definitely custom because I can't imagine anything like that being sold in a store.

"You caught me," the man admits. "I was looking for an excuse to talk to a pretty lady."

Heat floods my face, surely making me blush, and I can't tell if all the liquor or his simple compliment caused it. "That's very kind of you, but I can't accept you paying for my stuff. I have a boyfriend."

"A really big, scary one," Tyler chimes in from across the bar. "And he's right behind you."

My head whips around, and I spot Xavier standing just inside the door. His long hair is damp from a shower, and he's changed into a fitted T-shirt, a pair of jeans, and boots. He's no doubt here to find me since I haven't been back to his house since we fought.

Suddenly, I fear for the man sitting next to me because Xavier gets crazy jealous when it comes to other men speaking to me. I don't want him to go nutso on this guy who is trying to be nice.

The man, on the other hand, doesn't appear to be the least bit worried. Matter of fact, he doesn't even make an attempt to turn around and check out the man whom Tyler has warned him about. Instead, he fishes out his wallet from his back pocket and lays down a one hundred dollar bill.

My pulse pounds beneath my skin as Xavier's eyes meet mine, and then his gaze flits over to the man next to me. Even from across the room, it's easy to tell that his body has instantly stiffened. Then, he squares his shoulders and marches in my direction.

"Oh, shit," Tyler says from behind me. "Mister, you should leave."

The man shrugs. "I'll leave when I'm ready, and no one will make me do so otherwise."

"Your funeral," Tyler mumbles as he walks to the opposite end of the bar.

Xavier stands in front of me, but his eyes are fixated on the guy while he flexes his fingers in and out. "Let's go, Anna."

It's not a request but a command. After how he treated me today, I'm not ready to let his bossiness slide.

I fold my arms across my chest. "No. Maybe I'm not ready

to leave. I told you before, I can handle myself."

"Yeah, X. She said she's got it under control," the man taunts.

I know this isn't going to go over well.

Xavier's eyes narrow and his jaw muscle works beneath the skin. "Shut your fucking mouth before I shut it for you."

"Xavier!" I scold him, trying to grab his attention before he does something crazy and ends up in trouble yet again.

"Anna . . ." he growls my name in a sexy way.

At the moment, I refuse to admit how my body to reacts to him because I'm still mad at him.

"Let's go. *Now*," he adds.

The man turns around on the stool, wearing a shit-eating grin, and I want to order him to turn back around if he doesn't have a death wish, but the man seems to be amused by Xavier's obvious anger.

"What the fuck are you smiling at?" Xavier barks to the man.

I'm instantly on my wobbly feet to try to stop this argument from getting out of control.

"I will fucking end you right here, right now for fucking with what's mine."

I place my hand on Xavier's chest. "Don't. Nothing is going on. Let it go."

"The hell it's not. I see exactly what's happening here."

"Stop," I plead.

His gaze fixes on me.

"Let. It. Go," I say my words slowly so that, even in my drunken state, they come out with enough clarity, so he knows that I'm not joking around.

"Anna, this guy . . ." He trails off, like he's stopping himself from saying something that he really wants to say. "This fucker needs to be taught a fucking lesson."

I shake my head. "He doesn't. You need to control your temper."

He narrows his eyes, and I can see the tension is not going to go away until I remove him from the situation. That means I need to give in and leave with him.

"Just stop, and I'll go wherever you want."

His eyes leave me for a brief moment. He stares down at the man behind me, like he's debating on whether or not to walk away from the fight that's brewing. When his gaze meets mine again, he wraps his fingers around my elbow. "Let's go."

I stumble a bit, my feet a little numb from all the liquor I just drank, as he begins to lead me outside.

Supporting all my weight with ease, he releases a small growl as we pass through the front door. "You shouldn't drink without me. If I'm not there, what's going to stop some motherfucker from drugging you?"

We make it into the cool night air, and I swat his hand off me. "I had everything under control in there. No one in this place is going to hurt me, not with Quinn and Tyler on the lookout. You have to stop trying to save me all the time. This whole possessive thing is becoming a problem. Allow me to live, Xavier!"

His blue eyes narrow. "*Live*? If you call putting yourself in danger living, then excuse me for giving a fuck and for ruining your fun."

"Nothing was going on in there. If I were in danger, I would have known it," I fire back, completely angry that he sees me as a silly twit who cannot take care of herself.

"That's where you're wrong, beautiful. This cruel world is far worse than you can imagine, and you wouldn't know real danger if it bit you in the ass."

His words have a ring of bitterness, and while I might not have experienced the same levels of hell he did, living with my father was no picnic either. I feel like I've grown up so much since I left Portland, and I've gotten better at detecting danger.

I rake my fingers through my hair and attempt to take

a deep breath, but suddenly, I find it difficult to breathe, like I'm being smothered. "Maybe a few days apart will do us some good." The words leave my mouth before I even realize I've said them out loud.

Xavier's eyes widen, and I'm pretty sure I've shocked the hell out of him.

"Anna—"

"No, Xavier. I mean it. All we've been doing is fighting. You bite my head off when any man shows me the slightest bit of attention, yet you keep secrets from me all the time and basically tell me that another woman kissing you is none of my business."

I can't imagine living without this man, but I won't be the next woman he grows tired of and tosses to the side. He once told me to demand respect, so that's what I'm doing.

"It's not like that, Anna. I told you, she meant nothing to me."

He's trying to talk his way out of the situation yet again, but he still hasn't given me a real answer.

If he really loves me like he says, then he needs to come clean to me about what he was doing with Angie. We need to work this out before I leave for *Tension*. If I don't know the truth, my mind will run wild about what he's doing.

I fold my arms across my chest. "Then, tell me what she is to you."

"I explained that to you."

"No, you didn't. You've refused to tell me why you were with her," I snap.

He blows a rush of air out of his nose. "She gave me a ride back to my bike. That's it. You have nothing to worry about when it comes to her."

"How can I not worry? I'm about to leave town, and you're surrounded by women who want to sleep with you."

His eyes jerk down at me with a stare so intense that it

causes a shudder to ripple down my spine. "And you don't think I worry about that same fucking thing every minute of the goddamn day? Whenever we go out, all the male eyes around you can't seem to peel themselves away from you. What if, one day, you figure out what a son of a bitch I am and leave me for someone better? God knows I'm not worthy of you, so I'm waiting on the day when you realize that too."

His words sober me up, and I recall the conversation I had with Nettie.

I reach up and cup his face, so I can stare into his nearly see-through blue eyes. "I'll never leave you."

He closes his eyes as he leans into my touch. "You don't know how hard I pray for that. Losing you is my biggest fear, so that's why I fight like hell to keep you."

"You have to stop being afraid of that. Not everyone in this world is going to leave you," I whisper. "You have to allow yourself to have some good in your life. You need to let me in and trust me."

He gazes into my eyes as he cradles my face in his hands. "That works two ways, beautiful. Some things I keep from you would cause you more harm than good if I told you about them. I don't want you to worry, which is why I won't tell you about the details of today. Just know that I've never loved any-one the way I love you, and I'd never do anything to hurt you. I promise you that. I've not thought about touching another woman since I've been with you. Trust me when I say, every-thing I do is to keep you safe. I love you, Anna—only you—and I meant it when I said I want to keep you forever. I wouldn't do anything that might fuck this up between us."

The pleading I see in his eyes tells me that he's being sincere, that he didn't mean to hurt me. As angry as I was with him ear-lier today, I can no longer bring myself to be mad.

How can I ask Xavier to trust me if I don't give him the same courtesy?

He leans in and presses his forehead to mine, and then he closes his eyes. "Please, Anna. Don't frown. I can't stand to see you so upset."

"I'm not mad at you, but we need to be completely honest with each other if things are going to work out between us."

He sighs, and warm breath wafts against my lips. "I've never lied to you about anything, and I'll be up-front about everything with you—except for this. This, you don't need to know."

"By saying that, I'll only worry more."

"Don't." His finger slides under my chin, and he tilts my head up. "Things will be all right. I'll make sure of it."

"If you would just tell me what's going on, whatever problem you're trying to hide from me, maybe I can help."

He shakes his head, causing a lock of his dark hair to fall across his forehead. "Sorry, beautiful. No one can handle this but me."

I stare into his eyes, and I know Xavier well enough to know that when he decides something, there's no changing his mind. I have a sneaking suspicion that something from Xavier's past has come back to haunt us both.

I sigh. "Then, I'm afraid, until you trust me enough to let me in, I'm going to need some time to think about things, to think about us."

The worry in his eyes is clear as he processes what I said. "Anna . . ."

I swallow hard, and it takes every bit of my willpower to muster up the courage to take a step back, leaving the comforting warmth of his embrace. "I need time. You can take me to the airport tomorrow, but I'll be staying at Aunt Dee's tonight."

The sad expression on his face nearly causes me to crumble and give in to him, allowing him to keep me out of the loop, as long as I get to be with him. But if I continue to live in the darkness of his secrets, I will never forgive myself for not standing up to him and demanding the truth.

Tears begin to burn my eyes, so I turn and run back into the restaurant because the last thing I want is for Xavier to see me cry.

Chapter
SIXTEEN

Xavier

ONE OF THE HARDEST THINGS I've ever done is allow Anna to walk away from me without too much of a fight. She wants the truth. I completely understand that, but it doesn't mean I can give it to her.

I lace my fingers together and stare up at the star-filled sky, wishing there were some way to make everything better. It kills me to be at the center of what's causing her pain, and I seem to have been doing that a lot lately. If I were a better man, I would encourage her to leave me for a guy who wouldn't hurt her all the fucking time.

I just can't get this relationship thing right.

The door of the restaurant slamming shut catches my attention.

The shit-stain who was sitting next to Anna at the bar comes strolling out with a cocky grin on his face. "Bishop sends his regards."

Adrenaline is still flowing through my veins, and I dare this shit stain to step to me.

I know exactly why he was sniffing around her. The symbols on his shirt are ones Bishop brands on his crew. It's one of the marks on my forearm that I've tried damn hard to cover up with other tattoos.

Now that Anna's out of earshot, there's no need for all these fucking games.

"What the fuck did you just say to me?"

He rolls his shoulders back, like my threat doesn't affect him, but I know better. If he's a part of the Block crew, then he's heard of me, so he must be well aware of the damage I could inflict on him in a matter of seconds. Being so damn brutal is what made me Bishop's right hand. He knows, when I unleash on someone, it won't be pretty.

"Bishop's giving you one month to get shit together and make things happen, like he's asked you to do, or next time, we get even closer to your girl."

Heat washes through me. "You. Will. Not. Fucking. Touch. Her."

He smirks. "You can't be with her all the time, X. It was all too easy to track her down and get right up next to her. Don't think we can't do it again."

"I'll kill every fucking one of you. I swear to God."

He laughs, and my chest puffs up as I curl my fingers into fists at my sides. I lunge forward, and the smirk falls off his face as he lifts his shirt in one quick motion.

A gleam from the bar's sign shines off the solid steel tucked into the waistband of his jeans. "Don't fucking try it."

My eyes zero in on the gun, and then I glare at him. "If you think that will stop me from ending you, then that proves you don't know my reputation very well."

"You're not quicker than a bullet, X."

I fix my stare on him. "You don't want to test that theory. I can fucking assure you of that. If you know what's good for you, you'd walk away right now."

He takes a step back. "Last warning, X. Do what Bishop says, or we'll be back."

My top lip curls of its own accord. "If you come around again, it'll be your fucking funeral. No one will touch her. No.

One. You run and tell Bishop that."

The tension hangs in the air until the man backs away and hops into a black car. He squeals the tires as he pulls out of the parking lot.

The moment he's gone, my hands begin to tremble as I come down from my adrenaline high.

It seems as though I need to make good on my promise to be Anna's personal bodyguard and keep eyes on her twenty-four/seven anytime she's in Detroit. Whether she knows it or not, she truly is incapable of handling every problem in this city on her own, and she will need me to watch over her.

AFTER WAITING IN THE PARKING lot for Quinn's shift to end, I take care to follow Anna and Quinn home while keeping out of sight. It comforts me to know who's around Anna, and if she refuses to come back to the house on Sycamore with me, then I'll be forced to make sure she's safe in other ways. And that starts with finding a place to park my bike where the girls won't see it in her aunt's backyard because I plan on spending the night out here, so I can keep watch over the house.

Chapter
SEVENTEEN

Anna

XAVIER BEHIND THE WHEEL OF Quinn's compact Honda would be almost comical if he didn't appear to be so tired this morning. He's so tall and broad that he barely fits in the seat, but it was necessary to borrow her car to drive me to the airport. Suitcases don't exactly fit on the back of a motorcycle.

He's wearing the same clothes he had on last night, and judging by the bags under his eyes, he hasn't slept a wink.

I know the feeling because I tossed and turned all night, wondering if refusing to go home with Xavier last night was the right thing to do even though I needed to make it clear that I demand honesty from him.

After we go to the house on Sycamore to pick up my suitcase, we head to the airport. We haven't said much to each other. Some tension from the things we said last night is clearly lingering between us, and it seems neither of us is going to budge to compromise.

Xavier parks the car next to the curb in the passenger drop-off area. "Guess this is it."

"I don't want to leave you, but this is the best thing for us right now. I want to be by your side when this is over."

The sadness in his eyes is unmistakable, but surprisingly, he hasn't asked me to quit my job with *Tension* in order to stay with him. It's like it's finally clicked with him that I need to keep this job, so we can be together when his suspension is lifted.

He reaches over and touches my cheek. He opens his mouth, like he wants to say something else, but he quickly closes it. Instead, he sighs and then flips open the door handle of the car. "Better get your bag. Planes don't wait."

I swallow hard when Xavier leaves me alone in the car. It's hitting me that I won't see him until Wednesday. Four days apart doesn't sound like a long time, but we haven't spent one day away from each other since we've met. I don't know if I'll be able to do this without breaking down into a complete puddle of tears.

I haven't even left yet, and I'm missing him like crazy.

Xavier can't see me like this. If he sees me hurting, he'll ask me to stay, and I won't say no.

I take a deep breath and lift my chin before opening the door. Xavier's standing there with his hands shoved into his pockets with my suitcase by his side.

He sucks in his bottom lip before slowly pulling it through his teeth. "You got everything?"

Everything but you, I want to say, but instead, I run through the mental checklist I made when I was packing. "I think so."

He nods. "Just remember, stick with Brian and Liv. They'll help you out if you need anything."

"Got it."

There's a weird uncertainty between us, and I can't think of a way to make it any better because leaving is something I have to do. There's no time for a long heart-to-heart talk about what happened between us.

Xavier stretches his tattooed arms out toward me and then wraps them around me. He buries his face into my hair, and he inhales deeply, like he's trying to commit my scent to his memory. "I'll miss you every damn day. If you have any problems, call me."

I cling to him, feeling the heat of his skin against me. "I will."

He pulls back first. "Head in there before I make a huge mistake and throw you back in this car."

I run my fingers along his jaw, scratching his stubble from his day-old beard. "I love you. This won't last forever. The only thing that's permanent is you and me."

He nods and then leans in and presses his lips to mine. "Love you, too. Now, go." He takes a step back as I grab the handle of my suitcase. "Later, beautiful."

I head into the building, and when I turn to get a final glimpse of Xavier, he's already gone.

The flight from Detroit to Seattle takes forever. Last time I flew cross-country like this, I was thoroughly distracted by the sexy wrestler sitting next to me while he was busy attempting to get into my pants.

When I finally get off the plane, I make my way through the airport to the exit. Seattle is a little cooler than Detroit, but it's still a comfortable summer evening.

I search for a sign to point me in the direction of a taxi, but my eyes widen when they land on a familiar face.

Liv waves to me. "Anna!"

I head in her direction, rolling my suitcase behind me, and notice that she's completely alone. "What are you doing here?"

"Waiting for you. X texted Brian and asked if we could look out for you, so I took the liberty of picking you up once X gave us your flight information. Hope you don't mind."

"Of course not," I say as I lean in to hug her. "That's so sweet of you. Thank you."

She releases me. "You're welcome. Now, come on. Let's get you over to the hotel. I parked just over here."

Once everything is loaded into the back of Liv's SUV, we hop into the cab.

She weaves in and out of traffic until we're coursing down

the highway.

She adjusts her butt in her seat. "So, how's X holding up with everything? Brian's worried about him."

"He's handling it better than I expected actually. When Mr. Silverman dropped the suspension on him, Xavier freaked out a bit, threatening to quit if they made me go on the road without him."

She raises her eyebrows. "I'm assuming he's gotten over that since you're here?"

I nod. "We fought about it a lot at first, but me being here is for the best, and he realizes that. It's just hard for us to be apart."

"Young love, the kind where you can't seem to get enough of one another"—Liv sighs with a dreamy expression on her face—"it's a beautiful thing. I used to worry that those butter-flies I felt when I first started dating Brian would fizzle away one day."

I smile as I observe in the sappy look on her face. "I take it that you're still madly in love?"

Her lips twist into a smile. "That obvious?"

I hold my fingers up, putting my thumb and forefinger near-ly together, allowing less than an inch of space between them. "Only a little."

We both laugh. It feels good because I haven't laughed much since the whole suspension thing went down.

Xavier is always intense, so I've come to expect that from him, but with everything going on, it's been hard to get him out of his own head. He worries so much, and looking back, we've been having a lot of heated discussions lately. I hope that when all of this is settled and he's able to get back into the ring, playful Xavier will return. I miss that side of him.

We pull up to the hotel, and Liv drives under the awning of the building, but I don't see a sign for valet parking.

"You didn't have to pull up here. I can walk in with you after you park the car."

"Brian and I aren't staying at the hotel. We live not too far from here, so we prefer to stay home when *Tension* travels close. Kami sleeps better in her own bed, which means Brian and I actually get to sleep, too."

"Speaking of Kami, is she with Brian?"

She nods. "Yes. They rarely get quality time together. Kami keeps him on his toes."

I chuckle, picturing such a large man like Brian at the mercy of a little blonde two-year-old girl.

Liv pushes the button to pop the hatch on the trunk, and a bellhop in a burgundy suit makes his way to the back of the SUV.

"Call me if you need anything. I'm only about fifteen minutes away."

I smile, thankful for her kindness. "Thank you so much, Liv."

"Of course. What are friends for?"

My grin widens. It's nice to finally have some friends after so many years of being cooped up with my father's rules.

I hop out of the SUV and turn toward Liv. "I'll see you tomorrow at the show?"

"You can count on it. I'll be out there, front and center, to watch what they do with you, Anna Sweets." She winks at me after calling me out on my stage name.

I roll my eyes. "I doubt they'll use me tomorrow. Xavier isn't here, so there's no point in putting me in the show."

"I don't know, Anna. If they're paying you, they'll find a way to work you into the ring."

My stomach flips, and I suddenly feel uneasy at the thought of heading out into that arena without Xavier. I'm not sure if I can do it alone.

Liv tilts her head, and by the expression on her face, I can tell that I'm not hiding my worry very well. "Aw, Anna, don't be nervous. You'll be great."

"You think so?"

"I do. Don't give it another thought." Her cell phone rings from the console next to her. She glances down at the screen and shakes her head. "It's Brian. I'm sure there's an emergency, like a dirty diaper, and he's freaking out. I'll see you tomorrow."

I tell her good-bye, close the door, and then watch her pull away, laughing to myself as I think about Brian unable to handle Kami on his own.

"Checking in, miss?" the bellhop asks as he holds the handle of my bag.

"Yes. Thank you."

I follow the short, pudgy man into the hotel lobby. "Would you like me to bring your bag up?"

"I can manage."

He smiles and releases the handle. "Here you go. The front desk is straight ahead. Enjoy your stay."

Tons of people are milling about with cameras and cell phones in hand. Over the past few weeks, I have learned these people are wrestling fanatics. They follow the superstars on social media so that they can figure out exactly where the guys will be. Autographs and pictures with their favorite wrestlers are a hot commodity among fans.

I'm sure a lot of them are looking for Xavier. It's sad that he can't be here because he loves his fans, and I know he probably misses giving back to them, like he usually does.

I weave around the crowd, and then I hear the name that Tension dubbed me with being shouted.

"Anna Sweets! Is X with you?"

I shake my head, a little dazed that they know who I am. "Sorry, guys. He's not."

The collective sound of disappointed fans echoes around the lobby as I continue to walk around them.

A rather skinny man wearing a T-shirt with Tension's logo

on it steps in front of me while holding a silver Sharpie. "Will you sign my shirt?"

The corner of my mouth turns up. "I'm flattered. Of course I will." I scribble my name on his shirt, trying to be as neat as I can while giving my very first autograph. I re-cap the marker and hand it back to the guy. "There you go."

He smiles. "Thank you so much."

"You're welcome."

I walk away from the mob of people, completely overwhelmed and humbled and totally smiling like an idiot.

Steps away from the front desk, I'm in line, waiting to check in, when a familiar voice sounds, reminding me of nails on a chalkboard.

"Who would've ever thought that the fans would ask for your autograph? They're almost as pathetic as X with the way they're fawning all over you."

I turn to find Deena in a skintight blue dress, staring down her nose at me.

I fight the urge to roll my eyes at her and stick my tongue out like a five-year-old. "What do you want?"

She smirks and then throws her blonde hair over her shoulder. "Am I not allowed to make small talk with you?"

I shake my head. "I'd prefer if you didn't."

She lifts an eyebrow. "Well, we don't always get what we want in life, do we?"

It's not hard to tell that she's still hung up on Xavier blowing her off, but I refuse to argue with her.

When she sees that I'm ignoring her, she folds her arms over her chest and continues to talk without invitation, "What does X think about your upcoming storyline with Rex? I bet he's dying to watch you make out with another man on television."

"That's not going to happen."

"Of course it is," she says as she pretends to be occupied with her perfectly manicured nails.

"You heard Mr. Silverman the other night. It's going to be weeks before Rex is back in the ring."

"To wrestle," she corrects. "He said it would be weeks before Rex returns in the ring for a match. It doesn't mean that they can't put the two of you into the show. Rex has excellent mic skills, and that pumps the crowd up nearly as much as the high-flying maneuvers he does."

My brow furrows. "Are you telling me that Rex is here this weekend?"

Deena nods. "Of course he is, and I believe he requested a room right next to yours."

If I could see my own face, I'm sure I'd see that all the color has completely drained from my face. My plan was to ignore Rex as best as I could when he returned from his injuries. I thought that would be a few weeks from now. I never dreamed he would be around so soon.

Xavier and I aren't on the best of terms right now. Things are still so rocky between us. How is he going to handle knowing that Rex is back so soon and staying in the room right next to mine?

My panic must greatly amuse Deena. A catty witchlike laugh bubbles up from her throat as she turns and walks away, no doubt feeling like she accomplished her mission at getting me frazzled.

"Next? I can take the next person in line, please."

My attention snaps to the lady at the front desk, wearing a required smile.

"Hi. Sorry. Anna Cortez." I hand over my debit card and driver's license.

The dark-haired lady types my information into the computer. "Okay, found you. Seems you were added on to the reservation originally in Mr. Cold's name."

"Yes. Is there any way you can confirm if my room is next to someone else's?"

"Yes, ma'am. Name?"

"Rex Risen."

She types in a few more things and then nods her head. "Yes, ma'am. He's right next door."

I sigh. "I hate to be a pain, but can I be moved?"

"Let me check." Her eyes scan the screen. "Not at the price range you are currently in. Those rooms have all been checked in, but we can upgrade you to a suite for an extra four hundred per night."

I grimace, knowing that I need to be careful with what I spend. "That's okay. I'll stay where I am."

"Very well." The lady finishes checking me in and then hands me a room key along with my other two cards. "Enjoy your stay."

I make my way over to the elevator, and when the door slides open, a familiar face comes into view.

"Oh, good. Just who I am looking for," Jimmy says as he steps off the elevator. "I've got something for you." He opens the manila folder in his hands. "Here's your itinerary."

I take the paper, and there's a list of times and places written on it. "Mine?"

He nods and adjusts the white plastic sunglasses sitting on top of his mullet. "X texted me and asked that I show you the ropes while he's not here."

"That's kind of you, Jimmy."

He shrugs. "He's paying me, so don't think too highly of me." He glances down at my bag. "Well, I'll let you get settled in. As usual, dinner in the hotel restaurant is on *Tension*. Come down when you're ready."

"Okay."

Jimmy begins to walk away.

I throw out another, "Thank you," which only results in him raising his hand into the air in a weird wave while his back is still to me.

I sigh as I get on the next open elevator. This experience is so different from when I travel with Xavier. I can't wait for him to get back on the road with me.

Chapter
EIGHTEEN

Anna

AFTER DINNER, THE NEXT THING on the agenda was a meeting with the wardrobe department. I knock on room 507, and a little black lady with short-cropped hair and glasses answers the door.

She smiles, making her appear warm and inviting. "Anna Sweets, it's lovely to finally meet you. I'm Pearl, the entire wardrobe department. Come on in."

"A one woman show?"

"Exactly," she says.

I laugh as I step into the hotel room and notice that her it's packed with suitcases full of fabric. A compact sewing machine sits on the desk with a wrestler's costume.

"You weren't kidding. You really are a one-man band. You make everyone's costumes by hand?"

She nods. "I do. Every outfit you've ever seen on *Tension* over the last fifteen years has been one of my designs. That brings me to you. I can't have you out there, on the air, wearing just a plain old T-shirt and jeans."

I grimace. "You can't? I really don't plan on being in the ring much."

She lifts one eyebrow. "That's not the word that has been passed down from the top of the *Tension* chain. From what I hear, you'll be making an appearance on every show for the next three months, maybe longer, on Rex's arm."

I rub my forehead and squeeze my eyes shut. "Oh no."

She pats my shoulder. "X is gonna have to get over it, honey. If he wants you to keep this job, he knows better than anyone that you'll have to play along with whatever the big boss wants. Mr. Silverman has really been pushing the idea of a huge rivalry over you between X and Rex."

"Any idea what they want me to do when I'm out in the ring?"

"You're asking the wrong person for that. I only make the clothes for the storyline. They don't divulge more than minor information to me when it comes to the plot so I can make sure the outfits are correct. I've been asked to prepare a costume for you that goes along with Rex's."

The idea of matching Rex makes my stomach turn a bit. "This is going to end so badly."

"Maybe it won't. X is a smart guy. He'll get over it if he wants to keep you."

"Thank you." I sigh. "I guess we'd better get to work then."

Pearl takes a few minutes to measure every inch of my body, and then she sits on the side of her bed and begins sketching on a pad. Within a few moments, the vision she sees in her head for the outfit she wants to make for me comes to fruition on paper. It's basically the same as jeans and a T-shirt I usually wear. This time though, the outfit consists of tight pink leather pants and a white blouse with bright pink sequins that say *Anna Sweets* on top of a frosted cupcake.

I laugh. "Cute."

"Thanks." She smiles widely at her own artwork. "I think it plays up the whole sweet thing pretty well." She hands me the pad, so I can take a closer inspection. "You like it?"

I nod. "It's really great."

She smiles. "Good. Then, I'll get to work and have this ready for your appearance tomorrow night."

"Tomorrow?" My stomach flips again. The idea of being out in front of that crowd without Xavier terrifies me. "That soon?"

"You'll be great," Pearl encourages. She glances down at her watch. "Okay, it's almost time for my next appointment. I'll find you backstage to give you this outfit before you go live."

"Sounds good."

We exchange cell phone numbers, so she can text me when the costume is ready, and then I head back to my room.

While I wait on the elevator, I check my cell. I haven't had a chance to read messages since I texted Quinn and Xavier to tell them I'd safely landed in Seattle and got checked into my room. I have four missed texts.

I click on the message icon and chuckle. Quinn was the last person to text me, and without even clicking on the full message, I can see she's waiting on me to call her.

> *Quinn: Hello?*

> *Quinn: Call me every day while you're on the road. Does this ring a bell?*

I shake my head as I type my reply.

> *Anna: Sorry. Busy schedule since I landed. Heading to bed now. Will call in the morning.*

Even though it's only eight in the evening here on the West Coast, I'm still on Detroit time. I yawn as I click the next message. It causes me to bite my lip with anticipation since Xavier and I didn't exactly part on a happy note.

> *Xavier: Glad you're safe. Hope Liv found you okay.*

> *Xavier: Going to bed. Totally beat. I know the time change sucks for you, but if you need to talk, call anytime. Love you.*

His words make me smile. Even when we fight, he's still

sweet, making me miss him even more. If I were back in Detroit, I would have him cornered by now, forcing him to spill whatever it is that he's been hiding from me, the thing that's caused this weird rift between us. Once whatever it is comes to light, I know we'll be able to fix it together.

I shoot a reply to him, wanting to let him know I'm thinking about him.

Anna: I'll call you tomorrow. Get some rest. You looked beat today. Miss you like crazy and love you.

I stuff my phone into my back pocket as the elevator stops on my floor. I'm exhausted myself and can't wait to lay down. I fish my room card out of pocket, and when my eyes snap up to read the numbers on the doors, they lock on Rex's dark eyes.

My back stiffens when I see the one man I've been dreading to face ever since I discovered I would have to come on the road without Xavier. Rex's long dark hair is pulled back into a low ponytail. A yellow hue tints the underside of his eyes, a remnant of Xavier breaking his nose, and several small bruises are on his chin and arms. Other than that, he appears to be in pretty good shape. Rex should be thankful *Tension*'s bouncer, Freddy, was there to pull Xavier off of him before Xavier could inflict a lot more damage.

His eyes twinkle as an evil smile dances across his lips. "There's my girl."

"Stop it," I order. "I'm not your girl."

His smile widens. "Of course you are. For the next three months while Xavier is gone, you'll be on my arm while on camera . . . and off camera, too, if you play your cards right."

I roll my eyes as I attempt to step around him in the hall. "You disgust me."

"That's interesting." He smirks. "Xavier can fuck half the women in this company, yet I'm the disgusting one. I find that a little hypocritical coming from you."

Even though I know it's probably true, the mention of Xavier being with a lot of women turns my stomach. I don't enjoy that thought being thrown in my face. In some ways, I'm just as bad as Xavier in some ways when it comes to the jealousy department.

The thing about this conversation though is that I know Rex is trying to mess with me in a lame attempt at pushing Xavier's buttons even though he's on the other side of the country.

I try one more time to step around Rex, wanting nothing more than to get away from him. "Would you please stop getting in front of me?"

Rex defensively throws his hands up. "All you have to do is say please. I like it when beautiful women beg. It's my weakness."

I shove past him and don't even bother to engage in an argument.

I swipe my key in the door and then shove down the handle.

"Oh, Anna," Rex calls in a singsong voice, "I'll be right next door if you want to work on that kiss of ours that's happening tomorrow night."

"Fuck you, Rex." I square my shoulders and march into my room, cutting off my contact with the man that can get under my skin quicker than any other man I've ever met.

I waste no time in getting ready for bed. Tomorrow will be a busy day, and I know I'll need all the sleep I can get if I'm going to survive it.

I set my alarm on my phone for eight in the morning, and just before I place the phone on the nightstand, I notice a new text has arrived. I click on the phone and gasp.

It's been a long time since that name has shown up on my phone. My hand trembles a bit as I pull the screen up for a closer inspection. After I left him without so much as a word, Jorge is the last person I ever expected to hear from again.

Out of everything I left behind in Portland, the one thing

I regret is the way I left Jorge. Even though it was obvious we didn't love each other the way we should have in such an involved relationship, I did care for him, and he deserved at least an explanation from me. I wouldn't blame him if he hated me.

As I click on his name, I take a deep breath and prepare myself for the scathing message.

> *Jorge: I heard you're in Seattle. If I drive up there, will you see me?*

My heart does a double thump against my ribs as I read over his words more than a dozen times. I'm not sure what he'll say to me, but whatever it is, I need to woman up and hear him out. I owe him that much.

> *Anna: I'll be here until Wednesday morning. I have shows tonight and Sunday, but I have downtime on Monday until I do Tuesday's show.*

I chew my bottom lip as I hit Send and wait on his response. The phone chimes again, alerting me to a new message before I've even had the chance to set the phone down.

> *Jorge: Dinner on Monday night? We have many things to discuss.*

> *Anna: We do. Monday sounds great. I'll text you my hotel information, so you can pick me up.*

I send the information and lay the phone down on the nightstand. A sliver of light from the evening sun creeps through the crack in the curtains and streaks across the ceiling as I stare at it. So many things roll through my mind all at once. I find it difficult to focus. It almost feels as though everything is coming down on me at once—being on my own at the show, being away from Xavier, dealing with Rex, and now facing the messy past with Jorge.

I hope I can handle all the pressure because now is not the time for me to crack.

Chapter NINETEEN

Anna

THE DRIVER PULLS THROUGH THE gated section of the arena and stops near a back door where I recognize Freddy, the *Tension* bouncer who pulled Xavier off of Rex.

I push open the back door and slip out of the SUV.

I head toward the door. Freddy is standing there with his eyes are trained on me as I near him.

Immediately, his gaze checks behind me. "I see X took the suspension seriously since he's not with you."

I step up next to him, and his nearly seven-foot frame towers over me. "He did. He's still back in Detroit."

Freddy raises his dark eyebrows and writes something down on his clipboard. "I have to say, I'm a bit surprised that X didn't attempt to bend the rules, like he typically does, and show up with you here anyway. I expected that actually."

I shrug. "He knows this is only temporary. Hopefully he trusts me. There's no need for him to violate the terms of his suspension."

"X might trust you, but I know he sure as hell doesn't trust Rex. I don't care what line of bullshit the public relations department fed the press about the fight between them onstage being a part of the show. I've gotten between the two of them too many times for me to believe it wasn't real. Rex has been taunting X for far too long. It was all bound to come to a head at some point."

My lips pull into a tight line. "You're right, but if the story keeps X out of jail, I'll go along with it any day."

Freddy gives me a pointed look. "Is that why you agreed to the whole love-triangle thing with Rex?"

I tilt my head to the side. "How do you know about that?"

"Everyone does. This is Tension, Anna. Everyone knows everyone's business here." He sighs. "It doesn't help that Rex has been bragging about having you on his arm to everyone either."

"Great," I mutter. "I suppose he's already in there?"

Freddy nods. "He is. If he gives you shit, come find me."

"Thank you. I appreciate that."

"Not a problem," he replies coolly. "X is a good guy, and I know he only did what he did because he had been pushed, so I'd like to help him out as much as I can."

"You're a good guy, Freddy." I pat the smooth brown skin on his forearm.

He smiles. "I try. Now, let's get you back there before you're late."

He presses a button on the walkie-talkie hanging over his shoulder. "Security needed at the back entrance. I'm escorting talent into the building."

The radio squawks to life. "Copy that."

Freddy nods toward the door and then heads inside with me on his heels.

Backstage is the same as every other time I've been back here. Men and women of all shapes and sizes, wearing T-shirts with the word *Tension* on them, are buzzing around, pushing equipment in every direction.

Freddy stops at a set of open blue doors. "Catering is in here. I'll radio the writers and tell them where you are. I'm sure they'll send someone for you shortly."

"Thanks, again, Freddy."

"No problem, Anna Sweets. Take care of yourself."

When he leaves me standing there, I wrap my arms around myself and head into what Xavier loves to refer to as the Snake Pit. As always, several women dressed to kill are gathered around one of the tables, no doubt plotting on how to get their hooks into a professional wrestler.

Not one friendly face is to be seen in the place, so I make my way over to an empty tables and sit down. I drag my phone out and dial Xavier's number, but the line simply rings a few times before going straight to voice mail.

I wonder where he could be?

When the tone sounds, I leave a quick message. "Hey, it's me. I'm at the show and really missing you. I'll try to call you again later. Love you."

My heart sinks a little. It would have been nice to hear his voice and find a little encouragement or last-minute pointers from a guy who's been through this hundreds of times.

I sigh and then quickly dial Quinn's number, desperately needing the sound of a friendly voice to help me not feel so alone right now.

Quinn answers on the second ring. "Hey, chica! Nice to see you're taking my threat of calling me every day a little more seriously now."

I smile but roll my eyes. "When have I missed a day of talking to you?"

She clears her throat. "I can think of a few when you were with Mr. Sexy all the time. Speaking of, how did it go with him dropping you off at the airport?"

I nibble on the corner of my bottom lip as I fight back some tears. "It was rough. I hate fighting with him all the time. It's been extra hard, being here and knowing that there's this weird tension between us."

"When you get home, I'm sure he'll finally come to his

senses and figure out how to be more open with you."

"I hope so," I mumble.

"He's not an idiot, Anna. He knows you mean business now because you set your foot down. You're demanding respect from him. He'll come to his senses. He's a man, and sometimes, men are a little slow at figuring things out. Hell, look at how many times Brock and I fought over when we should get married before he came around and compromised with me."

My eyes widen as she lets me see a glimpse of something they fought over. She was always so secretive about it before, so it takes me aback that she blurted it out like that.

"Wait a minute," I say as things click. "Are you telling me that all the fighting between you and Brock that I witnessed at Larry's was over setting a wedding date? Quinn, I didn't even know you were engaged then."

"We weren't engaged until recently. Our fights were about that very thing though. I left him there for a while to pound it into his head that if he wanted to keep me around, he would need to really commit to me. That's when we got back together, when you first got here. I give you props, Anna, for standing up to X and sticking to your guns. We women need to stand up to our men and make them understand what we need in order to be happy."

The mention of Xavier causes me to wonder again where he might be. We haven't spoken, except through our texts, since he dropped me off at the airport. I miss him terribly, but if he needs some space from me, I have no choice right now but to give it to him, seeing as I'm on the other side of the country.

I shake my head, trying to rid myself of thoughts of Xavier before I break down into a puddle of tears with Quinn on the other end of the line.

I need to change the subject. "I got an interesting text last night."

"Oh?" Quinn says. I can tell her interest is piqued. "From

whom?"

"Jorge," I reply simply.

"What? Oh my God. What did he want?"

"He somehow knew I was in Seattle and asked to meet while I'm close to home. He says we have things we need to discuss."

"Are you serious? You're not going to see him, are you? X will shit a brick if you're out with your ex-fiancé."

I run my fingers through my hair, pushing it back from my face. "I know, but I feel like I owe it to Jorge to hear out whatever he wants to say to me. He was my friend, one I was promised to marry, and then I ran out on him without any explanation. He has a right to be upset with me."

Quinn sighs into the phone, and it's not hard to tell that she doesn't exactly agree with me. "You're a better woman than me, cuz. The best I would've agreed to would've been a phone call. I don't think I could bear to see an old boyfriend face-to-face, but your situation is different. Jorge wasn't just some guy you dated for a while who cheated on you or something."

"He's actually a great guy. He's just not the man I'm meant to be with, and I should've had the guts to tell him that before I left, but I didn't. I need to make things right between us. I need that closure."

"That's what makes you such a good person, Anna. You really do care about people."

"Thank you. I don't always feel that way about myself. Father always made me feel like I was the evilest thing in the world."

"Pfft," Quinn huffs. "Uncle Simon needs a reality check. By being his crazy, uptight self, he's missing out on what an extraordinary woman you have become. It's his loss, Anna, and you have to stop believing that what he said is true. He's the one who's wrong when it comes to how strict he's been with you. Hopefully, one day, he'll wake up and give you the apology he owes you."

I release a slightly bitter laugh. "That's never going to happen, Quinn. You and I both know Father doesn't work that way."

"You never know. He might surprise you after he realizes that you're not going to bend to his will anymore."

I open my mouth to repeat again that Father will never apologize, but the sound of my name being called over the low murmurs in the catering room catches my attention.

"Anna Sweet?"

"Right here." I raise my hand and then whisper into the phone, "Got to go, Quinn. I'll call you soon."

"Okay, love you," she says before we end the call.

I shove myself out of the seat and then follow the guy wearing a *Tension* T-shirt out of the room. I recognize the man as one of the stagehands. When the show goes live, he is responsible for fetching the talent to get them ready to head out and face the crowd.

We make it back to a set of closed blue double doors, and the man raps his knuckles on the steel just below a piece of paper that says *Writers*.

He twists the knob and then pops his head inside. "Anna Sweets for you."

"Send her in, Al," a female voice on the other side calls.

I instantly know I'm about to face Vicky.

Al turns to me with an expression on his face that can only be described as worry as the corners of his mouth pull down. "Good luck."

I lift my chin and step through the door, unsure of what I'm walking into.

The writers' room is set up identical as it was in Atlanta with the folding tables side by side and four writers sitting next to each other, typing furiously.

"Have a seat," Vicky orders. She doesn't bother to glance up at me from her computer.

My eyes flick to the blue plastic chairs in front of Vicky, and there, with a smirk on his face, sits Rex.

I sigh as I note he's strategically placed himself in the middle seat, leaving me no choice but to take a chair next to him.

He wiggles his eyebrows and pats the empty seat to his right. "Saved you a seat."

I roll my eyes and plop down on the edge of the seat next to him, doing my best to scoot the further away from him. He throws his arm around my shoulders, and my skin crawls.

"Ugh." I throw his arm off me. "Please don't touch me."

This amuses him. He leans in toward me and whispers, "Come on, Anna. You need to get used to me touching you because I'll be doing it a lot on camera."

I want to argue with him and tell him that there's no way that's going to happen, but Mr. Silverman has already made it perfectly clear that a romance with Rex on camera is in the cards for me.

I twist my head away from Rex, and he chuckles darkly as he settles back into his seat.

"Okay, Anna," Vicky says as she swivels her chair to face me. "I'm sure you know why you're here, so let's get right down to the storyline, shall we?"

"Okay." I fold my arms across my chest, knowing full well that I'll absolutely hate whatever comes out of her mouth.

"Tonight, we're going to send you out with Rex and another lady we've brought on as an employee. Rex informs me you've already met Deena."

Great.

When I thought things couldn't get any worse, Deena gets thrown into the mix.

Vicky awaits a response from me, but when she sees that she won't be getting one, she adjusts her black-rimmed glasses and continues, "The two of you ladies will accompany Rex out to the ring, and you both will be a part of the Fire Phenomenal X support group, being sympathetic to Rex. The three of you will be leading a fictional protest to get Phenomenal X out of *Tension* for good."

My mouth falls open. "That's the most absurd idea I've ever heard. The fans will hate that, and I will not—"

"Need I remind you, Ms. Cortez, that you are under contract? You must follow the script we provide, or we will have cause to remove you from the company."

Her threat is clear. I need to go along with this or get fired. And if I'm fired, Mr. Silverman will not allow me back into the building when Xavier's suspension is lifted.

I take a deep breath. Being a part of a group in this scenario is better than being in a fake relationship with Rex.

I clear my throat. "So, I just walk into the ring with Rex and Deena and stand there? Is that all I do?"

"For now," Vicky replies coolly. "Feel free to improvise if you think something will strengthen the plotline for the rivalry between X and Rex. We need to get the fans excited about an epic showdown between the two."

"Got it," I answer solemnly. "Anything else?"

She eyes me over the top of her glasses for a moment and then shakes her head. "That's it. You may go."

Without another word, I hop up from the chair and race through the door, relieved a little that I won't be kissing Rex tonight like he threatened, but I still have this looming feeling that I've only temporarily escaped it.

Chapter
TWENTY

Anna

MY CELL VIBRATES, ALERTING ME to a new text, so I quickly check the message folder.

Pearl: Your costume is ready. Come see me to get fitted.

My heart sinks when it doesn't end up being Xavier responding to my earlier attempts of reaching him. I know we've been bickering a little, but he's never gone this long without contacting me. The last time I heard from him was last night when he responded with the message that he was going to bed.

I fully expect him to call me before I go out solo on my first show, but so far, he hasn't, so I decide to try him again one more time.

Anna: Checking in. Hope you're all right. Super nervous about the show tonight. Would love to hear your voice before I go out there.

I stuff the phone into my back pocket as I head down the long hallway in an attempt to find where Pearl is set up backstage.

"You lost, Anna?" Brian's voice cuts through my thoughts as I pass by him, half-dazed.

I grimace. "Wardrobe?"

"Come on." Brian motions with his hand. "Pearl's set up

right down the hall." He casually tosses the championship belt over his shoulder as he walks with me. "How are you holding up without X being around? Anyone giving you any problems?"

Rex's and Deena's faces both immediately come to mind, but I decide to keep my run-ins with them to myself. "It's been tough without Xavier, but everything has been fine. I've had no issues."

"That's good." Brian raises his eyebrows.

I can tell he doesn't exactly believe me, but with me giving him nothing else to go on, he has no choice but to roll with what I've told him.

As long as I remain strong, Rex's and Deena's words are only words, and they can only do damage to me if I allow them to. If I let Brian in on them harassing me, he'll report it to Xavier and get him all riled up, causing him to do God knows what when I can control the situation by remaining levelheaded. If Xavier gets involved, knowing his temper, all hell will break loose, and I can't allow that to happen since he's already on thin ice when it comes to his job at Tension. Mr. Silverman doesn't seem like a man who gives many third chances.

As soon as Brian and I round the corner in the hallway, Pearl comes into view. She doesn't get an office to set up, like most of the other behind-the-scenes people do. Instead, she simply has her sewing machine propped up on a folding table with a couple of suitcases of fabric next to her.

"I'll leave you to it. Good luck out there tonight, Anna. Try not to stress too much. Filming Tension on the weekends is never televised, so they'll save all the crazy stunts until Tuesday when the show is live to the world," Brian informs me.

That's why I don't have to kiss Rex tonight. Vicky and Rex are saving that for when it'll be on live TV, and X will be sure to see it along with the rest of the world.

Brian notices the expression on my face, which I'm sure is a look of horror, and then he pats my shoulder. "You'll be fine.

Don't panic."

I take a deep breath, resolved to keep my anxiety to myself the best I can. "Thanks, Brian. I appreciate the words of encouragement."

"Anytime." He starts to turn away but holds in his tracks. "Liv wanted me to invite you to dinner at the house Monday since it's our day off. She's making meatloaf."

I smile. "Sounds great. Thank you for the offer, but I actually have plans. I'm from Portland, and I'm meeting a friend from home that night."

He nods. "No worries. I'll let her know. She didn't want you spending the day alone, so she'll be happy to hear that you've got family close." He takes a step back. "Catch you later, Anna. Break a leg tonight."

"Thanks," I call down the hall after him. Then, I step up beside Pearl. "You wanted to see me?"

After a few adjustments, the outfit Pearl designed on her sketchpad in the hotel room is the exact outfit that's on my body right now. It really does fit my personality, and it's not too far of a stretch from what I would actually wear—jeans and a T-shirt—except this outfit is skintight and made of some sort of spandex material.

"Looks good," Pearl says while appraising her work. "We're all finished. Let me know if you have any problems with the outfit tonight, and I'll make changes if needed."

"All right. Thanks, Pearl."

Unsure of what to do with myself now, I weave my way around the hallways again and find the catering room. The same women are still sitting there, only Deena is now mixed up with them. I'm not in the mood to deal with her right now, so I lean against the wall in the hall and check my phone again.

There's still no message from Xavier. Why is he avoiding me? Was our fight that bad that he's resolved to give up on our relationship?

The last thought hurts, and a weight settles over my heart while I entertain the possibility that we might not be together anymore. When I threatened he would lose me if he didn't change, I didn't think he would opt to be done with me instead of controlling his temper.

You don't so easily dismiss someone you love, do you?

I glance up from my phone, and my eyes land on Al, the stagehand, as he marches toward me at a brisk pace.

"Anna, you're up next." He pokes his head inside the catering room. "Deena, you're up."

The sound of her chair scraping against the tile floor echoes into the hallway. "Excuse me, ladies. A star is about to be born."

Hearing Deena make a smug statement causes me to roll my eyes hard. You've got to be kidding me.

Deena struts out of the room in one of her typical too tight body-hugging dresses and smirks when she spots me. Her eyebrow lifts as she takes in my outfit. "You look like a toddler."

I glance down at my sparkly shirt and shrug. "At least I don't look like an uptight bitch." The words leave my mouth before I realize I've said them out loud. Normally, I would never speak up like this, but being around Quinn, who constantly pushes me to stand up for myself, coupled with how Deena gets on my last damn nerve have caused me to deviate from my overly sweet good-girl personality.

Deena's eyes widen, but I don't give her time to say anything in response.

Trying to find the quickest way out of the situation, I immediately turn to Al. "Lead the way."

When Al takes us to the black entrance curtain, I spot Rex. He's not wearing his typical wrestling getup tonight. This time, he's dressed in a suit with a white dress shirt that's unbuttoned halfway down, so his chest is exposed.

The only things that ruin the somewhat sophisticated look are the still yellow marks under his eyes from where his nose was broken.

Deena immediately cozies up against his side and then kisses his cheek. I, on the other hand, stand back and fold my arms.

Rex chuckles. "Well, at least one of you has your part down pat. Anna, if you want to make it in Tension, you'd do well to take some notes from Deena. She understands how the game is played."

"No, thanks. Being trampy isn't my thing."

Deena narrows her eyes at me. "I'm sick and tired of your shit, Anna. Call me a slut one more time—"

I resist the urge to do as she asks, but Rex interjects.

"Ladies, ladies, save it for the ring. The tension between the two of you will make an entertaining show, so don't unleash it on each other until we get out there, and make sure the fans perceive it as the two of you fighting over me."

"That's never going to happen," I snap.

Rex levels his stare on me. "It has to. It's scripted. We are all actors, remember? You'd better follow the script if you don't want your pretty little ass canned."

His words bring forward a bit of a reality check for me.

He's right. Damn it, I hate that he's right.

I have to figure out a way to stand my ground yet coexist with these two assholes if I want to be with Xavier when he goes back on the road—that is, if he still wants me around.

It's hard to know what's going on between Xavier and I, seeing as how he has yet to respond to any of my attempts to contact him. If he doesn't answer me by the time I'm finished with my portion of the show, I'm going to be pissed.

Rex's entrance music blasts through the arena, and he extends his elbow to me. "Shall we?"

I lift my chin and then hook my arm through his. "Let's get this over with."

Rex leads Deena and I through the black curtain and out onto the steel grating stage. When we're facing the audience, the crowd ignites in a roar of applause and cheers.

Rex's expression is smug as he walks us down the ramp and then up the steps leading into the ring. He sits on the ropes, holding them open for me and Deena to squeeze through.

Stepping into the square ring without Xavier is a surreal experience. I don't want to be the center of attention. It was much better when I was out here with Xavier because all eyes were on him.

A stagehand runs up to the ring, hands Rex a microphone, and then dashes out of sight.

Rex takes a moment to stare out at the crowd while Deena struts around the ring, showing off her legs, eliciting catcalls from some of the men in the crowd. I do my best to be invisible.

"Well, well, well. I bet you all didn't expect me to be back so soon. Thought Phenomenal X messed me up real good, didn't you? Well, as you can see, I'm doing quite well." Rex waves his hand up and down in front of himself, as if to say, Check out my body. "In fact, I'm doing so well that I'll be back in the ring when we film Tension live on Tuesday night."

This statement causes the crowd to go nuts.

"So, this Tuesday, live, right here on Tension, you all will get the pleasure of watching me go one-on-one with Brian 'Razor' Rollins with the championship on the line!"

The decibels shoot up tenfold at this announcement.

My eyes widen. I didn't expect for him to say that at all, considering I was told he had some broken ribs.

Rex smiles as he gives the crowd a few seconds to calm down, but instead, they all begin chanting the word, "Tonight," over and over again.

He brings the mic back up to his lips. "I would love nothing more than to take on Razor tonight, but where's the fun in that? I want Phenomenal X to witness me taking something that he wants so much. Speaking of . . ." His voice trails off just before he reaches over and hooks his arm around my waist, drawing me to his side. "You all remember Phenomenal X's lady, Anna Sweets, don't you?"

Whistles erupt around the crowd—approving the way I look, I suppose. Never have I felt so much like a piece of meat on display.

"Mark your calendars, people. You won't want to miss the fireworks that are coming because I'm about to crush Phenomenal X's dreams live, right before your very eyes, by taking everything in this world that's important to him." Rex laughs darkly into the mic before dropping it on the blue mat.

"Come on, ladies." He extends one elbow to Deena and the other to me. He escorts us out of the ring and to the backstage area, much in the same manner as when we came in.

The moment we're away from the eyes of the crowd, I jerk my hand away from Rex, causing Deena to snap her head in my direction.

She narrows her eyes at me. "You'd better learn how to be a team player. You did absolutely nothing out there to sell the idea that you are Team Rex now."

"That's because I'm not on it. I'll walk out there with him because I have to in order to keep this job. Doesn't mean I'll be lovey-dovey with him—pretend or not."

I turn to walk away, but the second I pivot, something catches my feet, sending me flying forward. Pain shoots through my hand as I land awkwardly on my left side.

I glance up, only to see an evil snarl showing up on Deena's face, and it's clear that she caused me to fall.

What is it with all these bitches tripping me?

"Anna?" Brian bends down next to me. "You all right?"

I stare at the pinkie finger on my left hand, and it's beginning to bruise already.

Brian grimaces. "Let's get you to a trainer. Someone needs to take a look at that." He helps me to my feet. "I'll show you where it is. I've got a little time until my main event."

"Don't worry," Rex chimes in. "You won't be the main attraction for much longer. Come Tuesday, I'll be taking that belt."

Brian's lip curls back, and it's easy to tell that he'd like to rip into Rex.

But Brian exhibits perfect self-control and simply says, "The only reason you'll be getting it is because I'll be giving it to you willingly. If this were a real fight, you and I both know you wouldn't have a shot in hell against me."

Rex's nostrils flare, but he doesn't argue with Brian.

"Come on, Anna. Let's get you looked at."

Brian's quiet as he walks me to the trainer, and as soon as we get there, he alerts the doctor to our presence. "Looks like a busted little finger, Doc."

The tall redheaded doctor stands up and walks over to me before gingerly inspecting my hand. "How the hell did this happen?"

"I fell backstage," I answer, leaving out the details about Deena tripping me.

Doc sighs. "All right. Let me get you some paperwork to fill out. We'll need to take a urine sample to test for drugs and pregnancy—you know, the standard workplace accident protocol—and then we'll get you X-rayed."

"Good luck," Brian says before he ducks out of the room.

After I complete all the paperwork and pee in a cup, Doc checks out my hand. "Well, you want the good news or the bad news first?"

"Bad news," I answer firmly, wanting to get the worst part of whatever he's going to tell me out of the way.

He sighs. "Your little finger is sprained." He opens a kit and lays out a few supplies. "We'll need to splint your finger, so you won't be able to wrestle for a couple of weeks."

I laugh. "I highly doubt Tension ever planned on me doing that, considering I've never been trained."

"Okay then, I guess that news wasn't too horrible for you."

"Nope," I tell him. "So, what's the good news?"

Doc gets busy wrapping my finger in some gauze. "You're pregnant."

My eyes grow wide, and I slightly shake my head. "Excuse me? I don't think I heard you correctly. Pregnant?"

He nods as he keeps working. "I'm not an OB/GYN, but that's what the test says. I highly recommend you make an appointment to confirm it."

My mouth falls open, and all I can think of is telling Xavier.

How is he going to react?

One thing's for sure, this isn't the kind of thing you leave a message about. Suddenly, I'm anxious to call him because I need help digesting the information myself.

Doc secures the gauze tape around my finger. "Okay, that should do it. Ice on for fifteen minutes and then off for swelling. Take some Tylenol for pain and swelling, and you should feel better in the next few days."

"Thank you," is all I can manage to get out because I'm still reeling from the shock of the news of being pregnant.

I walk out of the training room, and the world around me floats by in a fog as I make my way through the maze of hallways to find the women's locker room. I quickly change into my street clothes and carry my ring outfit outside with me.

"Need a car, Anna?" Freddy asks.

"Please," I reply. Then, I lean against the wall next to Freddy.

"You okay?" he asks.

"Fine," I lie. "Just tired."

He nods. "A good night's sleep will do wonders after a stressful day."

A black SUV pulls up, and Freddy opens the back passenger door, allowing me to climb inside.

"I'll see you tomorrow," I say.

"Yeah, okay. Bye." He shuts the door, and the car begins to

move.

I fish my cell phone out of my back pocket and frown when I notice there's no new message from Xavier. I'm unable to stop myself from calling him.

His phone rings twice and then goes straight to voice mail.

"Xavier, if you don't call me back tonight, I'll know we're finished."

There's so much more I could say, but I decide what I've said is clear and concise. If he doesn't call back after that, I'll have my answer.

Chapter TWENTY ONE

Xavier

THE DISTINCT AROMA OF GINGERBREAD cookies fills the entire house, and it makes me smile. Today is going to be a good day. Whenever Mama makes her special cookies, no matter the time of year, she's always in a good mood.

I step into the kitchen, and my gaze lands on a freshly showered woman wearing a yellow sundress with a grin on her face and a twinkle in her eyes.

Mama notices me watching her and waves me to come farther into the room. "Want to help me? I'm making gingerbread cookies, your favorite."

I nod as she reaches down and pats my cheek. "Okay then, go get your hands washed. Cleanliness is next to godliness."

I rush over to the sink and stand on my tiptoes to reach the faucet and soap. Mama says I'm tall for a seven-year-old and that I get my height from my father. I like when she tells me things about him because I don't have many facts about him.

I hold my hands up for her inspection. "All clean."

She nods and then gives me the cookie cutter in the shape of a little man. "You can cut out the next batch."

She kisses my cheek and then nuzzles her nose in the spot her lips touched, causing me to giggle. It's times like these when I'm truly happy.

More and more often, Mama's been taking medicine to make her sadness go away, but today she's happy without using it.

We are on our third batch of cookies when the front door of our apartment flies open, and my grandmother comes flouncing in, wearing her favorite flower dress, which means she came from church.

Grandmother steps into our tiny kitchen and removes the oversize hat from her head. "Gingerbread cookies in the middle of the summer, Gina? You do realize those are intended to be Christmas treats."

Mama waves her off. "Who says? They're Xavier's favorite, so we can make them anytime we want. We don't follow rules around here."

Grandmother lifts her chin. "Rules maintain order. Without them, there would be chaos. Speaking of which, have you thought any more about what I said to you? I think you would do much better staying clean if you moved back home where I could keep an eye on you."

"You mean, smother me, don't you?" Mother retorts. "I've told you, Mother, I'm done living under your rules."

"Gina, don't be ridiculous. I don't—"

"Yes, you do. You've always managed to chase off every man who's ever been important to me, and then you try to control every aspect of my life."

"I just want what's best for you. Living life by the good book and finding a man who's suitable to marry aren't such bad things for me to want for my only daughter, is it?"

Mother sighs as she rolls out the last batch of dough before her. "No, I guess not, but all the men you pick for me are boring, and I don't find them the least bit attractive."

Grandmother's nostrils flare. "And I suppose that monster who got you pregnant was better? Remind me where he is again. Oh, that's right. He ran off and left you after his spawn was born."

Mother slams her hands down hard onto the table. "His name is Xavier. He is your grandson, and if you can't love him the same way you love me, you can forget about me ever moving back home with you."

Grandmother's cool blue eyes lock on to me, and I slink down, trying my best to become invisible to rid myself from the weight of her stare.

"By bringing him along with you, perhaps we'll get to know one another better."

That sounds nice, but I know she hates me. The only reason she tolerates me is because she loves Mama. When she's not around, Grandmother calls me names and shoves me.

I tried to tell Mama about it once, but she explained to me that Grandmother has a right to discipline me when I misbehave while she's not around. After that, I never told Mama about anything that went on when she left me alone with her. I would do my best to make sure I was never alone with Grandmother though.

Mama sighs. "No. I like being on my own."

"You don't want to come live with me? Fine." Grandmother slams her purse on the counter beside Mama and then fishes a rectangular piece of paper out from it. "Then, understand this, Gina. There will be no more money from me. I will not pay another penny on this apartment of yours, so when you decide to go out on a binge again and lose this new job of yours, don't ask me for another handout. The only way I will continue to help you is if you move back home, where you belong."

Grandmother tosses the check at Mama, and it flutters down to the floor as Grandmother grabs her purse and disappears through the front door as quickly as she came in.

It's quiet in our kitchen for a few minutes before Mama begins humming "Jingle Bells" and continues to cut out little gingerbread men. She bumps her hip into mine. "Sing with me."

She smiles at me as we both sing, and when we're through, she gently pinches my chin. "You have your father's eyes, and I know you're going to be just as handsome as he was. Only promise me that you'll be a better man than him. Promise me, when things get hard, you won't run away and leave me like he did."

"I promise," I tell her. I mean it with my whole heart.

I stare into her eyes, and I don't know how she get the idea that I would ever leave her when my biggest fear in this world is losing her, the only person in this messed up world who loves me.

"Such a good, strong boy," Mama whispers. She bends down to kiss my cheek.

A gasp so deep comes out of me that it wakes me from a dead sleep. I sit up, stiff as a board, in my makeshift bed on the floor.

Heat still lingers on my cheek from where my mother kissed me in the dream. I clutch my shirtless chest as I attempt to slow my breathing down, but it's no use. Even though this wasn't a nightmare, it still yanks me back to the past, back to the place where all I can do is think about my mother.

I roll over onto my belly and begin to do vigorous push-ups, counting out loud as I work my body into pain so that I'll forget.

"One hundred twenty-seven . . ."

I keep going, but the pain isn't bringing my normal relief.

I twist my neck, focusing on the couch. I can't forget my past while I'm in this house, while I'm surrounded by every painful memory throughout my lifetime.

Nothing good has ever come of this place. Coming here was a mistake.

I lift my head and realize the fifth of Jack I killed before going to bed is still flowing through my veins. Even through my drunken haze, I can't even bring myself to sit on the stupid fucking couch. Every time I see it, I see Mother's face. Her dark hair and brown eyes are burned into my memory, and I don't understand how she couldn't love me more than the high she always sought out. Life was so good when she was clean. It was just her and me against the world.

It's a fact that Mom never received the abuse from Grandmother that I did, so that couldn't have been the reason Mom never wanted to live in the moment. Grandmother treated my mom like a princess, always telling me that her Gina was perfect, until the evil infection, which was my monster father's seed, found its way into her daughter.

Maybe Grandmother was right. I do seem to fuck up everything I touch, and if I don't stop myself soon, I'll destroy Anna's life, too.

I close my eyes as tears slip down my cheeks.

My Anna. My sweet Anna. I'm losing her.

I'm not good enough for her, and it was selfish of me to ever believe that I could keep someone as loyal and loving as her to myself.

I am a fuckup.

I am evil.

I don't deserve her goodness, no matter how badly I crave it.

I do nothing but put her in danger, which is why I haven't answered when she calls. Maybe distance will be good for us, and she'll figure out what a waste of her time I am and leave me. The only way I can make sure she's safe is to keep her as far away from me as possible.

I eye the couch, desperately needing it out of my face because I can't take much more of reliving the shit of my past, the past that's still ruining my life. I march over to the end of it and bend at the knees to pick it up. It easily lifts off the floor, and I drag it to the front door. I twist the knob and kick it open before I grip the middle of the couch and hoist it over one shoulder and my head. I step out onto the porch and toss the couch into the yard, and an audible crack echoes down the deserted street.

My thoughts run wild, and the only thing I can think of is how I want to be rid of this thing because of what it represents. I run back into the house and head straight for the kitchen to the drawer where Grandmother always kept a lighter for her candles. My fingers curl around the first one I see, and I sprint back outside and then down the steps to the couch. I drag it out to the middle of the street. With the flick of my thumb, a flame dances on the lighter, and I crouch down and hold the fire to the edge of the burlap material poking out beneath the plastic. It takes a moment, but eventually, flames take ahold of the fabric and lick their way around the couch before the entire thing is engulfed.

I take a step back, and relief washes over my chest at the very thought of never seeing this couch again. Now, I have to figure out a way to expel every other bad thing that plagues my life. It's time to purge these fucking demons.

Soon, the only thing left of the spot where my mother died is a pile of smoldering ash. Watching the fire has sobered me up. Good thing, too, because the flickering of red and blue lights in the darkness catch my attention as a police car rolls up to where I'm standing.

Jesus. Just what I fucking need.

My body tenses. Every time cops come my way, there seems to be trouble.

I stand still as a statue and continue to face the fire. There's no way I'll be able to deny that I did this. Grandmother's house is one of the only ones occupied on this street, so no one else would have a couch to drag outside but me.

My eyes flick over to the squad car as the door pops open, and my body quickly relaxes when I notice the cop getting out of the car is Cole.

"Shit, Cole. You scared the fuck out of me," I tell him as he approaches me.

He slips the stiff hat off and then rubs the top of his head. "What the hell are you doing, man?"

I fold my arms over my chest. "Redecorating."

"I can see that, but did it really require starting a fire in the middle of the street?"

I shrug. "Seemed like a good idea at the time."

He shakes his head. "I have to call this in, so we can get it cleaned up. You should take off."

I nod. "Thanks, man."

"What are friends for?" he answers simply.

"I owe you one."

He slaps the hat back on his head, and his face lights up with a half-smile. "If that's the case, can I collect tomorrow?"

I suspiciously eye him. "Depends. What is it?"

"I've got this kid I've been working with, and I really think he has something special, X. He's just rough around the edges. Reminds me a lot of you actually."

"So, you want me to come down and check him out? Show him a couple of moves?"

Cole nods. "I know it would mean a lot to him. The kid's had it rough and never caught a break. Hearing from you that he has some talent and can actually make it in professional wrestling might be the thing that will keep him off the streets and out of Bishop's crew."

I raise my eyebrow. "If he runs with Bishop, I don't want any part of the kid."

Cole frowns. "That's the thing, X. He's not with them, but they are trying their damnedest to recruit him. He's built, and he has a lot of rage—the perfect weapon for Bishop."

When Cole says that to me, he might as well have been describing me all those years ago when I found refuge with Bishop. If I can do some small thing to keep this kid out of living the same hell the Block put me through, it'll be worth my time.

"I'm in," I tell him. "Have him at Tough's at noon."

Cole smiles. "Will do. Thanks, X."

I turn to walk into the house to grab the keys to my bike. There's no way I can sleep inside this fucking house after all this. I stuff my cell, containing voice mails I have yet to listen to from Anna, into my pocket, and I set out for the one place that really feels like home—Nettie and Carl's diner. Hopefully, I can figure out what the fuck is going on with my life.

Chapter
TWENTY TWO

Xavier

THE SOUND OF BOXES CRASHING to the floor jerks me out of a deep sleep. I gasp and sit up ramrod straight in the twin bed I found sanctuary in last night after letting myself into the diner with my key.

"Sorry, sugar," Nettie says as she stacks the boxes back onto the stockroom shelf. "We needed more ketchup out front."

I stretch and then rub the heels of my hands against my closed eyelids. "What time is it?"

"Close to noon," Nettie informs me as she comes over to sit next to me on the bed. There's concern in her eyes. "You okay?"

I nod. "Yeah. Rough night in the house, is all. It's hard being there, alone."

She pats my shoulder. "Anna will be back before long."

I sigh and then pinch the bridge of my nose. "I'm not sure she'll be back."

Her brow furrows. "Why would you say that? That girl loves you."

"And that's the problem. She shouldn't love me."

"You deserve love, Xavier. You have to learn to open up and let her in. She'll stand by you, no matter what, if she really loves you."

"What if she doesn't?" That's the thing that scares me the

most. I fear the possibility that she might leave me.

Nettie frowns. "You'll never know unless you open yourself up and find out." She pats my leg. "Want me to have Carl make you some breakfast?"

"A quick sandwich to go would be great. I have to head over to the gym to work with a kid Cole thinks might have a real shot in professional wrestling."

She pushes up from the bed. "That's great. It'll take your mind off things a bit."

"Yeah, maybe," I tell her. But I know getting Anna off my mind won't be easy.

"I'll get that sandwich going." Nettie pauses at the door and turns to me. "Make sure you take a shower at Tough's. I can still smell the Jack on you." She winks at me before she disappears.

I down the sausage-and-egg sandwich in about four bites and head out the door to my bike. I ride down the street to the house on Sycamore and am surprised to see only scorched concrete where the couch burned last night.

I park my bike, take a deep breath, and then dash inside to change into workout gear. I do my best not to allow the house to get to me, but when I rush past the door upstairs to get to the bathroom, I eye the lock on Grandmother's door.

God, that woman really hated me and did anything to keep me at a distance.

After brushing my teeth and slapping on some deodorant, I rush back out the door and head toward the gym.

I hate being late.

My bike roars as it comes to a halt in front of Tough's Gym, and then I sprint up the stairs.

When I open the door, the sound of jump ropes slapping against the wooden floor is the first thing I hear. The gym is packed today, but after a quick glance around, I spot Cole talking to a man about my height. He has sandy-blond spiked hair, and he's covered from the neck down in tattoos.

Cole spots me and raises his hand in the air. "X!"

A lot of the heads in the gym turn and notice me there, but they go back to training almost instantly.

The guy next to Cole smiles and extends his hand to me as I approach. "What's up, X? Thank you for doing this."

Now that I'm up close, I can tell this guy is really young, probably no more than twenty-one.

"No problem. What's your name, kid?"

"Corey Trulove," he says proudly.

I raise my eyebrows. "Real or fake name?"

"One hundred percent real, bro."

Cole laughs. "Almost as good as Xavier Cold, huh, X?"

I nod. "Almost." I turn back to the kid. "Okay, let's warm up, and then we'll step in the ring and see what you've got."

After about fifteen minutes, we're loosened up and in the ring, bouncing around on our toes.

I widen my stance and wave Corey at me. "All right, kid, come at me."

Corey shakes his hands out at his sides and then charges at me, but I easily sidestep him and push him down on the mat.

He jumps up and smacks his hands together. "Damn it. Again!"

I raise my eyebrows and then glance at Cole, who gives me an I-told-you-so nod.

I admire people who don't give up in the ring. It's what makes a good wrestler.

We go at it again and again for nearly two hours, but the kid never gets me in any holds. I can see the frustration growing on his face, and I want to make sure I don't break his spirit or make him doubt his abilities too much.

I step back and hold my hands up. "I think that's enough."

"No, wait. I can do better. Please give me another shot."

I can see panic in his eyes because he believes he's failed.

"Kid, calm down. We're not finished. We're just done for

the day. I think you've got something, and while I'm here, I'll work with you."

His eyes light up. "You will?"

I nod.

Corey jumps in the air and pumps his fist. "Hell yeah! I'll see you tomorrow."

He runs off toward the locker room, and I smile.

Cole nudges my shoulder. "You're doing a good thing. This means a lot to him."

I shrug. "It's not that big of a deal."

"It is to him. Remember, little things mean a shit-ton in this neighborhood."

He's right about that. I was all too happy to accept the handouts Bishop had offered even though what he demanded in return turned me into a thug.

I don't want Corey to end up in that same boat.

After a shower, I head out of the gym with Corey flanking my side, asking me a million questions about what it's like to be a part of *Tension*.

I'm about to answer another question for Corey, but I stop when I spot Kai leaning against the front of the same SUV he was in once before.

"Fuck," Corey mumbles next to me. "They've been coming around more and more, wanting an answer from me about doing some work for them."

I turn to him and say, "You fuck with the Block, and our training days are over."

"That won't happen," Corey says. "I've been doing my best to avoid them, but those fuckers are relentless when they want something."

I want to say, *Tell me something I don't know*, but the less people who know about the threats Bishop's crew has made toward me and Anna, the safer Anna will be. God knows I don't need anyone getting any ideas to join in on the action in order to prove loyalty to Bishop.

I know it makes me a fucking asshole for not taking Anna's calls, but I'm doing it for her own good even though it's killing me to let her go.

Chapter
TWENTY THREE

Anna

IT'S BEEN TWO DAYS SINCE I found out I'm pregnant, and the shock hasn't worn off yet. The passing days also mean it's been two additional days since I heard from Xavier.

I guess my threats of the certain demise of our relationship if he didn't call me back weren't enough to motivate him to reach out to me.

A tear slips down my cheek, and I quickly bat it away as I finish curling my hair. From the beginning, Xavier warned me that he wasn't a good guy and that I shouldn't trust him, but I didn't listen.

Through it all, I thought a good guy who had a heart of gold was beneath that tough exterior. It seems my gut was wrong about him because here I sit—alone, in a hotel room, across the country from the city I call home now—and Xavier hasn't even had the decency to call and check on me. He's the only person in the world I want to talk to about this baby and all the emotions I'm feeling—happiness, sadness, fear—but he's making that impossible.

It crushes me that he could be so cold. Why would my heart allow me to fall in love with someone who didn't really care about me like I'd thought? Turns out, he's an excellent actor in and out of the ring.

I talked to Quinn, and I almost confided in her about the baby, but it wouldn't be right if she knew about me being pregnant before Xavier did.

My cell rings, and I answer and put it on speaker, "Hello?"

"Hey, Anna. I'll be there in about fifteen minutes. Would you like for me to come to your room to escort you to the vehicle?" Jorge asks, his manners ever present.

"That's sweet of you, but I'll meet you downstairs. They charge an arm and a leg to park at this hotel because it's downtown."

"You sure?" he asks with a bit of skepticism in his voice. "It's really no trouble for me to come up and make sure you're safe."

"I'm positive." I shut off my curling iron and add the last minute touches of makeup. "This hotel is perfectly safe."

"All right. I'll see you in a bit."

We end our call, and it finally hits me that I'm about to face Jorge after running away from him. A jitter passes through me, but I quickly shake it off, reminding myself that it's okay to be tough and live life the way I want and not by the rules my family set forth.

I double-check the modest black cocktail dress I'm wearing and hope I'm not overdressed for wherever Jorge is taking me for dinner.

After waiting in the lobby for a few minutes, Jorge's blue Audi cruises the drive in front of the hotel. I smile, but I'm still completely terrified as I step outside, and Jorge gets out of the car.

He rounds the front of the car in a few long strides and makes his way over to me. His black hair is a touch longer than the normal crew cut he usually sports, but it's not out of place with the gray suit he's wearing. If anything, he's more stylish.

Jorge's dark eyes roam over me before moving back up to lock on my face. "Wow, Anna. You look amazing. You're practically glowing."

I smile, knowing he really means the compliment because Jorge isn't one to stray from the truth. "Thank you. You do as well. I love the hair. It's really working for you."

He grins, and his perfectly white teeth practically sparkle as he runs his fingers through the strands on the top of his head. "Thanks. It's the longest it's been in years. My father hates it."

I laugh. Jorge's father is the pastor of my family's church and has some strict rules when it comes to the appearance of his children. Jorge's rebellion with the hair has to be getting under his father's skin.

Jorge reaches down and opens the passenger door for me. "Ready?"

I nod and slide onto the seat.

Jorge puts the transmission in drive, and we set out on the busy downtown Seattle streets, making small talk, until we pull up next to a fancy-looking steak house where he gives his keys to a valet. He extends an elbow to me as we head inside.

The place is posh, decorated head to toe in expensive curtains and table linens, and it's clear it will cost a pretty penny to eat here.

The hostess, dressed in a white button-down shirt and black vest, smiles at us from behind a podium. "Welcome to Alma Maria. Name on the reservation?"

"Elizondo." Jorge's last name rolls off his tongue with ease.

The woman nods after scanning a list of names. "Ah, yes. Here you are. Elizondo, table for two. Right this way."

The hostess stops at a small table and lays thick book-like menus down for us. "Enjoy."

Jorge pulls out my chair and then slides into the seat across from me. He unfolds the white cloth napkin onto his lap.

Before we even have a chance to speak, a man approaches the table with a white towel draped across his forearm while holding a bottle of wine. "Good evening. I'm Matthew. I'll be your waiter tonight. May I start you off with a sample of our finest house wine?"

"Absolutely," Jorge says as he nudges his empty wine glass toward the edge of the table.

"And for you, miss?"

The man begins to tip the bottle to pour some for me, but I quickly hold my hand over the opening of the glass.

"None for me. Thanks. Can I just have water instead?"

"Not a problem, miss. I'll have that right out to you."

He disappears, and once he's out of earshot, I glance up at Jorge, who is suspiciously watching me.

"No wine? I figured, now that you were away from Simon, you'd be partying it up."

"Being able to drink and have fun aren't the reasons I ran away from home, Jorge."

He licks his lips. "Was it being engaged to me that freaked you out?"

"No . . . yes—I mean, it wasn't you per se. It was the idea of being with someone who I didn't have fire with that scared me."

He raises his eyebrows and sighs. "I see."

Suddenly, I feel bad about being so open with him. It obviously hurt his feelings. I might not be in love with him, but it doesn't mean that I want to hurt him either.

"I didn't mean it like that."

His brows furrow. "Then, what exactly did you mean when you said you felt no fire with me?"

I rub my forehead. This is harder than I thought it would be. I don't like it when people are upset with me because it rattles me.

My goal in meeting with Jorge tonight was to be honest with him and eliminate any anger he might have against me because our fathers are still close.

"I apologize for how I chose to end things with you. I didn't mean to hurt you, but deep down, we both knew that we weren't right for one another, that we were never really in love."

"No. We were. In fact, I think I still love you, despite what you did."

"But how do you know you love me?"

"I just know."

"That's not a good answer," I tell him. I hope that what I say next will make him understand that he simply loves me out of obligation and not because a passion inside us pushes us together. "Have you missed me since I left?"

His face softens. "Of course, I have."

"Did it kill you? Did it crush your soul to think we would never be together again?"

That takes him off guard, and when he doesn't say anything for a moment, I can see the wheels turning.

"If you have to think about it, that's how you know. If you'd ever truly had your heart shattered, you'd know it. It's a feeling that doesn't go away."

Jorge nods. "Sounds like you're speaking from experience."

My mind wanders to Xavier and how it's been days since I've heard from him and how much it hurts.

"I am," I whisper. "And getting your heart broken hurts like a bitch."

Jorge's eyes widen, and he nearly chokes on the red wine he was sipping. "I never expected profanity to come out of your mouth."

I laugh. "I've changed, Jorge. Leaving Portland a few months ago has really made me grow up and see the world in an entirely different light. Growing up the way we did sheltered us, Jorge. The world outside of the church isn't so bad. There are a lot of good of people out there, and it doesn't make us better than them because we attended church on a regular basis. ."

He sighs. "Were our lives so bad?"

"No. But truthfully, I wasn't happy."

He eyes me over his wineglass. "And are you happy now?"

His question is meant to have a simple answer, but it's difficult for me to give him one. On one hand, I'm ecstatic about the freedom I've gained since I left home, but on the other hand, I'm dealing with the loss of Xavier and the cruel reality that I might end up being a single mother, struggling to take care of a baby all by myself. All in all, I'm happy with a whole lot of scared shitless mixed in, but I don't regret making the decision to leave home.

"Yes, I'm happy."

He raises his glass to me. "Then, that's all that matters."

The rest of our evening is far less intense. Our converstation flows easily, and he even fills me in on how my mother and father are doing since they haven't spoken to me in a while.

"You should visit them while you're in Portland next week. It would mean the world to your mother to see you. She's been missing you like crazy."

"I don't think that's such a good idea. Father and I didn't part on good terms."

Jorge nods. "I heard. Your new boyfriend got in his face?"

I twist my lips. "That's not *exactly* what happened, but yes, they did have some heated words. But Xavier wasn't wrong for standing up to Father."

He sighs. "Simon can be hotheaded, but he really does love you, Anna."

My eyes burn as I think of my parents. If we keep fighting like this, they'll never know their grandchild. None of that makes a difference though because Father will never accept me, especially after finding out that I got pregnant outside of wedlock.

"Don't cry, Anna." Jorge hands me the cloth napkin he unfolded. "If you miss them so much, go see them and fix things before they get too out of control to be made right again."

I sniff as the fear of facing Father races through me. "I'll think about it."

Jorge smiles. "Let me know if you want to see them. I'd be happy to chauffeur you around."

"I'll have to think about it."

"Please do. With Tension staying so close, it might just make more sense to stay in the Pacific Northwest for a while. You could use the next couple of weeks to spend time here with your family."

What he said makes sense. With no word from Xavier, what would be the point in rushing across the country for only a couple of days in Detroit between shows unless it was to check on him and make sure he was all right?

My mind instantly begins rolling with a ton of thoughts.

What if Kai hurt Xavier?

What if he's not answering because he can't?

Panic shoots through me, and I pop up from the table in such a quick manner that it startles Jorge and causes heads to turn in my direction.

"You all right?" Jorge asks.

"Yes, fine. I need to make a phone call. I'll be right back."

"Okay . . ."

The confusion on Jorge's face morphs into concern, but I don't explain the situation any further before I turn and rush away from him.

My fingers fly over the buttons on my phone as I search for the number for Nettie's Diner, and then I quickly hit Call as I pace back and forth in the hallway leading to the restrooms.

The phone rings three times before it's picked up. "Nettie's."

"Hey, Nettie. It's Anna. I know this might sound strange, but have you seen Xavier lately?"

My heart pounds as I wait on her to say something. If she's seen him, it means he's fine, and he is truly ignoring me, but if she hasn't, then another type of panic will set in.

The chatter of the people in the restaurant sounds in the

background as she speaks, "I sure have. He stayed here last night."

My heart drops as I receive my answer. Guess it was silly of me to worry about his safety when he's clearly able to take care of himself. This information tells me where we stand.

I grip the phone tighter in my hand and lift my chin. "Can you please deliver a message to him for me?"

"Sure, honey."

"Tell him I got his point loud and clear, and I won't bother him ever again."

"I swear, that boy . . ." Nettie tsks, and I'm about to tell her good-bye when she says, "Don't give up on him, Anna, even if you want to."

I sigh, understanding what she's asking, but I won't allow my heart to keep going through this. "I can't do that, Nettie. Not anymore." My lip quivers, and I can feel the tears coming on, but I don't want to cry while I'm on the phone with her. "I've got to go."

"No, Anna. Wait—"

I don't give her time to finish her sentence before I end the call and lean back against the wall, shutting my eyes to hold in the tears.

This is the last sign I needed to give up on Xavier.

You don't treat someone you love like this.

I have to find the strength to move on with my life.

Somehow, I manage to make it through dinner without completely breaking down. Jorge knew something was bothering me, but in typical Jorge fashion, he didn't pry into my business for fear of being rude.

We don't say much on the way back to the hotel. When the car comes to a stop in front of the door, I'm fully prepared to end our evening, but Jorge opts to have the attendant park his car.

I give him a curious look as he opens my door. "What are

you doing?"

He extends his hand to me and helps me out. "You look like you need a friend."

That's so like him—always giving. It's in his nature.

"It's not necessary. I'll be okay."

He gives me a pointed look. "Anna, I know you. You're hurting, and even though we are not together, I still consider you one of my best friends. Talk to me if it will make you feel better."

I bite my lower lip, unwilling to part with what's truly bothering me. I don't want my parents to find out from someone other than me that I'm pregnant. Talking things out with Jorge is dangerous. I need to keep this to myself for a bit longer, even if I want some advice on what to do in this situation.

My lips pull back into a tight line. "I'm sorry, Jorge. I can't tell you about this."

He swallows while his eyes search my face. "I've really lost you, haven't I?"

I nod as a tear rolls down my cheek. Loving Jorge would be so simple—a natural fit in the life I used to lead—but I'm a different person now, and I will not settle for lukewarm love. I want full-on passion or nothing at all.

He swipes away my tear with his thumb. "It's okay, Anna. I always knew I would someday. You have more zest for life than anyone I've ever known. I'm not the right guy for you to find adventure with, but I'll always be your friend."

His sweet words cause a sob to rip out of my throat, and I throw my arms around his neck, hugging him as I cry. It's then I finally realize how much I've changed. No matter what happens from this point on, I can no longer go back to the perfect church girl that Father always groomed me to be—not with a baby on the way. I have to figure out how to stand in this world on my own two feet.

Chapter
TWENTY FOUR

Xavier

MY CELL CHIMES WITH A new text, and I motion to Corey to continue practicing the drills I gave him while I check my phone. I swipe the screen, and Deena's name pops up with an attachment symbol next to it. I roll my eyes and click on the button.

This bitch doesn't fucking give up.

I probably shouldn't even look at whatever she's sent because it's most likely going to piss me off.

Curiosity wins out, and I open the attachment. It's a photo, and when it loads, my heart nearly stops dead in my chest.

There, plain as day, is Anna hugging another man, and it's not just a polite hug. She's clinging to him while her face is buried in his chest. I shake my head, as if to clear my vision, and then lean in for a closer look.

Fuck.

She's in a nice dress, and she has heels on while he's in a suit. Were they on a fucking *date*?

I curl my fingers around the phone and fight the urge to chuck it across the room and shatter it into a million pieces.

It's one thing to believe in the idea of letting her go, but it's another when the fact that I'm no longer the man in her life is shoved in my face.

My nostrils flare as rage overtakes me.

I turn toward an empty punching bag and ram a hard right hook into it as I roar, "Goddamn it!"

I've fucked up.

I take back every thought I've ever had about letting Anna go because I can't do it. She's mine. I will do whatever it takes to get her back.

FOR THE NEXT TWO WEEKS, I try to call Anna every day, but my calls go unanswered. I guess this is payback for me treating her the same way. She hasn't been back to Detroit, and the only thing I know for sure is that she's been staying at Brian and Liv's house on her downtime while Tension tours the Northwest. The only ways I have to check on Anna now is through Brian or the times I've seen her on television.

I hate seeing Anna with Rex in this fucking stupid anti-Phenomenal X campaign that the writers have come up with to amp the drama between Rex and me, but I appreciate Tension putting her in the show. It makes it possible for me to gaze at her face, other than in my dreams.

One thing is clear. If I'm going to get Anna back, I need to get Tension to allow me to be back around her.

Chapter
TWENTY FIVE

Anna

BRIAN AND LIV ARE AMAZING people. In the past couple of weeks, they've taken me in during *Tension's* downtime to help me save money. I confided in Liv that Xavier and I aren't exactly on the best terms right now.

Liv sets a cup of coffee in front of me and slides into the seat next to me. "Are you sure you and Xavier won't make up? He's been ringing Brian's phone off the hook."

I frown, knowing I have close to a hundred missed calls from Xavier on my phone. "He should've answered instead of blowing me off when I tried to reach him before."

"Don't get me wrong when I say this, Anna—because, believe me, I would've been pissed if Brian ignored my calls—but is it possible for you to forgive Xavier? He knows he screwed up."

I sigh. "I don't know. Right now, I need distance from him. He hurt me really bad. I'm not sure I can trust him not to do it again, which is why I know I won't be able to keep this job for much longer. I can't work in a place where I'll see him often and not be with him."

"Leaving *Tension* is a pretty big deal. Many people would kill to work there."

I take a sip of the warm liquid and then set my cup down.

"I'm sure there are, but being a professional wrestler isn't something I see for myself. I would quit now, but I want to save some money and get my own apartment when I move back to Detroit."

The one thing I've decided is that the first step in making it by myself is to get a place of my own, one where I could bring my baby home and he or she would have its own room. Working for *Tension* until they lift Xavier's suspension will allow me to build up enough money to get a modest two-bedroom place and then furnish it.

"What will you do for money?"

There's concern in Liv's voice, so I do my best to make her aware that I do have a plan to take care of myself.

"The other night, my cousin told me that I could get my old waitressing job back in Detroit."

Liv sighs. "Sounds like you have it all mapped out. It makes me sad that things didn't work out between you and Xavier. The two of you seemed to be so in love."

"I thought the same thing. I was too naive to believe we'd ever split up."

"Do you still love him?"

"Of course, I do," I answer. "But I don't think he loves me—or at least that he loves me enough. You don't abandon the people you love."

She gives me a small smile and then reaches over to pat my hand. "Sometimes, people get things wrong. No one's perfect, and perhaps, he's realized his mistake. Speaking to him and hearing what he has to say might be therapeutic for you even if you decide not to take him back. Closure is always a good thing."

I nod, thinking of how I finally felt better about the whole Jorge situation after he and I spoke. Liv could be on to something. Maybe I should give Xavier a chance to explain himself.

After our show in Portland, I'm going to fly back to Detroit. It will be good to hear what he has to say and inform him that he's about to become a father whether he's with me or not.

Chapter
TWENTY SIX

Xavier

I TAKE A DEEP BREATH as I dial the number to the talent manager of *Tension*, and I say a little prayer that this plan of mine works.

It's been over two weeks since I talked to Anna. I don't blame her for not answering any of my calls. I would've given up on me, too. As hard as I've tried to get her out of my head, I can't. Even if I'm not with her, I need to be around her to make sure she's okay. I need to get back on the road in order to do that because being here in Detroit and not being able to see her is driving me fucking nuts.

On the second ring, a voice answers on the other end of the line, "Seaborne."

I clear my throat, and for the first time in a long time, I'm nervous. "Hey, Chip. It's X."

"X, my man. What can I do for you?"

Next to Mr. Silverman, Chip Seaborne is the highest in the chain of command when it comes to what goes down at *Tension*, as far as the talent is concerned. If I can get him on board to take Corey on and allow me off my suspension so that I could train him, I'll be able to be with Anna again—away from Bishop and the danger he poses to her.

"I wanted to talk to you about lifting my suspension."

Chip sighs into the phone. "The boss was clear about you being off the show for a while. Besides, the storyline for your rivalry with Rex has already been set into motion."

"I realize that, but I'm not asking to come back to get into the ring just yet."

"Now, you've piqued my interest. Continue."

"Well, since I've been off, I've been training back at my old gym in Detroit, and I think I've found a kid who has some talent. He's still pretty green, but with the right training, I think he's got the stuff," I explain.

"And how does this involve you?" he questions.

"I'd like to help train him, but in order to do that, I need to get my formal suspension removed, so I can come back into the areas where Tension will be. Some one-on-one time with the trainers and some pre-show shadowing with me to get the feel of the business aspect of wrestling will be imperative for this guy."

Chip is quiet for a few moments, but then the sound of a rush of air hits the phone. "All right, I'll make it happen, but, X, I'm sticking my neck out here, so this kid had better be worth it."

"Thanks, Chip. I appreciate it. I'll have him at the next show in Portland." I hit the button to end the call.

I turn to where Corey and Cole are sitting on the edge of the ring, waiting for me to give them the verdict.

Corey leans forward, every inch of him anxious to hear the news. "Well? What did he say?"

My mouth pulls up into a one-sided grin, and I can't hide how fucking happy the news makes me. "Pack your bags, asshole. We're going to Portland."

Corey pumps his fist in the air before he runs over and throws his arms around me in a huge bear hug. "Thank you. This never would have happened without you. I promise to make you proud."

It feels good to help him in this way. I see a lot of myself in Corey, and if it hadn't been for people helping me out in this fucked-up world, I would probably be dead by now.

I thump him on the back just before he releases me. "I know you will."

EVERYTHING FROM THE PLANE RIDE to being in a taxi is a new experience for Corey. The kid's never been out of Detroit, so every little fucking thing amazes the kid. I swear to God, he would be poking his head out the window like an excited dog if I allowed it.

"Wow, look at how fucking green it is here," Corey says as he stares out the window of the cab. "All you see in Detroit is concrete and garbage."

I've traveled the world with Tension, but it was only about ten years ago when things were new to me, too, so I let the kid have his moment.

We pull up to a motel about fifteen blocks away from the place where all the other talent is staying, and we get out of the cab. Staying in a run-down dive won't bother Corey in the slightest because he lives rougher than this, but it's hard for me to go back to the roach motels after growing accustomed to the finer hotels in the city.

We check in and toss our bags in the room, so we can head down to the other hotel and catch a free ride over to the arena where Tuesday *Tension* will be tonight.

When we walk up to the hotel, I spot the black Escalade that usually drives me around. I nudge Corey's arm and point at it, indicating which one we need to get in. "There's Tension's shuttle."

I tap the glass on the passenger side window. Tim, a heavy-set man with a mustache, unlocks the vehicle when he spots me, allowing me to slide into the back.

"Hello, X," Deena's voice purrs next to me. "I didn't know you were back already."

The muscles in my back tense, and I hop out of the backseat, wanting to get as far away from her as possible.

There's no way in hell I'm going to sit next to that vindictive bitch.

Corey tilts his head, and I jerk my thumb over my shoulder as I open the front passenger door. "You take the back."

Corey shrugs and gets in, having no idea that he's about to sit next to a fucking dragon.

I slam the door a little harder than I meant to, and then the vehicle begins to move, taking us in the direction of the arena.

"And who might you be?" Deena asks.

I resist the urge to tell her that it's none of her damn business and that she needs to keep her hooks out of the kid.

"Corey Trulove," he answers proudly.

Without even seeing his face, I can tell that he's grinning.

"That's cute," she tells him in the fake flirty tone she once used on me.

Deena has a killer body, and until you get to know the true evil that lives inside her, she has a way of fooling people into believing that she's actually a pleasant human to be around.

The Escalade pulls up to the back door, and I get out of the SUV as fast as I can, wanting distance between Deena and me before I snap on her bitch ass.

Freddy grins when he notices me. "What's up, X? I saw your name on the roster today. I knew you wouldn't be able to stay gone for too long. It's good to see you. Rex is about to get on my last damn nerve, bragging on how he's taking the belt from Brian. Now that you're here, hopefully, he'll shut his damn mouth."

I laugh. "Don't even trip, Freddy. Rex might have the belt for a minute, but you know I'll be coming for his ass as soon as I'm allowed back in that ring. I didn't quite get to finish the job last time."

"We'll see about that," Deena cuts in as she passes by Freddy and me with a wicked smile before making her way inside the building.

"She's such a fucking bitch," I mutter when the door closes behind her. "Why in the fuck did I ever mess around with that?"

"Beats me," Freddy answers. "No piece of ass is worth her shit."

God, is he ever fucking right about that. She's been nothing but a fucking headache since I slipped her my dick.

"Yo, you tapped that?" Corey asks as he flanks my side with an expression of awe on his face. "Bro, she's a fucking ten."

I lift one eyebrow. "Easy, kid. That one might look good, but her bite is pure venom. Stay far away from her."

Corey nods with a serious expression on his face. It's nice to see that he takes my words as gospel.

While I have his attention, I feel an introduction is in order. "Kid, this is Freddy, the eyes of *Tension*. He knows everyone, and he's an excellent judge of character. Freddy, meet Corey Trulove."

Freddy chuckles as he shakes Corey's hand. "I'm only about ninety percent right when it comes to people. Occasionally, I misjudge young punks from Detroit, especially one who calls himself Phenomenal X. I had that guy pegged as a douche bag, and he proved me wrong."

I laugh. "Ninety percent? Are you admitting that Rex was your other mistake when you told me he was a good guy?"

"He *was* until he got so hung up on having the world championship attached to his name."

I shake my head as I remember when I actually considered Rex to be a friend—that was, until he started playing dirty, cheating his way through matches. "He changed big time, and I owe him another ass-kicking to bring him down a couple of notches."

"Careful, X," Freddy warns. "Don't go fucking up your career. Mr. Silverman might have pulled some strings to make shit disappear for you, but I highly doubt that he'll do it again. He's not exactly known for being the forgiving type."

No matter what the media and the rest of the staff at Tension are led to believe about what happened in the ring back in Atlanta, Freddy knows all too well about the real shit between me and Rex. He was the guy always making sure things didn't get out of control between us.

I pat Freddy on the back. "I've got myself under control now. Fighting for real—I've tried to tame that shit. My temper has fucked up a lot of good things for me."

"Good." He rubs the scalp on his bald head. "I'm getting too old to keep breaking up your fights. You're a strong son of a bitch." Freddy checks his clipboard and then allows a couple of more wrestlers who I recognize into the building. After they pass, he turns to me. "You going inside or what?"

I nod toward the door, and even though I need to keep my distance, I can't help but ask, "Anna already in there?"

Freddy shakes his head. "Not yet, but she typically comes in only a few minutes early, not hours like most of you others who want to get workouts in before the show."

I smile, knowing Anna isn't into pumping iron in the weight room with the rest of us. She'd only sit and watch me. "Then, if it's all the same to you, I'll wait out here with you. The kid can go in and explore if he wants though."

Freddy nods as he pulls a backstage pass out and hands it to Corey. "Go ahead, kid. Knock yourself out."

"Fuck yeah!" No one has to tell him twice. Corey slips the lanyard over his head and heads inside.

I stand next to Freddy as I await Anna's arrival.

If I'm being honest, I'm nervous as fuck about what she's going to say when she sees me after I ignored her calls the way I did. She's going to be pissed—that's a given—but I pray to God that it's not too late to earn her forgiveness. At least, I hope she'll let me back into her life as a friend. I need her in my life some way even though I'm not the right man to claim her.

Freddy glances down at his watch. "I'm sure she'll be here any minute."

I nod, knowing Freddy's sensing my tension and attempting to calm me down, but it does nothing to curb my anxiety.

I lean back against the wall and fold my arms over my chest as a blue Audi pulls up to the back entrance. At first, I don't pay it much attention because it's not a *Tension*-owned vehicle that shuttles the talent to and from the hotel, but when the passenger shoves her dark brown hair over her shoulder, it immediately catches my attention.

Anna is sitting inside the car, speaking animatedly with the driver. I squint my eyes to focus better on the driver, and when I realize it's the same guy I saw her hugging in the photo, I curl my hands into fists and march over to the car. My jealousy completely takes over and throws my promise to myself to control my goddamn temper right out the fucking window.

Chapter
TWENTY SEVEN

Anna

JORGE IS DEFINITELY DUE SOME credit. He's been a good friend to me since I've been hanging around this part of the country. He's texted me a few times to check on me, and tonight, he picked me up from Liv and Brian's to take me to Tuesday *Tension*, so he can watch the show.

When we pull up to the arena, Jorge asks, "Am I going to see you wrestle tonight?"

I laugh. "No. I'm what they call a valet. I only escort wrestlers out to the ring."

"Will you be with Phenomenal X again?"

"No. He's actually been suspended for the past few weeks, so I've been assigned to Assassin."

"Oh, is he any good?"

I shrug. "He's the current champ. He won the belt when we were in Seattle."

"Wow. The champ? Impressive, Anna."

"Not really," I mumble. "He's an asshole. I can't wait until Xavier comes back, so he can kick Assassin's butt and take the belt away from him. I'll be cheering like this." I pump my arms in the air, as if I'm lifting the roof.

Jorge chuckles. "Not a fan, huh?"

"Definitely no—" I can't even get the words out because his

driver's door flies open, and two large hands reach inside.

"Xavier, no!" I shout.

It doesn't faze him as he curls his fingers into the fabric of Jorge's once perfectly pressed polo shirt.

Xavier leans down in the car, so he can get face-to-face with Jorge, who is pinned to his seat by both his seat belt and fear. "What the fuck are you doing with my girl?"

Jorge's eyes widen as he defensively holds his hands up, and his voice shakes as he says, "We're friends."

Xavier pulls him up and then slams him back on the seat. "Don't lie to me. I know more than that is going on. You fucking her?"

"Xavier! Stop it! You'll hurt him." My plea for him to end this before it gets any further out of control seems to fall on deaf ears. It's as if he's lost in a rage haze, unable to recognize anything outside of his anger. I need to do something drastic, something to snap him out of it. "I'm pregnant!"

That does the trick because Xavier's eyes snap to me. "What did you just say?"

Tears stream down my face as I lock my gaze on his. "I'm pregnant."

"No, you're not."

My mouth drifts open as his words feel like a slap in the face, but I refuse to let him make me feel bad about this. He might not want this baby, but I do.

"I am," I whisper. "And it's yours. And . . . I'm keeping it. You can either be a part of its life or not—it's up to you—but I'm going to be a mother."

Xavier releases Jorge's shirt from his grasp, and his eyes soften. "Anna . . . I . . . I can't. I'm sorry."

He steps back, and yet again, he's running from me because things are hard, but I refuse to let him turn his back on me so easily.

I jump out of the car and chase him down to the edge of the

gated lot where I grab his arm. "You can't keep walking away from me," I tell him.

"You don't understand, Anna. This changes everything. I came here to beg you to come back to me because I'm a selfish bastard who can't stand the thought of losing you, but now, I know I was doing the right thing by letting you go. It's one thing for me to ruin your life because you can leave me anytime you want, but a baby? If it's stuck with me, it has no choice. I won't ruin my kid's life. I'm too much of a fuckup to be a father."

"No, you're not. This baby deserves to have you in its life."

I can clearly see the struggle in Xavier's eyes, and as he takes another step back from me, I know I'm losing the battle in making him see he's a good man.

"Don't," I whisper. "Don't leave me again. It's now or never, Xavier. I won't keep playing this game with you. Either you want to be with me or not. Choose."

Tears flow freely from his eyes. "I'm sorry, Anna. I can't."

He walks away from me, and I drop to my knees on the asphalt of the parking lot. No air gets to my lungs as I gasp for breath between sobs.

He's gone.

This time, I feel like I've really lost him.

I'm not sure how long I stay kneeling in the parking lot, but Jorge is there, putting his hands around my shoulders and urging me to get up.

"Come on, Anna. The bouncer guy says he'll cover for you and tell your bosses that you were throwing up all over the place. I'll take you to the hotel, so you can get yourself together."

I nod and then stand up on my feet. My legs feel like they're made of Jell-O as Jorge leads me back to his car.

Freddy is standing by the car with a deep-set frown. The pity he feels for me is clear, and I'm sure I look like a pathetic mess because that's exactly how I feel.

"Take care of yourself, Anna."

I stare up at the big teddy bear of a man who has always been so kind to me. "Thank you."

"Come on." Jorge nudges me to get inside the car.

As soon as the door closes, the sobs start again, and I don't see them stopping anytime soon.

LATER THAT EVENING, I'M STILL crying while lying on the bed. No matter how hard I try, I can't stop the tears from falling.

Jorge has been pacing the floor nonstop over the last couple of hours. He's never been through something like this, so I'm sure he has no idea how to handle a heartbroken woman.

A knock at the door causes me to gasp. I'm not ready to see Xavier right now, if that's him.

Jorge releases a relieved sigh as he hustles to the door. "Finally," he mutters.

The door creaks open, and the distinct sound of Mother's voice wafts into the room. "Where is she?"

"In here. But—" Jorge begins to tell her, and the door hits the wall like she's forced her way past Jorge.

I push up into a sitting position in time for her to make it down the short hall of the room. My heart thunders in my chest as she stands there, staring at me. She looks just the exactly like she did as the last day I saw her. The same dark hair is perfectly pulled back into a low-set ponytail, and her make-up has been flawlessly applied. All of that coordinates with the black dress slacks and red blouse she has on.

I'm going to kill Jorge for calling her.

Her head tilts, and her eyes soften as she rounds the bed and sits down next to me, wrapping her arms around me in the process. "My baby," she whispers.

I instantly begin crying again.

After she holds me for a long time, she pulls back and inspects my face, tucking a loose strand of my hair behind my ear. "He's done a number on you, hasn't he? Jorge says you're pregnant."

My eyes cut to Jorge, and he knows he's betrayed my trust by telling her that.

He raises his hands in surrender. "I panicked. They were the only people I knew to call who could help you."

"They?" I question. "What do you mean, *they?*"

"Don't be angry at Jorge, dear. He did the right thing by calling us. We're here to help you. Your father is downstairs, and he forgives you—"

"Forgives me? I did nothing to him. He's the one who was smothering me," I tell her.

Mother licks her lips but continues to stare at me with her beautiful green eyes. "Perhaps we are guilty of sheltering you too much, but you have to believe that we did it because we had your best interests at heart. When you left the way you did, it hit us that you weren't a little kid anymore. You're a grown woman, capable of making your own decisions. If you come back home with us, we promise we will do our best to lighten up and give you freedom."

I wipe under my eyes. "I love you, Mother, but I can't live at home again. Father will never stop seeing me as a little girl he can control unless I stand on my own two feet."

She pokes out her bottom lip. "But with a baby, Anna, life will be difficult without help."

"I know," I tell her. "But I'll manage. I'm ready to accept the responsibility."

Mother pinches my chin between her forefinger and thumb as she sighs. "My little girl is all grown-up and going to be a mother. I can't believe it."

She smiles, which makes me smile.

Somehow, I know that Mother and I will find a way to work out our differences. My father, on the other hand, will be a different story.

Chapter
TWENTY EIGHT

Xavier

I'M SITTING ON THE EDGE of my bed, bawling like a fucking baby.

It killed me to walk away from Anna, but how can I be a father?

I'm not cut out for it. I don't want to be the reason the kid eventually turns into a monster like me.

But what I do want is for Anna to be happy. I swore, I would never make her frown and that I would be a good man to her, yet here I am, breaking those promises.

I wish I were different.

I wish I were better.

I wish I could give her the happily ever after that she craves, like the ones in those romance books she reads.

It's then, in the confusion in my head, I do something I haven't done in a long time. I fall to my knees in the middle of my motel room and fold my hands to pray.

I raise my head up toward the ceiling. "God? I know I stopped talking to you after you took my mother away from me, and you probably don't give a shit about me either way, but I need your guidance. I need a sign to tell me what I need to do. I love Anna. God, I love her so much that it scares me to lose her. She's my everything, but I'm willing to let her go if it's the right thing to do." Tears drip down onto my shirt. "What should I do?"

A gentle knock at the door causes my head to snap in its direction. No one knows where Corey and I are staying, so having a visitor startles the hell out of me. Corey probably forgot his key.

I hop up onto my feet and then dry my face with the sleeve of my T-shirt.

I open the door, and at first, I don't see anyone until I drop my gaze about four feet. Standing there is a dark-haired little girl, wearing a pink dress and clutching a teddy bear to her chest.

"Da-da?" is all she says. Evidently, she's still in the babbling phase of her communication skills.

I furrow my brows just as a woman from down the hallway scoops up the child into her arms.

The woman grimaces as she stares up at me, obviously intimidated by my towering frame. "I'm so sorry. No, no, Anna. Stay with Mommy."

My mouth falls open, and for the first time in my life, I swear, I've witnessed a miracle. I asked for a sign, and the man upstairs sure as hell provided one for me.

At that moment, it's clear to me what I'm supposed to do. I need to find a way to make things work with Anna and to say to hell with all the things that could happen. I'll fight to keep her and my baby safe until my last dying breath.

Anxious to see Anna and groveling for her forgiveness, I sprint all the way back to the hotel where I know all the wrestlers are staying.

I burst through the doors and cut in front of the line at the concierge desk. "What room is Anna Cortez in?"

The woman, who is visibly put off by my behavior, looks at me with a resting bitch face. "We cannot give out that information. Now, if you don't mind, please step away from the counter."

"Fine," I say. "If you don't want to tell me, I'll just go up and down every hallway, searching for her. I think I'll start here in the lobby. Anna! Anna?" My voice commands the attention of the entire room, and every head turns in my direction.

"Sir! Lower your voice. *Please*, sir!"

The woman keeps trying, but I ignore her and begin walking toward the elevators when a man I vividly recognize from Atlanta steps in front of me.

"What are you? Crazy? You can't go around, yelling for my daughter like that."

I stare down at Anna's father. "What are you doing here? She doesn't want to see you."

He narrows his eyes at me. "I could say the same thing to you. I heard what you did. Got my daughter pregnant and then ran out on her. What happened to all that preaching you did to me, huh? The same rules don't apply to Mr. Superstar?"

He's right. I did give him the third fucking degree for not treating her right, and I haven't been doing much better myself lately.

"You're right. I've been screwing up. But I'm going to do my best to beg her for forgiveness."

Mr. Cortez sighs and rubs his chin. "My daughter will forgive you because she's a good girl, and she knows the words of the good book. Forgive, and you will be forgiven."

When he quotes the line of scripture, I remember reading that passage over and over as a kid, wishing Grandmother would apply that rule to herself every time she told me she hated me.

"Luke—six, thirty-seven."

He lifts his eyebrows in surprise. "You know *his* word?"

I lift my chin. "I do. And I believe he put the two of us together for a reason. She's my angel, and she has been saving my life since the day I met her."

He smooths back his dark hair as he contemplates what I said. "She's in room four thirty-two."

We are far from friends, but it seems we have an understanding now when it comes to the type of relationship his daughter and I share.

My lips pull into a tight line, and I nod. "Thank you."

I turn and head for the elevators and jump into the first one that opens, pressing the button to the fourth floor. I make it up to her room and take a deep breath before I raise my hand and knock on the door.

When the door opens, it's not Anna who opens it but the guy I was so ready to kill earlier, and he doesn't look too pleased to see me.

I shove my hands deep into my pockets, so he knows I'm not here to cause any problems. "Anna here?"

The man doesn't make a move to clear out of my path, and I'm impressed that, even after what I did to him, he's willing to stand his ground.

"I don't think she wants to see you right now."

I swallow hard. "I know I fucked up. At least let me come in and apologize to her."

He shakes his head. "You hurt her enough. Why don't you—"

"Jorge," Anna calls from inside the room. "It's okay. Let him in."

Jorge? The same Jorge she was supposed to marry?

I eyeball the guy, and it's understandable why her father picked a guy like that for her. He's the complete opposite of me in every way and probably more deserving of her than me, but I refuse to allow him to have her.

Jorge steps back, and I pass by him.

Anna's sitting in the middle of the bed in her room. Her legs are curled underneath her, and her face is red and swollen from crying.

Jesus, I'm a piece of shit for doing that to her.

A woman with the same dark hair and green eyes as Anna pushes up from the bed and approaches me with her hand extended. "I'm Maria Cortez, Anna's mother."

I nod, easily seeing the resemblance between Anna and her mother. "Xavier Cold."

"I figured," she replies. "My daughter is a good girl. Make this right with her." She turns back to Anna. "Call me if you need me, *mija*. Our offer for you to come home always stands."

Anna nods. "Okay."

Maria kisses the top of Anna's head and makes her way toward the door. "Come on, Jorge."

"You don't think we should stay?" he questions as she walks by him.

She grabs the door handle. "No. They can handle things from here."

Jorge sighs, and it's easy to see that, while Anna might be over him, he's not over her, and it kills him to leave her unaccompanied with me.

But he's an obedient guy and does as he's asked. "Good-bye, Anna."

When we're alone in the room, I clear my throat. "When did you find out about the baby?"

"After my first show on Tension. I fell and had to get checked out by the trainer. They drug-tested me and gave me a pregnancy test." She is quiet for a moment. "I tried to call and tell you, but you never answered me."

Things begin to click. Not only was she upset because she thought I was blowing her off, but she was also going through some real shit, and I wasn't there for her.

"I'm sorry, Anna. For everything. I handled it all wrong. I wish I could go back and have a do-over."

She doesn't even look at me, and I know I've hurt her bad, but I need to see her eyes, so I can tell what she's thinking.

"Anna . . ."

"I'm sorry, Xavier. I can't—"

Before she has a chance to finish that sentence, I drop to my knees by her side. "Whatever you're going to say, don't. Please, don't. Anna, look at me."

She reluctantly shifts her eyes in my direction.

"Don't end this. Don't end us. I'll do whatever you want to make you stay with me. I can't live my life without you, Anna."

Her lips twist as she stares into my eyes. "Then, tell me the truth, Xavier. Tell me everything that you've been hiding from me. Help me understand you and why you keep pushing me away."

I lock my fingers together on the bed in front of me and then drop my head onto my arms. Telling her everything might change the way she sees me. I don't want her pity—I never wanted that—but if exposing the demons of my past is what will make her stay, then she's about to get an earful.

I raise my head and take a deep breath. "Where do you want me to start?"

"At the beginning," she whispers. "Talk to me instead of getting angry all the time."

And so it begins.

I launch into my earliest childhood memories of all the good times I spent with my mother and then how things got really hard when she figured out my father—whoever he was—was never coming back. I tell Anna about all the drugs, living with Grandmother, the beatings she inflicted on me, and lastly, about the times I lived on the streets, doing things for money that made me a monster.

I'm lying next to her on the bed, facing her, as I pour my heart out, telling her things I've never told anyone else before, and she's listening to everything.

She never makes a move to judge me. She just listens, and it feels good to get all this off my chest.

The last thing I tell her is the one thing I was trying hard to keep from her. Nothing is held back this time as I tell her about the day Kai took me to see Bishop. "That's why I was with Angie that day. Bishop threatened to hurt you unless I did as he asked. I'm not getting back into business with him, so the only way I could keep you safe was to keep you away."

Anna pushes my hair back off my face. "So, that's why you were trying to break things off with me—to keep me safe?"

"Yes. I knew I had to. The night you went to Larry's and drank, one of Bishop's flunkies was the guy next to you, trying to pay your bill. They were showing me that they could get to you anytime they wanted. I couldn't handle it if they hurt you. You're my reason for living. The only problem is, I can't make it without you.

"When you told me you were pregnant, I lost it, believing I would drag a kid down and make it a monster like me, believing you—both of you—would be better off without me."

She stares into my eyes. "I'm better when I'm with you, and I know our kid will be, too. You're good, Xavier. It's time you start believing in yourself, seeing yourself the way I do. You deserve to be happy. You deserve to have a family, and I'm willing to give you that chance, but you can't check out on me again, no matter what happens."

"I'll never leave your side again. I will control my temper—that, I promise. It's cost me too much in my life, and I have more to lose now than I ever have." My hand covers her entire stomach as I cradle my unborn child. "I'll love both of you with every inch of my soul until my very last breath on this earth. I swear to you, from here on out, no more secrets. I'll tell you everything. Nothing will get between us. I love you, Anna."

Tears fill her eyes. "And I love you. Forever."

I crash my lips to hers while relief floods me. I've finally found my heart again.

Chapter
TWENTY NINE

Xavier

WALKING BACK INTO *TENSION* WITH Anna on my arm feels damn good. For a while, I doubted if this would ever happen again, but now, after everything, we're stronger than ever.

Freddy lifts his chin when he spots us, knowing this is a big change from the last time he saw us together. "Sup, X?"

I throw my hand up to him.

Walking toward us is Brian with his hair pulled up in a ponytail. He's holding Kami on his hip, and Liv is nestled up to his other side. "The two of you back together?"

I nod. "We are. I couldn't stay away."

I kiss the top of Anna's head, and she smiles when she looks up at me.

"You two look good together," Liv chimes in.

"So, you back permanently?" Brian asks.

"Not yet. The suspension is lifted, but I'm not allowed to have any matches."

Brian squints a bit as his mouth twists. "Don't get me wrong when I ask this because I'm happy as hell to have you back around, but why are you here then?"

As if on clockwork, Corey comes around the corner, brightly displaying the backstage pass Freddy gave him yesterday.

I nod behind Brian. "I found a kid I think would be a good

fit for the *Tension* Training Program. I met him back at my old gym in Detroit. The kid is fast. He has flare and that *it* thing that makes a good wrestler."

"So, Silverman lifted the suspension because you brought the kid?"

"No. Chip took care of it, but he couldn't do anything about the matches."

"That's a damn shame. I hated handing my belt over to Rex. It should've been you."

I sigh. "Maybe I can change that soon."

"Wow," Corey says as he steps up next to me with wide eyes. "You're Brian 'Razor' Rollins."

"I am," Brian confirms. "You must be the kid X was telling me about. He says you're good."

There's a question in Anna's eyes, so I fill in the gap for her. "Anna, this is Corey, the kid I've been training. Corey, this is my beautiful Anna."

"Nice to meet you." Corey reaches out and shakes her hand. "X here has been showing me some of his moves."

"That's awesome." Anna snuggles into my side. "I'm proud of you for helping others," she says to me.

I shrug. "It's not a big deal. Besides, bringing the kid here is the reason *Tension* took me back."

"You're not back yet. The kid still needs to prove he's worth the shot he's been given." Mr. Silverman's voice cuts between all of us.

The appearance of our boss causes everyone to stiffen a bit.

I haven't spoken to him since the night he got me out of jail and told me to stay away from this place for three months. He's probably not too happy about me defying that demand and weaseling my way back here much sooner.

The boss's gray eyes flick to me. "I'll be expecting a demonstration of these skills after the show tonight."

Corey's grin widens, but I can tell by the tone in Mr.

Silverman's voice that a huge catch is coming.

"If he doesn't impress me tonight, you are to leave the building immediately, and I don't want to hear another peep from you over the next two months while you finish out the remainder of your suspension in Detroit."

That's a steep penalty, but I'm willing to take that risk because I know what Corey can do. "And when he impresses you, I want to be fully reinstated, and I want to move my match with Rex up to the next live *Tension* event."

He narrows his eyes into tiny slits. "Done."

I fight back the smile that's threatening to expose how elated I am. I know, after tonight, Rex's ass will be mine.

THE ARENA IS EERILY QUIET as I step into the ring with Corey. The only people in the huge room are the two of us with Mr. Silverman and Chip sitting in the stands, waiting to judge Corey's talent level.

"All right," Mr. Silverman calls out, "impress me."

"You heard him, kid. Make me look good and help us both out." I shake my shoulders loose and rock my neck a few times. "Now, come at me exactly how we practiced at Tough's."

Corey nods, and just like every other time we've stepped inside the ring, the playful demeanor he typically sports is long gone and is now replaced with an expression of pure determination.

We are on our toes, anticipating the other's first move, when Corey strikes first. He slams into me, attempting to twist me around and get me into a simple neck hold, but I easily get out of it before shoving him away.

"You've got to do better than that. He wants to be impressed, remember?"

Corey gives me a slow nod and then comes back at me with three times as much force. It's like a fire has been lit under him because the way he's moving shows hunger with the need to prove himself.

I give in this time and let him get a few holds on me—not because I'm allowing him to win, but because he's putting on a hell of a show and he deserves for me to help him look good.

Corey grabs my arm and tosses me into the ropes where I bounce off of them and then run straight into his perfect form clothesline. His forearm collides with my chest, and an audible crack echoes around the arena.

I have to admit, it hurts, like a million bees are shoving their stingers into my skin at once.

I lie there on the mat, and Corey bends down to yanks my hair before pulling me back up onto my feet.

He draws back, as if to punch me, but my boss orders, "Enough!"

Corey releases me, and we both stand there, in the middle of the ring with our hands by our sides, while Chip and my boss whisper among themselves.

"What do you think they're saying?" Corey asks in a hushed tone.

I shrug. "Beats me. I gave up a long time ago on trying to figure out how these upper-level people think."

Finally, Chip nods, as if he's in agreement, and then both men face us again.

The owner of the company pushes himself up from the seat. "You're in, kid. Be over at the training facility in Dallas next Monday morning."

My heart pounds in my chest. "Does that mean I'm back?"

Chip glances over to our boss.

Mr. Silverman nods. "The ratings have been down since you've been gone, and the fans have been blasting our social media for suspending you. The people have dubbed you their real champion, and they refuse to get behind Rex, so we need to get him out of the spotlight before he ruins my company."

Corey pumps his fist and lets out a yell that people in the next state could probably hear, "Hell yeah!"

"And, X?" Mr. Silverman adds. "You've got your match against Rex. It will be right here in Portland on Tuesday night."

This time, I feel like yelling, but I manage to keep myself restrained. I hope Rex is ready because I'm coming for him sooner rather than later.

SITTING IN A CONFERENCE ROOM to go over the script with the writers is a new experience for me. Most of the time, we meet in whatever room the writers have been thrown in, as we bounce from arena to arena.

Rex stares at the belt laying on the table in front of him with Vicky next to him and Deena flanking his other side.

I reach under the table and thread my fingers through Anna's. It feels pretty fucking sweet to have her by my side right about now. It's a great way to show Rex that, no matter how hard he tried, he couldn't break us.

No one says a word while we wait for the boss to show up. He never attends these meetings, so this is serious shit.

Mr. Silverman steps into the room, and I straighten in the chair.

He takes a seat at the head of the table and smoothes his tie. "Let's get down to business. Vicky, take us through the play-by-play."

She adjusts her glasses, pushing them up from the tip of her nose. "To close up the storyline with Anna being on Rex's side, she'll accompany him out to open the show. Rex will call X out, and then we'll have Rex accuse her of conspiring with X and then kick her out of the ring."

"I don't like that idea," Rex interjects. "I think Anna being on my side will keep the fans involved."

"Agreed," Deena adds. "If it helps, I can be in X's corner."

Anna squeezes my hand, and I'm sure she hates their ideas just as much as I do.

"No," the boss answers. "No more games. Anna belongs to X, and we are going with that. X gets the belt tonight."

"That's not fair! I just got it. You can't take it away from me," Rex argues with a whine in his voice.

The boss slams his fist on the table. "You had your shot, and now, it's up. If you don't like the way we're doing things, don't let the door hit you on the ass."

I smirk. It's about time this company put Rex in his place. They've let him get away with far too much for far too long. Things are finally going to be the way they are supposed to be.

Chapter
THIRTY

Xavier

ANNA COMES FROM THE FEMALE dressing room, wearing the tight stage outfit I've seen her in as of late. I appreciate the way it hugs every curve of her body. The cupcake sparkling under the word *Sweets* has me thinking about what I would like to do to that sweet body of hers.

I wrap my arms around her. "Damn, beautiful. You're smoking hot. I'd like a little taste of your cupcakes."

She giggles as I kiss her lips. "You are so bad."

"Cut the shit," Rex snaps. "It's time to head out to the ring."

I lift my chin and force myself to bite my tongue. I'm so close to getting everything I want. I will not allow this shit stain to push my buttons.

Rex tosses the belt over his shoulder as he stares me down. "Come on, Anna. Let's give the fans a show."

Anna's muscles tense as I'm still holding her in my arms. It's like she's unsure of what's about to happen. I don't want her to be stressed, so I have to show her that I'm cool.

I pat her butt. "Go ahead. It's time to put an end to the time he's had you by his side."

"Okay," she whispers before giving me a quick kiss.

Anna leaves us, and Rex smirks at me one last time before he takes off after her.

Never in a million fucking years did I ever think I would be stuck backstage, sitting on the sideline, while my woman is being made to parade around with another fucking man on national television. My nostrils flare as Rex escorts Anna out to the ring with Deena on his other side. The cocky grin on the bastard's face tells me how much enjoyment he's getting out of this moment, knowing I'm sitting back here, seething.

Rex sits on the ropes, allowing the girls to slip inside the ring.

He casually leans against the ropes and stares into the camera. "Well, all you people here in Portland tonight are in for a treat. Phenomenal X is back in the building tonight, and I've decided I'm ready for that rematch."

The crowd goes nuts, shouting my name over and over, "X! X! X! X!"

Those cheering for me remind me that, even though I don't have the belt, I'm the people's champion. I have to find ways to curb my rage and earn the championship to make them proud.

"Shut up! All of you! X isn't here. I'm here! I'm the one who matters!" Rex shouts.

The fans continue to support me, and Rex's expression turns dark. It's not hard to tell that he's pissed off because people aren't behind him.

Without warning, he grabs Anna, dips her back, and presses his lips to hers.

I growl and instinctually curl my hands into fists. "I'm going to kill that fucker."

Anna pounds against Rex's chest until he finally releases her. Her eyes narrow as she pulls her hand back and smacks the shit out of Rex's face. His head snaps sideways, and he rubs his cheek as Anna slides out of the ring.

A collective sound of, "Ooh," echoes around the arena, and then they immediately launch into chanting, "Anna," but she doesn't seem to notice because she's so focused on getting backstage.

Brian shakes his head as he stands next to me. "What a dick. He loves getting under your skin."

"I'm convinced he has a death wish," Freddy chimes in.

I stand near the curtain, and when Anna pushes through it, her face is red.

I reach for her, but she shakes her head.

"I need a minute. I have to find something to bleach the slimeball off my lips."

I hold my hands up, knowing what it's like to need a moment of privacy when something has pissed me off. "I'll wait for you right here."

Deena's throaty laugh floats through the curtain just before she and Rex waltz through it. When they make eye contact with me, they both wear nearly matching evil smiles.

My instinct is to launch at Rex and tear him a new asshole, but I promised Anna I would learn to control my temper, so I'm going to do my best to keep that promise.

I roll my eyes. "You two are pathetic."

Rex gingerly touches his bottom lip. "Her lips were so soft. No wonder that pussy of hers had you ready to throw away your career. I bet it's just as smooth and silky."

I lunge forward, but Freddy grabs me from behind.

"Don't, X. He's baiting you, trying to get you to fuck up again."

My jaw muscle flexes as my mind runs through how this scenario played out last time and how I was the loser in the situation. I won't allow Rex to fuck this up for me.

Rex smirks and adjusts the belt on his shoulders. "See you in the ring, asshole."

"Count on it, motherfucker." My nostrils flare, and I take a deep breath in an attempt to calm myself down.

This learning-to-control-my-temper thing is a lot of fucking work. It's way harder than simply punching the object of my rage square in the motherfucking face.

A sarcastic laugh bubbles out of Rex as he turns and walks away from me.

Once he's out of sight, Freddy slowly releases me. "When is that asshole going to learn to stop poking the bear? One of these days, I won't be around to save his ungrateful ass."

"He needs to back the fuck off me." I smooth my hair out of my face. "I'm really trying to turn things around and keep my shit in check."

"That's good because you're about to be the champ—the rightful one. Don't fuck shit up again and allow him to come between you and that belt. It's yours for the taking. All you have to do is keep your head in the game and your ass out of trouble."

"I'm working on it, Freddy. Believe me."

The last thing I want to do is fuck up my livelihood again, especially with a baby on the way now.

I will be the champ.

I will make my dreams come true.

Tonight, I will remain in control.

Chapter
THIRTY ONE

Anna

XAVIER'S HEAD HANGS DOWN, HIS long hair falling around his face like a curtain, as he stares absently at his hands. He flexes his fingers in and out, causing the tone muscles of his arms to work beneath his tattooed skin.

This match is the biggest one of his life, both in his professional career and his personal struggle to reinvent himself by controlling his temper.

He walked away from Rex's taunts, which was a huge deal for him. Xavier has never been known for turning the other cheek when he's angry.

The biggest question on his mind has to be whether he can continue to harness that anger and still be able to pull this match off.

The last thing he needs right now is a repeat of what went on in Atlanta. If he loses it, it will probably be the end of his wrestling career with the largest company in the world. This job means a lot to him, and now, with a baby on the way, he must feel even more pressure to keep it.

I lean my chin on his shoulder. The scent of soap and something distinctly Xavier wraps around me as I quietly sit with him. I want him to know, just like always, I'm here for him.

Xavier blows a rush of air out of his nose and then whispers,

"What if I fuck up again? What will happen to us?"

"Nothing," I say. He turns to look at me with those crystal-blue eyes of his, and I repeat, "Nothing because you will be in control this time."

"What if I'm not?" The question he's really asking is, *If I don't change, will you leave me?*

I need to keep reassuring him. It's the small role I have to play to in order to bring Xavier to a better mental health state so that he knows he doesn't have to lash out to express his fears, that talking to me is always a better choice.

"I believe in you." I touch his cheek with the tips of my fingers. "I love you, Xavier. *Nothing* is going to tear us apart. You're well on your way to showing the rest of the world the good man you've kept locked up all these years, the one I've known has been in there all along."

He cradles my face in his hands. "I love you, beautiful. Thank you for being my angel in the dark."

He presses his lips to mine, but before our kiss can get too heated, Al, the stagehand's voice cuts into the empty room. "X, you're up."

Xavier pulls back and stares into my eyes. "I want you in my corner. You belong there."

I smile. "Then, lead the way."

Pandemonium erupts as Xavier's entrance music starts. The fans have been waiting anxiously for his return, and now, they are about to get what they've wanted. Tonight's sold-out crowd is insane. Faces are everywhere I look. I move back and watch Xavier do his thing. My eyes rake over him as he stands there, staring out at the crowd. His chiseled arms are on full display, and the fabric of the black tank top he's wearing is straining against his toned chest.

His face shows no emotion, and it's intimidating. Rex had better be on his A game because Xavier is all business.

Xavier crouches down and then jumps up in perfect time as

fireworks shoot up from the stage. He throws his head and his shoulders back as his signature howl erupts from his throat.

My God, this gets me every time.

My heart flutters at the sight of my powerful man.

He grabs my hand and then struts down the ramp, like a warrior entering battle.

"The following match is scheduled for one fall," the announcer calls. "Making his way to the ring, from Detroit, Michigan, weighing two hundred and sixty-five pounds, is . . . Phenomenal X!"

"Stay right here." Xavier kisses my cheek and then climbs inside the ropes. He continues putting on a show for the crowd by running from corner to corner, throwing a victorious fist in the air.

The announcer introduces Xavier's opponent, "Making his way to the ring, from Hollywood, California, weighing two hundred and thirty pounds, your *Tension* champion, is . . . Rex 'Assassin' Risen!"

Rex and Deena take their time in making their way down the ramp. Deena glares at me from the opposite corner as Rex steps inside the ring and holds the belt in the air.

The two men stare each other down, and the crowd goes electric, thrusting up lots of signs with Xavier's stage name written all over them. There's no question whom the fans are backing tonight.

Bright lights flicker overhead, and a bell rings, signaling the beginning of the match.

Xavier and Rex circle each other, and I grab the corner of the mat and shout encouragements to Xavier. My breath hitches the moment they lock up. Part of me doesn't want to watch, but the other part of me wants to see Xavier unleash on Rex. Nervous energy passes through every inch of me because I have no idea what's about to happen.

I just pray that Rex doesn't do something stupid that will

get him killed. Xavier has promised to work on his temper, but I think, at this point, his intention to keep a calm head can only be tested so much before he loses his mind.

Rex's taunts earlier tonight didn't help, but I have faith that Xavier will somehow dig deep inside himself and find a way to do this.

Rex twists around and catches Xavier in a headlock, but Xavier quickly shoves Rex off and grabs his wrist before landing a kick to his side. This time, Xavier wraps his arm around Rex's neck and grunts as he pulls tight. Rex's arms wildly flail around, and then he elbows Xavier in the ribs, causing him to let go.

Xavier doesn't give up though. He grabs Rex's arms and flings him into the ropes before landing a clothesline, knocking his opponent to the mat so hard that the ring shakes.

Rex pushes himself up and waves Xavier on. "Is that all you've got?"

"Spear! Spear! Spear!" the crowd chants over and over, egging Xavier on to use one of his finishing moves on Rex.

Xavier bends at the waist and puts his hand on the mat in a football-player-three-point stance, and then he charges full speed at Rex. Cameras flash the moment Xavier makes contact, and both men go flying.

A collective, "Oh," sounds through the massive room as Xavier tackles Rex down to the mat and punches him once in the face.

Rex doesn't make an attempt to get up, but Xavier isn't finished with him yet. He crawls over to the corner of the ring and climbs up the turnbuckles until he's balancing himself on the top rope. A six-foot-four man towering this high over the ring is really a sight to see. It's spectacular.

Xavier stretches his arms out and then sends his body toward Rex. An audible crack echoes around the room, and I gasp. I've been around wrestling enough lately to know that sound means real pain, and I pray Xavier is all right.

I resist the urge to jump into the ring to check on him be-cause doing that will only stop the match, so I wait with bated breath to find out if Xavier is okay. I can barely watch to see what happens next.

Chapter
THIRTY TWO

Xavier

THE MINUTE MY ELBOW MAKES contact with Rex's chest, he grunts in pain. Granted, we aren't trained to actually land with that much force on our opponent, but this motherfucker deserves all the pain I can inflict on him.

The lights overhead are nearly blinding when I stare up at them for too long. The mat is hard beneath me as I lie here, attempting to catch my breath.

I roll over and then push myself up to my feet. Pinning Rex so early isn't good business. The fans are expecting a show, and it's my job to give it to them.

I stumble over to Rex and grab his hair, forcing him back up. "On your feet, fucker."

"Kiss my ass. I won't help you take my belt."

He grunts as I elbow again him in the ribs. As much as I want to unleash my anger, I hold back and maintain perfect control of my temper. This asshole will not ruin this title shot for me again, no matter how much he tries to get to me.

Rex shoves me, and I stumble backward to sell it to the crowd. We face each other, both of our chests heaving, as we wait on the other one to make the first move.

"Come on!" Rex screams out of frustration.

I rush at him.

Our arms hook up in a test of strength, and he tries to push me back. I plant my feet, and a cold smile crosses my face when he realizes that I'm not budging.

His eyes widen as I slam a forearm across his chest. The wind gushes out of him as I pin him against the ropes.

I growl, "This is my house, motherfucker, and you will respect that."

I hit him once more, and he wobbles on his feet. It's clear that he's losing the will to fight. It's time to finish this.

I rush back against the ropes and bounce off of them with momentum that could rival a freight train. Rex braces for impact as I launch myself at him before spearing him to the mat with enough force to shake the whole ring.

The crowd chants my name, "X! X! X!"

Rex moans as he lies next to me, and I know he can't take much more punishment.

Energy surges through me, and I seize the moment to hook my elbow around his leg, effectively pinning him to the mat.

The referee falls to the mat and smacks it hard as he counts out loud.

"One!" the crowd chants along with the referee.

"Two!"

"Three!"

I lie there, stunned. I've finally done it. I'm the motherfucking champion.

The referee hands me the belt and then helps me onto my feet. The gold on the belt glistens beneath the lights above the stage as I hold it out in front of me.

I've worked so hard in my career, punishing my body nearly to its breaking point, for this moment—the chance to hold this championship belt in my hands. I've earned this. I've gone through hell for this belt, and I finally feel like I deserve to happy.

"Your new heavyweight champion, *Phenomenal X!*" the

announcer shouts over the crowd.

My name echoes around the room.

Rex slams his fist into the ground, like a spoiled child throwing a fit, but him being pissed over the situation isn't my problem. This is how things were always meant to be.

I stare up at the crowd, and every single person in the place is on their feet, cheering and chanting my name. It's a fucking rush. I raise my hand in victory while I clutch the belt against my chest.

I walk over to the corner of the ring and extend my hand to Anna. "Come on, beautiful. Share this with me."

She takes my hand, and I pull her up into the ring. She wraps her arms around me, and I bury my face into her hair.

"We did it," I say.

Anna pulls back and shakes her head. "No, *you* did it."

There's no way I could've done this without her, and it's high time she knows just how much she means to me.

I turn to the referee. "Get me a mic."

Within seconds of my request, a microphone is shoved into my hand, so I can address the crowd. "Last time I was in this ring, I left in handcuffs. This time, I walk out of here as the champ."

The fans get so loud that I swear, the roof of this place is about to blow. After a couple of minutes, they quiet down enough for me to continue.

"Assassin tried to take away everything that was important to me, but that dumbass couldn't figure out that you can't mess with fate. I've got my belt, and I've got my woman."

Anna stares up at me with a wide grin and mouths the words, *I love you*, to me.

I gaze into her eyes, knowing this woman is my soul mate, the one I can't live without. Our relationship is permanent. "This woman has brought me out of the depths of my darkness. She's my light, my everything, and I want the world to know she's mine." I drop down to one knee in front of a sold-out crowd and millions of people watching at home. "Anna . . . will you marry me?"

Her hands cover her face in shock. She wasn't prepared for this, but she should know by now that I never do what's expected.

Tears flow from her eyes as she smiles and nods, repeating the word, "Yes," over and over.

I hop to my feet, drop the mic, and cradle her face in my hands. "I love you, Anna. Always have and always will."

I thread my fingers into her hair as I crash my lips onto hers and get lost in the moment.

ANNA CURLS HER FINGERS INTO my shirt and yanks me into the elevator with her. We've been celebrating my victory all evening, and it looks like the party is going to continue in her room.

As soon as the doors close, I pick her up and press my lips to hers.

She wraps her legs around my waist and grips handfuls of my hair. "I want you."

Fuck. I nearly come apart every time she says that to me.

This woman is fucking perfection. Everything she does turns me on, like a fucking light switch, and I can't wait until I get her sexy ass in bed.

I glance up at the elevator numbers and realize we're stopping on her floor. Excitement for what I know is going to be amazing sex builds inside me. "Patience, baby. We're almost there."

The doors open, and I carry her with ease down the hall. Her lips are still connected with mine when we arrive at her door.

I pull back. "Room key?"

She reaches into her back pocket and then slips it into the slot on the door. It opens on the first try, and we push inside.

The lights remain off as I walk over to the bed and toss Anna onto it. She scoots to the middle with her eyes trained on me, her hair wild from our elevator make-out session.

I crawl toward her like a predator. "Ever been fucked by a champion?"

She bites her lip. "No . . . but I have a feeling that I'm about to be."

With a firm hand, I push her down onto the bed and then slide her tank top up. I kiss the warm flesh of her stomach and stare up at her through hooded eyes. "Did I mention how fucking sexy you looked tonight? You have no idea how tempted I was to drag you to a dark corner somewhere and have my way with you."

A blush immediately creeps into her cheeks. "I would've liked that."

My tongue darts out, and I lick around her navel. "Don't tempt me, beautiful, or next time I have the urge to take you, I'll just do it and not give a fuck where we are or who can hear you scream out my name when I make you come."

I crawl up next to her and then prop my head up with my left hand. I trace the smooth skin on her exposed shoulder before I lean in and nip it, causing her to giggle. I hook my finger around the hem of her shirt and lift the fabric higher, exposing the white lacy bra covering her breasts. I run my index finger along the curve of her breast, enjoying the feel of its silky softness.

My cock jerks inside my jeans, begging for her attention.

Anna kisses my lips and then knots her fingers into my hair. Taking things slow has never been on our sexual menu. It's like, the moment we start, we can't get enough of each other.

She touches my cheek, and I kiss her wrist, inhaling the sweet scent of her soap and perfume.

"I love you, Xavier."

"I love you, too." It's surprising how saying this to her now comes with such ease.

Before her, I was lost in the darkness, battling demons all alone. I'm nowhere near healed, but with her light, I know I'll be able to find my way out of my own self-destructive path. She is my angel, and she's giving me something I never thought I would have—a family.

"You okay?" she whispers as she gazes into my eyes.

I press my lips to hers. "Never better."

"I'm sure that's not totally true," she taunts. "I can think of something else that will make you feel a whole lot better."

I grin wickedly, loving how dirty her mind has become. "I see my naughty Anna has come out to play."

"What can I say? You make me horny." The blush on her face deepens. "I can't believe I just said that to you."

I push her hair back off her shoulder. "Honesty always, right? Isn't that our new rule?"

She nods. "It is."

"Then, you should never be afraid or embarrassed to tell me how you feel. Otherwise, how will I ever know what you want from me?"

She swallows hard. "Make love to me, Xavier."

"I will happily grant that request." I turn over and pin her to the bed. "Ready to go one-on-one with the champ?"

She giggles. "Absolutely."

Anna pushes my shoulder, rolling me over onto my back. "How'd you like that reversal?"

"Impressive." I grab her hips as she straddles me. "Got any other moves?"

She bends down and presses her lips to mine before she begins her delicious tease of slowly kissing a path across my face. "A few."

I lick my lips. "Show me."

She leans back and shoves my shirt up before running her hands down my torso. The button of my jeans pops open with ease, and she snakes her hand inside to grab my cock.

"Jesus," I hiss, not used to her taking such control but loving that she's asserting herself with me.

I sit up and wrap her in my arms, crushing my lips to hers, before I plunge my tongue inside her mouth. She rotates her hips, and a soft moan emits from her throat. My cock strains against my jeans, missing the warmth of her hand and needing her touch again.

Her dark hair floats around us as she throws her head back, giving me better access to drag my lips down her throat.

"I need you."

Her plea for me to take her is heard loud and clear.

I rip her top off the rest of the way and push her bra down so hard that a distinct tearing sound can't be missed. Anna works quickly in pulling my shirt over my head. It's like she can't get her skin against mine fast enough, and I fucking love knowing how bad she wants me.

"Pants," I mutter, needing them off before I lose my fucking mind.

She crawls back onto her knees and yanks the rest of her clothes off as I remove my own. We watch each other with lust-filled eyes as we get naked, and it's as if we're waiting for the bell to go off so we can attack one another.

When everything is gone, I flip her onto her back and spread her legs out wide before me. I slip a digit between her folds, feeling her swollen clit. "Damn, beautiful. Always so wet and ready for me."

She stares up at me. "Because my body always craves you."

I kiss her again. Taut nipples rub against my chest as I press my body to hers.

This woman is fucking perfect and all fucking mine.

I finger-fuck her pussy until she's writhing beneath me.

"You ready, baby?"

"Yes," she hisses. "Please, God, *yes*."

I bring my fingers up to my mouth and taste the sweet juices of her arousal. "Tastes so fucking good. Sweet, like you." I lean in and whisper, "Mine. You're all mine, Anna, now and forever."

I swivel my hips, coating myself with her wetness, and then I enter her in one quick thrust. "Fuck me. Being inside you never gets old. It feels so fucking good."

I pull out and then pump back inside again and again until I'm pounding into her so hard that the sound of our skin slamming together fills the room.

Anna reaches up and curls her fingers around my forearms. "Oh God. Oh God. Xavier . . . *oh!*"

I gaze into her eyes as she falls apart.

Her mouth drifts open, and she digs her nails into my skin as she cries out, "Xavier!"

Warmth spreads over my body. I'm nowhere near ready for this to be over, but there's no way I can fight it, knowing I'm deep inside the most beautiful fucking woman in the world while she's panting from coming around my cock.

My entire body shudders, and I slip into sweet ecstasy as I fill her full. This woman is my destiny, and I will never allow anything else to come between us.

Chapter
THIRTY THREE

Anna

IT'S ODD, SITTING IN THE back of Mother and Father's minivan with Xavier. It shocked the hell out of me when Father sent a text this morning, asking if they could drive us to the airport.

The clicking sound is the only thing to be heard inside the cab. None of us have made the first move to say anything, and the ride is the most awkward experience of my life.

Father pulls up to the passenger loading area. "I'll get the bags."

"I'll help him," Xavier says before jumping out to assist.

Mother turns around in her seat. "Anna, I know this is hard for you. It's hard for your father, too. But give him a chance. You might be surprised by what you hear."

I nod and take a deep breath in an attempt to calm my pounding heart.

I make it to the back of the vehicle, and my eyes land on Father shaking Xavier's hand.

"You take care of my little girl. I'm trusting you to protect her with your life."

Xavier gives him a half-smile. "She's in good hands, sir. Nothing will happen to her on my watch."

He seems to accept that because he nods curtly. As he

releases Xavier's hand, his eyes fall on me. "I've missed you."

My lips twist as I stare at the man who I believed hated me. "You have?"

"Of course I have. You're my daughter. I care deeply about you and your future, which is why I got so crazy before you left home. I thought you were heading down the wrong path because it wasn't one that I laid out for you, but I've done a lot of praying and talking with my pastor since the day you left." He bats away a tear from the corner of his eye. "I've come to see that what I was doing was wrong, that I shouldn't try to control you. No one should. You should always be your own person and find your own happiness even if I don't like how you've found it. I'm sorry, Anna. Can you ever forgive me?"

Tears roll down my cheeks. I can't believe what I'm hearing. Aunt Dee told me that this might happen, but I never expected an actual apology from my father. He's not the type of man who usually admits when he's wrong, so I know this was hard for him to do, and he wouldn't have done it unless he meant it.

I rush over to Father, and he wraps his arms around me.

"I forgive you," I say.

We stay in each other's arms, crying together, for a long time, and finally, everything feels complete again.

FLYING BACK TO DETROIT IN first class, sitting next to Xavier, I'm on cloud nine. There's no doubt that we went through some hell to get here, but we made it—together.

We've been given a second chance, one where Xavier and I are honest with one another and there are no more secrets.

Quinn was right about one thing. Without trust, a relationship will never survive.

Xavier threads his fingers through mine as the plane lands on the runway. "Do you feel up to apartment-hunting as soon as we get off the plane?"

I nod. "Of course. We can have Quinn drive us to your grandmother's house, so we can get your stuff first and get a hotel. Then, we can head out."

He leans his head back against the headrest and sighs. "We need to borrow a car."

I tilt my head. "Something wrong with the bike?"

He rolls his head against the seat and gazes down at me. "No. I just don't want you on the back of it. I've got to keep you and my baby safe."

I bite my bottom lip to keep myself from jumping his bones. When he gets all protective like this, it's sexy, but it's even more attractive now because he's worried about the baby too. I like that he's fully invested in this pregnancy with me.

I kiss his lips. "Okay, *Daddy*."

He gives me one of his best panty-soaking grins. "Keep it up, and I'll have you calling me that when we're alone with your legs over my shoulders."

I giggle. "I wouldn't exactly call that a threat."

He leans in and nips my earlobe. "God, I want to fuck you so bad right now," he growls.

He takes my hand and lays it over the crotch of his jeans. There's no mistaking the hard cock that's standing up, waiting on my attention.

"Maybe we should skip the apartment-shopping and spend the rest of the day in bed."

Heat from where his lips kiss the soft skin beneath my ear causes a tingle to rip through my body.

"Sounds like a plan to me. I'll take a day buried inside that sweet pussy of yours anytime."

I squirm in my seat, trying to ease the ache between my legs.

Xavier chuckles. "Patience, baby. Save it all for later, and I assure you , I'll give you the best toe-curling sex you've ever had."

"Promise?" I whisper, loving it when he makes guarantees

of pleasure.

"Yes."

It feels like it takes forever to get off the plane, gather our bags, and then make it outside to where Quinn is waiting next to her Honda for us. I shield my eyes from the setting sun as we head over to her.

"There's the champ!"

Xavier grins, and it's easy to see the pride on his face. Winning the belt has been a dream for him, and it was an amazing experience to be by his side while it happened.

"Oh my God, I can't believe you're engaged! I should totally start a matchmaking business. I called this from the start," Quinn rambles on a mile a minute, her excitement clear. "You two looked great on television last night, by the way. Anna, I especially liked when you smacked that Rex guy in the face. It looked real."

I laugh as I hug my cousin. "I rather enjoyed that part myself. It's good to see you, Quinn."

"I liked that part, too," Xavier interjects from behind us.

"I'll bet," Quinn adds. "The guy had it coming. He's been a complete asshole to you."

"Yes, he has, but now that Xavier's won the belt from him, I don't see him looking for a rematch anytime soon. He knows he'll never beat Xavier in a fair fight."

"I agree," Quinn says as she pops the trunk for Xavier to load our bags. "I think Phenomenal X will be the champ for a long time."

"He does make a pretty great champion." I wrap my arms around Xavier's waist after he closes the trunk.

"So, when's the wedding?" Quinn's eyes flit from me to Xavier and then back again. "You seem *different*. Is there anything other than the engagement I should know about?"

I glance up to Xavier, as if to ask his permission to tell my cousin about the secret we're keeping.

He smiles and nods. "Tell her."

"Oh, shit. There is something. The suspense is killing me," Quinn whines.

I lock my gaze with Quinn's, and instantly, I'm smiling. "I'm pregnant."

Her mouth drops open, and her eyes widen before she launches into a full-on scream. "Oh. My. God! A *baby?*"

I nod, and without warning, she lunges forward and throws her arms around me and Xavier.

"Congratulations! This is amazing. Wait until Ma finds out. She'll be thrilled." Suddenly, she gasps and pulls back to search my face. "Does Uncle Simon know?"

I take a deep breath. "They know. They came to see me in Portland."

Her mouth pulls down on one side. "How'd that go? Was there a lot of yelling this time?"

I sigh, and Xavier tucks me in closer to his side.

"Surprisingly, no. Don't get me wrong. They still don't think it's fantastic news that their only daughter is pregnant and unmarried, but they do seem to understand that Xavier is the man I'm with, and nothing they do will change that. I think things will eventually work themselves out."

"That's great news. I'm so excited for the both of you."

Xavier clears his throat. "Now that you know, my next request won't sound so odd."

Quinn raises one eyebrow. "What's that?"

"Can I borrow your car for the next couple of days? I want to take Anna apartment-hunting and ring-shopping, and being on the back of my bike isn't safe enough for her anymore."

My mouth drops open, and at the same time, Quinn covers her mouth with her hands.

I stare up at Xavier. *"Rings?"*

He nods. "Of course. A ring will make it official. I want everyone in the world to know you're mine and an expensive piece of jewelry will remind anyone who sees it that you're taken."

He leans in and crushes his mouth to mine, and I know this is just the beginning to the rest of our life together.

XAVIER PARKS QUINN'S HONDA IN the driveway of the house on Sycamore. This house, it creeps me the hell out of me now. It's a wonder Xavier was ever able to step foot back in here after all the things that had happened to him.

He sighs and cuts the engine. "I won't be long. I'll run in and get my things, and then we'll go find a hotel to check in to." He leans over the console and kisses my cheek.

I smile. "I'll be right here."

I release a content sigh as I lean my head back against the seat and close my eyes. I finally feel like things are going my way, that things are working out the way they are supposed to.

My door yanks open, startling the crap out of me, and my eyes snap open along with it. The minute I look over to see who opened the door, I slink back into my seat.

"Get out of the car, bitch," Kai snarls as he points a dull black gun in my face. When I don't move, he shouts at me again, "You think I'm playing? I'll blow your fucking head off if you don't get your ass out of this motherfucking car."

My hands shake uncontrollably as I hold them out in front of me. "Okay, okay. I have to unbuckle my seat belt."

He shoves the gun against my temple, and my stomach drops. "Well, unhook the motherfucker."

My left hand slips down, and I press the button, freeing me from the car. Kai reaches in and yanks me by the arm out of the car.

I stumble and fall to the ground, but he grabs the hair on top of my head and forces me back to my feet.

"Let's go."

"Xavier will be back out here any minute," I threaten as Kai continues to push me at gunpoint toward the black SUV parked down the street.

Kai laughs darkly. "I hope he does because I'm going to kill that bitch-ass sellout."

The moment he says that, Xavier's voice calls out my name.

Kai turns to look back just in time to see Xavier jumping off the porch. Before Xavier's feet fully land, another man who was hiding on the other side of the porch tackles Xavier midair. He grunts as he hits the ground. From neighboring yard, an additional man sprints over and kicks Xavier in the gut.

"Xavier!" I scream.

Kai backhands me across the face. "Shut up!" he orders as he turns back to watch the attack.

A metallic taste covers my tongue, and I clutch my face as it stings like fire.

I've never felt so helpless, so lost on finding a way to Xavier, while I'm forced to stand there and watch.

Both men beat Xavier while he lies on the ground, and then one of them kicks Xavier in the face, instantly knocking him out.

"No!" I scream, not caring if it earns me another hit from Kai. Tears pour out of my eyes as Kai tightens his grip on my arm. "Xavier, get up!"

The two men back away from an unmoving Xavier.

"Fuck!" Kai shouts. "You dumb shits. You weren't supposed to kill him here. Our prints are all over that fucking house."

"What do you want us to do?" the bigger of the two men asks.

Kai dismissively waves his hand. "Burn this shit to the ground, and leave him."

The men nod, and as if Kai is a general and they are foot soldiers, they go into the house to, no doubt, carry out orders.

"Come on." Kai shoves me forward while still holding the

gun on me.

He shoves me into the backseat and slides in next to me.

Within a few minutes, an unmistakable orange light flickers out onto the darkened lawn, and the two men run toward the truck.

As we drive past the house, Xavier's body is still lying in the same place. I lean my head against the window, unsure of what's about to happen to me. But, without Xavier, I don't care either way. Without him, my world means nothing.

Chapter
THIRTY FOUR

Xavier

A VOICE COMES THROUGH THE fog of my brain and tries over and over to wake me up, but it's a real struggle for me to open my eyes.

"Xavier? Can you hear me, man?"

My eyelids drag open, and I attempt to cure the blurry vision. "Where is she? Where's Anna?"

Cole's face comes into focus, and his brows furrow. "There's no one here but you."

I lean up onto my elbows, and light from the flames licking their way up the sides of Grandmother's house illuminates the entire block. "Holy shit!"

I rush to get up, but Cole puts his hand on my shoulder. The light catches the gold of Cole's badge, and the swirling red and blue lights from the top of his cruiser flash across his face.

"Easy, big guy. You need to stay put."

I shove his hand away and push myself up onto my feet. "Cole, they've taken Anna. I'll kill them before I allow them to hurt her."

Anger boils over inside me. I will get her back.

Cole steps in front of me. "Hold on, X. Let me call for—"

"There's no time for that shit."

"Then, let me go with you."

I keep walking. "I can't have you to risk your life, too. Call the fire department and take care of this. I'm going to get Anna."

I don't give Cole time to argue anymore. I sprint to Quinn's car, hop inside, and crank the engine to life. The tires squeal against the asphalt as I back out of the driveway, and then I slam the transmission into drive.

There's only one way to handle this—the only way people like Kai and Bishop handle problems—with brute force. That's how I'm going to take back what's mine.

The wheels on the little silver car damn near fall off as they scream through the streets of Detroit, finding the way to Nettie's. I rush through the front door, and at first, Nettie smiles at me, ready to greet me, but then she takes in the expression on my face.

"Xavier?"

I don't answer her.

I sprint to the stockroom and lift the twin mattress that I slept on for years to locate an old shoebox. Inside, I uncover the Beretta I used to carry when I worked for Bishop. I pick up the gun, double-check the magazine to make sure it has bullets, and then load it back into the gun.

Nettie walks in just in time to see me shoving the gun into the waistband of my jeans. "What the hell are you doing?"

I frown, hating that I'm disappointing her, but this is the only way to handle the situation. "Bishop has Anna."

Nettie's eyes widen. "No, Xavier. Don't go there alone."

"I have to, Nettie. They'll kill her if I don't."

Nettie swallows hard, and tears fill her eyes. She knows better than anyone that there's truth to what I'm saying. She's seen the violence created by Bishop and his gang, the Block, and she knows that the body count they've racked up means they aren't afraid to kill.

I hug Nettie and kiss the top of her head, and then I rush

out the back door of the restaurant to get my bike.

I fire up the engine, and it roars through the streets until I pull up to the building where Kai took me when all of this began. The bike is loud, and I'm sure it's signaled my arrival, but I don't give a shit. Nothing will stop me from getting to Anna.

I go in the same way Kai took me through. Only, this time, I don't make it to the bar Bishop built inside. When I round the corner, sitting in the middle of the empty warehouse, tied to a chair, is my Anna.

I rush over to her, and I immediately drop to my knees and untie her ropes. "Where are they, Anna?"

"I don't know," she whimpers. "They brought me here, and I haven't seen them much since then. I think they went into some room behind me."

I glance over her shoulder and spot the door to the club. Can freeing her really be this easy? It's unlike Bishop to leave bait unattended like this when he really wants to get to someone.

"You okay? Did they hurt you?"

"I'm fine. Just get me out of here."

Relief floods me, and I work faster to untie the last knot. When it's finished, I grab Anna's hand and kiss her lips. "Come on."

Before Anna makes it out of the chair, a slow clap sounds from behind me.

"We were beginning to wonder if the boys really did kill you. It took you a while to get here."

I turn slowly to find Bishop, Kai, and two other men. "I don't want any trouble. I just want to take Anna and go."

Bishop rubs the scruff on his chin. "Well, that's the problem now, isn't it? People always tend to want what they can't have. You haven't agreed to what I want from you, yet you expect me to hand over what you want? You and I both know the world doesn't work like that, X."

"I told you the truth before. I don't have any money to start a business with you."

Bishop shakes his finger at me. "It's not nice to lie to an old friend. I read your tax statements. You made nearly four hundred thousand dollars last year. You're good for it."

"Did you also read that half of that went toward my travel and business expenses, and the other half went back to Tension in fines?"

"So, you have nothing?"

"Like I told you, I. Don't. Fucking. Have. It."

Bishop sighs. "That's a shame because I can't let you go now. I can't have you pinning a kidnapping charge on me and my boys, so I'm afraid you can't leave." He pushes the glasses on his face up the tip of his nose as he turns to Kai. "Kill him. Kill them both."

Hearing his order, I reach for my gun and yank Anna behind me. I point my weapon directly at Bishop. "If he pulls that trigger, I will kill you. Hell, I should anyhow for trying to take away the thing I love most in this world."

Bishop grins. "There's the old X again. I have to tell you, I like him much better than this new let's-talk-everything-out X. Old X knew how to get shit done."

"Old X was a hotheaded idiot who fucked up his life all the time because he couldn't control his temper."

Bishop chuckles. "You really believe you've changed that much?"

"Yes," I say with the sternest tone I can muster.

"Prove it. Walk out of here without throwing a single punch."

I lift my eyebrows. "What?"

"I don't buy this whole nonviolence bullshit act, so prove me wrong. If I'm convinced, I might let you go."

"Just like that?"

He nods and confirms, *"Just like that.* I want to see this new X in action because the X I knew would've ripped my head off and spit down my throat for less. I don't believe you're any different from the man I once knew, from the hungry, angry kid I met all those years ago."

I clutch Anna's hand tighter, but I still keep my gun drawn as I pull her toward the men. I tiptoe around them, and he's right. I would love to tear into these motherfuckers, but I know getting Anna out of here in one piece is more important.

Once we've made it all around them, I keep walking backward toward the exit. "This ends here, Bishop."

This is the first time in my life I've ever walked away from a fight. It's baffling even to me, considering this is the one time I've ever had a good reason to go berserk and rip someone's head off.

"I still don't believe you," Bishop says.

I choose to ignore him.

As I turn away from him, Anna releases a blood-curdling scream. "He's got a gun!"

My eyes widen.

This could be the moment when it all ends.

This could be the moment when my world turns black.

I point the gun at Bishop, waiting to see if he's going to force me to pull the trigger.

The sound of my pulse thudding inside my head is the only sound I hear as everything around me seems to move in slow motion as Bishop and I stare one another down.

"Make your move, bitch," Bishop taunts.

My chest rises and then falls as I ask God to protect my family.

The sound of glass crashing jerks all of our attention behind Bishop.

Police, with the word *SWAT* written across the backs of their black uniforms, storm through the windows. The men land all around us. "Everyone, get on the ground!"

I grab Anna's hand and pull her down with me. In these

situations, it's best to comply even if you aren't the person doing anything wrong.

"What's happening?" she cries as cops come over to us.

An officer kneels beside me and removes his helmet and glasses. "You all right, X? Anna?"

I raise my chin and spot Cole wearing black tactical gear. "What in the hell's going on, Cole?"

He reaches down and helps Anna and then me up off the concrete floor. "I've been working on busting Bishop for years. When he kidnapped Anna, it was the last piece we needed to takc him down."

I glance over to where officers are cuffing Kai, Bishop, and his goons.

"Federico Bishop, you are formally charged with kidnapping, attempted murder, assault, racketeering, felon in possession of a firearm, drug possession . . ."

The list of things he's being charged with seems to be never-ending.

Something tells me that Bishop and Kai won't be getting out of prison anytime soon. That should make this neighborhood a hell of a lot safer for everyone in it, including Anna and me.

As Anna clings to me, I kiss the top of her head. "You all right?"

She nods. "I'm okay."

Cole's radio squawks. "Code ten fifty-four at house fire located at ten twenty Sycamore."

Cole's gaze flicks to me. "Why the fuck is there a dead body in your place, X?"

My eyes widen. "*What?*"

"That's what that code means. Was there anyone in that house, other than you and Anna, when it caught fire?"

"No," Anna speaks up. "Kai had the two guys who were just in here with him set the fire after they knocked Xavier out."

"No one was in the house when I was there," I confirm.

Cole raises his eyebrows. "Then, I suggest you get your ass over there and see what's going on. I'll handle all this."

"You sure?"

He nods. "I'll even walk you out."

"Thanks, man. I owe you one." I shake his hand.

"I'll remember that when I need people to testify against Bishop."

"Abso-fucking-lutely count me in on that shit," I tell him. "I'll do all that I can to help."

ANNA AND I RACE BACK to Grandmother's house on my bike. It wasn't my first choice to put her on the back of my ride, but seeing as the situation is an emergency, I had to get over it.

After I park my bike, I rush under the yellow police caution tape.

"You! Stop right there," one of the officers orders.

I point toward the house where smoke is still rolling out of the front door, but the visible flames are long gone. "This is my house. I own it."

The heavyset cop motions me toward him. "Shit, man, what happened to your face?"

I wave him off. "It's nothing."

Gauging by his reaction, I must look pretty rough. I will probably feel just how much Kai's men fucked up my face in the morning, but for now, my adrenaline is pumping so hard that I don't feel much pain at all.

He shrugs. "Follow me." He leads us over to a tall, skinny man wearing a suit, standing next to an open trunk on a police cruiser. "Detective Greyson, this is the homeowner."

The lanky detective with sandy-blond hair gives me a once-over and then flips out a notepad without asking about my injuries. "Name?"

"Xavier Cold."

His suspicious eyes jerk to me. "Age?"

"Twenty-eight." I lift one eyebrow. "What does this have to do with anything?"

Detective Greyson sighs. "The fire did not completely destroy the upstairs area. During the sweep of the house, the firefighters entered a bedroom that was padlocked from the outside. A body was located in the closet of that room, behind a false wall. From the looks of things, the mummified body had been there for quite some time, making it unidentifiable, but it was well preserved in several layers of plastic. Ironically, the corpse did have identification. The name on the ID was Xavier Cold."

My head jerks back. "What? It had my name on it?"

"Not exactly." He reaches into his trunk, pulls out a plastic baggie labeled *Evidence*, and holds it up for my inspection.

Inside the clear plastic is the state ID he's talking about. The picture staring back at me might as well be my own reflection. A man with long dark hair, crystal-blue eyes, and a smirk is a man named Xavier Cold, born in 1968.

"Oh my God," Anna murmurs next to me, seeing exactly what I see. "Is that your father?"

I bite my lower lip. "Looks that way. I never knew his name or saw his picture. Mom always said he ran off."

"We also found a diary in the same closet." He holds up another baggie. "We found this page especially incriminating, so we left it open as we put it in the bag because it clearly tells us who killed this man. Can you tell me if Irma Winslow had any mental health problems?"

"Who is Irma Winslow?" Anna asks.

"That's the name inscribed inside the diary," Detective Greyson says.

"She was my grandmother," I confirm for her. Then, I turn to address the detective. "She was an evil bitch, but I don't know of any diagnosed problems."

"Well," he says, "if you ever had any question if she did or not, check out what's written here."

He points to the open pages, and I lean in to read the scribbled mess.

Today was the day. I ended him, God, just like you said to do. I couldn't allow the evil monster to take away my Gina, so I stopped him.

The only problem is, his evil seed is already implanted in my daughter, so I have to figure out a way to get rid of his spawn. Gina won't believe me when I tell her about the devil. She doesn't believe that Satan tried to take her away from me, but I do.

I slowly blow a breath between my pursed lips as the things she wrote sinks in.

"Heavy shit, right? If she's referring to you in this insane rambling, you're lucky you're still here." The cop pulls the baggie away and puts it back into the evidence box. "The coroner will be able to give us an approximation of how long the victim has been deceased and the cause of death, but I'm guessing this man has been in that closet for a long, long time."

"Probably over twenty-eight years," I mutter, still in shock. "No wonder Grandmother hated me. I was probably a constant reminder of the evil thing she did to the man she locked in her closet. This . . . it explains so much."

Anna rubs my back. "Yes, it does."

Finally, all the lingering questions I've had my entire life have answers. My father never abandoned me and my mother. He was killed, murdered, by my Grandmother who spent the rest of her life concealing her evil from the public. But I knew the truth about her, and now, so will the rest of the world.

Chapter
THIRTY FIVE

Anna

I SET MY COFFEE DOWN on the desk and then creep over to place a cup on the nightstand by Xavier.

He didn't sleep well last night. We had stayed up, discussing the things found in his childhood home. It was hard for him to digest everything that had occured. It was a heavy load to take in, but at least, we're at a point in our relationship where he feels comfortable enough to talk to me about the things he's feeling.

I attempt to tiptoe away, but Xavier's hand snakes out from under the covers and snatches my wrist.

"Where are you going?" He playfully pulls me down onto the bed with him and then wraps his arm around me, snuggling against me. "You smell good."

"I showered." I giggle. "It's called soap."

"Mmm . . . maybe we shouldn't go out today. I still owe you a day in bed."

I trace the ridge of his nose with the tip of my finger, careful not to touch the swollen areas on his face. "We could do that, but I think finding an apartment before we leave for *Tension* might be a better option."

He nods. "You're right. And we need to find you a ring."

"We don't have to do that today."

"Yes, we do." He nuzzles his nose into my hair and kisses my neck. "Since I'm not allowed to fuck up assholes for checking you out anymore, a ring on that finger of yours will be the next best thing to let every man in the world know you're taken."

"I don't need a ring for that. All they would have to do is look into my eyes and see a woman whose heart has already been claimed."

Xavier touches my cheek. "I love you, beautiful. You're the best thing that's ever happened to me. You're my angel, my *everything*, and I'll never let you go again."

EPILOGUE

Anna

THE LIST OF THINGS NEEDED for Quinn's wedding is tattered like an old, worn-out book. I've kept in my purse during the last eleven months, afraid I would forget something. I must have triple-checked it over a hundred times, making sure this will be the best day ever for my cousin.

Quinn rips several tissues out of the box sitting on the table and stuffs them under her arm. Then, she repeats the scenario for the other armpit. She looks ridiculous in her wedding dress with tissues poking out from her underarms.

"It's hot as Hades in here," Quinn complains.

I laugh. "It's not that bad in here. You're just nervous."

"Am not. Why would I be? I'm marrying the man I love, and we're going to be together for the rest of our entire lives. No pressure."

I've noticed Quinn tends to rattle on when she's a bit panicked.

I stand up and grab her hands, trying to calm her down. "You're going to be fine. There's nothing to getting married."

"Easy for you to say." She rolls her eyes. "You and X didn't get married in a church full of people watching your every move."

"No, we didn't. But getting married at city hall was the

quickest way we could get it done."

I smile, thinking about our spur-of-the-moment wedding. We didn't tell anyone we were doing it. But after what had happened with Bishop, we decided that life was too short, and we wanted to officially make our love eternal.

A knock sounds on the door. I cross the small room the church provided for the bridal party to get ready in and pull open the door.

Xavier stands there, cradling our baby boy in his massive arms. He looks dapper in his three-piece black suit with his hair slicked back into a bun. I'm convinced my man looks good in anything he wears.

Xavier grimaces. "Sorry, I know this is girl time, but someone wanted to see Mommy before she had to go perform her maid-of-honor duties."

I pull the blanket away. "He's sleeping."

Xavier grins. "I didn't say Simon needed you."

"You're too much." I lean in and kiss his lips. "Are my parents and my brother here yet?"

"Yep. We're sitting in the second row together."

I bend down and place a light kiss on our baby's forehead and then kiss Xavier one more time. "I'll see you at the reception. I'll be the one in the puffy bridesmaid dress."

He steps back and checks out what I'm wearing. "Is it easy to get out of?"

I grin. "You'll find out tonight."

He wiggles his eyebrows. "It's a date. Later, beautiful." He turns and heads back out to the chapel where everyone else is waiting.

I turn to Quinn. "You ready to do this?"

"Yes," she confirms as she begins heading toward me.

I grimace and then point to her shoulders. "The tissues?"

She quickly jerks them out and tosses them into the trash can. Then, she takes a deep breath. "Let's do this."

I follow her out the door, and it hits me that I have a pretty great life. It was a long, hard road to get here, but together, Xavier and I made it out on the other side, stronger than ever. Things had tested us along the way, but learning to lean on each other had helped us get through everything, especially testifying against Bishop and Kai. Thanks to me and Xavier taking the stand, Bishop and Kai are serving nearly seventy years between the two of them. The streets of Detroit are a lot safer without them around.

Deena and Rex are still pains in our asses from time to time when Xavier and I are on the road, doing Tension, but once word got around that I was pregnant, they decided it was no longer worth their efforts to break us up. Since Simon was born, Xavier's been gone a lot without me for the last two months because we didn't want to Simon to fly right away, but as soon as our boy's a little bigger, we plan on taking him with us until it's time for him to start school.

My mother offered to babysit for us if we moved to Portland, but I explained that Detroit was home for us now.

In place of rebuilding the house on Sycamore, Xavier has built a recreation center for underprivileged youths in the neighborhood. Cole, Nettie, Carl, and Quinn have pitched in a lot to get the project off the ground, and they run it for us when we're on the road. It's been a personal project for Xavier. He loves the idea of providing a positive place to keep kids off the streets.

I've never seen Xavier happier.

I couldn't have asked for a better husband and father to our son than him. Having his own family has truly brought him out of the darkness, and now, the rest of the world is beginning to learn what I've known all along—that Xavier is a good man with a huge heart. I am so proud of him, and I know that our lives together will just keep getting better and better.

Acknowledgements

THE FIRST PERSON I WANT to thank is you, my dear readers, for waiting patiently for the conclusion to Xavier and Anna's story. Thank you all for loving them as much as I do. I hope you know how much I appreciate each and every one of you.

Jennifer Wolfel, I seriously don't know how I could ever write a story without your input. Your love, support and never wavering faith in me and my work truly means the world to me. Thank you for being your amazing self.

Emily Snow, thank you so much for helping me with this book. It seriously helped me a ton!

Jennifer Foor, Holly Malgieri, Heather Peiffer, and Jessica Mobbs, thank you all for being there for me over the years. I treasure the friendship I have with each of you so much!

Jenny Sims and Jovana Shirley, thank you for being an amazing editors and working so hard on this project. My timing was crappy, but you two pulled through for me. Thank you so much!

Christine Borgford, you are simply amazing and are truly a wicked awesome human being. Thank you for putting up with me.

My beautiful ladies in Valentine's Vixens Group, you all are the best. You guys always brighten my day and push me to be a better writer. Thank you!

To the romance blogging community, thank you for always supporting me and my books. I can't tell you how much every share, tweet, post, and comment means to me. I read them all, and every time I feel giddy. Thank you for everything you do. Blogging is not an easy job, and I can't tell you how much I appreciate what you do for indie authors like me. You totally make our world go round.

Last, but always first in my life, my husband and son: thank you for putting up with me. I love you both more than words can express.

About the Author

NEW YORK TIMES AND *USA Today* bestselling author Michelle A. Valentine is a self-professed music addict that resides in Columbus, Ohio, with her husband, son, and two scrappy dogs. When she's not slaving away over her next novel, she enjoys expressing herself with off-the-wall crafts and trying her hand at party planning.

While in college, Michelle's first grown-up job was in a medical office, where decided she loved working with people so much she changed her major from drafting and design to nursing. It wasn't until her toddler son occupied the television constantly that she discovered the amazing world of romance novels. Soon after reading over 180 books in a year, she decided to dive into trying her own hand at writing her first novel, and she hasn't looked back. After years of rejection, in 2012 she self-published *Rock the Heart*, her tenth full-length novel written, and it hit the *New York Times*. Her subsequent books have gone on to list multiple times on both the *New York Times* and *USA Today* bestseller lists.

Michelle loves to hear from her readers!
To Contact Michelle:
Email: *michelleavalentinebooks@gmail.com*
Website: *www.michelleavalentine.com*
Facebook: *www.facebook.com/AuthorMichelleAValentine*

Michelle's Latest Series Release!

The King Always Gets His Way.

Women, business, pleasure: When I want it, I get it.

I'm never denied.

Including her.

I will break her.

I will show her who the king of this city really is.

The Feisty Princess of Manhattan will learn I am not a man that can be tempted.

No matter how damn bad I want her in my bed.

Book one in a three part erotic romance series from NY Times and USA Today bestselling author Michelle A. Valentine (Rock the Heart, Phenomenal X, Wicked White, Demon at My Door).

Naughty King

(A Sexy Manhattan Fairytale: Part One)

Feisty Princess

(A Sexy Manhattan Fairytale: Part Two)

Dirty Royals

(A Sexy Manhattan Fairytale: Part Three)—Coming Soon

9625

Made in the USA
Middletown, DE
30 March 2016